A LESSON IN DESIRE

"Feel the motion," William instructed. "Make the sword an extension of your arm. Extend your stroke all the way out to the tip of the blade. Let the sword do the work."

She swallowed at the feel of his hard body against the softness of her own.

"I'll move you through the basic motions. Keep the balance of your weight on the balls of your feet."

She took each movement into herself, feeling as though they were dancing, not fighting.

"That's it. Let your body flow." He leaned more intimately against her. Her heart beat harder. "Get in close. Stay inside." Then he changed his motions, moving in tight irregular steps. "Confuse your opponent. Focus. Stay balanced."

Siobhan followed his every move. The two of them flowed together as the sword came up, then down, blocking their imaginary opponent. Behind her, she could feel his breath against her ear—short, sharp bursts that changed with the intensity of their swordplay. His body brushed against hers, then retreated. She tried to concentrate on the sword in her hand.

The long, hard muscles of his body pressed against her back, and the heat of him enveloped her. She swayed back against him, overwhelmed by her own desire. How could he continue to stand, when her own legs felt as though they would dissolve beneath her?

"Ms. Russell has created two strong characters able to rise above all that fate and nasty fathers can throw at the them . . . But the journey to the breathtaking conclusion gets more and more intriguing. The primary relationship . . . takes center stage with the suspenseful plot, but the other characters and the questions of loyalty and redemption of past deeds adds to the richness of the whole."

—Romance Reviews Today

THE WARRIOR TRAINER

"Russell . . . debuts with an action-packed, emotion-driven story that immediately captures your attention. Readers yearning for strong heroines and masterful men will find them here, along with a carefully plotted story. Russell's fresh voice secures her a place on the to-buy list."

—*RT Book Reviews*

"*The Warrior Trainer* is a romantic, action-packed story. Scotia is as hard as stone, except when it comes to those she loves. The characters are lovely and the story line will keep you coming back for more. I highly recommend this debut novel from talented new author Gerri Russell."

—Fresh Fiction

"*The Warrior Trainer* is an intelligent, heart-wrenching historical romance that convincingly and seamlessly weaves actual history and mythical fiction together in a work of literary craftsmanship. Gerri Russell has succeeded in rendering emotions, both ecstatic and agonizing, onto the written page. Pangs of joy and grief will linger long after the read is done. *The Warrior Trainer* is a wonderful gift from a very talented author."

—Romance Junkies

"Gerri Russell provides a strong fictional twist to the authentic history. The story line is action-packed from the start. . . ."

—Book Crossing

GERRI RUSSELL

To Tempt a Knight

LEISURE BOOKS   NEW YORK CITY

For Nancy Northcott.
What a treasure of a friend you are.

A LEISURE BOOK®

September 2009

Published by

Dorchester Publishing Co., Inc.
200 Madison Avenue
New York, NY 10016

ISBN 10: 0-8439-6259-3
ISBN 13: 978-0-8439-6259-8
E-ISBN: 978-1-4285-0727-2

The name "Leisure Books" and the stylized "L" with design are trademarks of Dorchester Publishing Co., Inc.

Printed in the United States of America.

10 9 8 7 6 5 4 3 2 1

Visit us online at www.dorchesterpub.com.

To Tempt a Knight

The Spear of Destiny was born of a white-hot bolt of lightning.

So legend has it . . .

The Spear of Destiny wields the power to alter the destinies of men and of entire nations.

So legend has it . . .

But legend, like history, can fade with time, be robbed of the truth and distorted. It is the gift of imagination that breathes new life into legend, giving it wings once more.

Chapter One

Scotland, 1331

The sound of thunder filled the air as twenty armed Knights Templar rode toward the town of Douglas at a breakneck pace. Peter had been captured. No matter how useless the world considered their Order, Peter was still one of them—a Templar hiding in a dangerous world.

Anger erupted, hot and primitive, in William Keith as he pushed his horse and his body to the limit. They were still so far away. Too far. William bent low against Phantom's neck, praying for more speed.

Someone had discovered Peter's connection to the Templars, that he had been the squire to James "Black" Douglas. That connection could very well cost him his life if they didn't hurry. William cast a quick glance at the man who raced beside him—Simon Lockhart, his longtime friend.

Simon responded with a look that said "Hold steady." That was Simon. So filled with hope, despite the danger and desperation.

The party of armed men rounded a bend, and the town of Douglas came into view. A reddish aura rose into the sky as a slender column of choking gray smoke coiled above the town square. Pain cut through William at the sight of the flames licking a pile of burning wood. The scent of burning flesh filled the air, and for a moment his stomach roiled as he made out the human shape within the cruel bonfire.

Too late. They'd arrived too late.

Please, God, why am I always too late . . . ?

His stomach knotted with shame. He squeezed his eyes shut waiting for the agony to abate. It only intensified. William sucked in a desperate breath, forcing himself not to gag. "*Damn you forever*, Pierre de la Roche." What right did a Frenchman have to dispense such horrendous justice on Scottish soil?

William choked back his pain, took a deep breath and focused on the flames that engulfed Peter. He knew the answer to his own question. With a child king on the throne, it seemed anyone who wanted to enforce his own brand of justice in Scotland, could.

"Fly, Phantom, fly," William coaxed his horse. He put his heels to the beast's flanks, encouraging even greater speed. He couldn't save Peter, any more than he'd been able to save the others. But he could retrieve what was left of the young squire for burial. De la Roche might have taken another Templar from this world, but he wouldn't win this fanatical war he'd started, not if William could stop him.

The Frenchman had arrived in Scotland only a sennight ago, and already he'd hastened twelve—nay, thirteen— Templars out of hiding and to their deaths. He'd tortured or burned them all.

William crashed Phantom through the village square and the crowd that gathered there. Two slashes of his sword took down the guards closest to the flames. Two more guards advanced. Simon and the other riders guided their horses into place, taking up their swords.

The battle raged all around them as William reined Phantom a hairsbreadth from the flames. He knocked the burning branches away with his sword until he could reach Peter's body. Another slash released the bindings at Peter's wrists. He grasped Peter's arm before he could fall, and with a tug, William caught the ravaged, sooty body in the folds of his thick cloak. Pain twisted his chest at what remained of the youth. William's only comfort was the thought that Peter was beyond pain now.

"Give me my brother," Lucius Carr demanded, bringing his horse alongside William's.

William recognized the pain and desperation in the young monk's eyes. "Nay, Lucius."

"He's dead?"

At William's nod, Lucius's face hardened. "De la Roche will pay for this."

With as much gentleness as possible, William wrapped his own cloak about Peter's body. "Revenge will come, Lucius, but not here or now. We mustn't risk anyone else's capture."

"Too late for that," a foreign voice drawled. De la Roche, along with a contingent of men, emerged on horseback from behind the billowing smoke. He looked straight at William, an odd smile twisting his mouth. "Kill the others," de la Roche shouted over the raging battle. "This one is mine."

William gazed into a pair of pale eyes. "What is it you want? Peter can give you nothing more precious than his life."

A bitter laugh sounded over the clang of steel upon steel as the Templars and de la Roche's men engaged. "I'm doing what no one else has done here. I'll rid the world of your kind. Heretics don't deserve the holiest relics of the world."

"You care nothing for religion. You've proved that today. You're after the treasure."

De la Roche drew his sword. "And now I know where to find it."

Peter would have never revealed the secret of the treasure. Would he?

A shiver of uncertainty crept over William at de la Roche's triumphant grin.

"The Spear of Destiny will be mine." De la Roche's grip tightened, his sword raised slightly.

Before de la Roche could charge, William jerked his horse back out of reach. He tightened his hold on Peter's body. His task was not to fight, but to deliver the young Templar to the monastery and his eternal rest.

Simon moved in on horseback to engage de la Roche and cover William's retreat. With a tug on Phantom's reins and a thump of his heels against the horse's flanks, William turned his horse. He surged through the village square, heading once again for the mottled shadow of the woods.

"You will not escape me," de la Roche roared. "You'll be next to burn, Keith." Heavy hoofbeats followed in rapid pursuit.

Phantom soared over a fallen tree that lay across the path and came to earth again, flinging clods of grass and mud helter-skelter in their haste. Spiteful twigs plucked at William's legs and clawed at the flapping cloak that held such ravaged cargo.

At the sound of hoofbeats behind him, William twisted back. De la Roche was close on his heels.

William urged his gelding on. Swiftly they flew among the thinning trees. An open field lay ahead, well lit by the afternoon sun and raggedly cloaked by drifts of mist. The open territory held the promise of an easier path where his horse could be urged into its fastest gait.

He pressed his heels into the horse's side. Phantom responded with a surging bound, lifting his hooves to clear a low spot where the mists had gathered. William headed for a fallen tree that sat five feet above the ground. Phantom, William knew, could easily clear the blockade with room to spare. The gelding took flight.

William had heard tales enough about de la Roche to know the man would attempt to clear the blockade. Pride would never allow him to slow down and find a way around the obstacle. A heartbeat later, a bellow and the shriek of a horse sounded behind him as de la Roche's horse failed to clear the fallen tree. "I'll find you, Keith. When I do, you'll meet a bitter and painful end. On that you have my word. I know all the Templars who yet remain."

Plunging ahead, William drew comfort from the knowledge that he had left de la Roche and his horse behind. The world swam, swirling around William as his eyes focused on the lifeless form in his arms. A bitter, painful end was what Peter had endured.

For what reason? He had served his king and country well, and in return he was labeled a heretic and hunted by vigilantes like the fanatic Frenchman who had taken his life. William had sworn to protect the young squire. As he'd sworn to protect all of the survivors who'd returned from their failed journey to the Holy Land. A last mission for their revered king Robert the Bruce had gone very wrong.

William's chest tightened, making it difficult to breathe. He drew a shuddering breath. He forced his thoughts away from the pain in his soul and focused on strategy, on what could be done to keep his fellow Templars safe.

Had they not already suffered enough since that fateful day in 1307 when the Templars were arrested, tortured into confessions as heretics and burned at the stake in France?

William turned his horse to the northeast, heading

for Crosswick Priory. He forced his attention to the road that would lead them home. In truth, he had no home. The monastery was the closest thing to one he'd had in years.

The Brotherhood of the Scottish Templars was his family. It was up to him to keep them alive. He was known as the Guardian for a reason. Whether at war or at peace, it was up to him to protect those who remained. He would find a way to stop the villainy and take de la Roche down.

Rain. Miserable rain. William turned his face up to the sky. Gray clouds billowed overhead, bathing the world in a strange half light. He always felt caught somewhere between this life and the next in the kirk yard.

Rain pressed against his cheeks, rolled down his neck beneath the heavy monk's robe he wore. William stared up into the falling water. Why could it not have rained before the flames had engulfed Peter's body?

With a sigh, he lowered his gaze to the stone tomb where he'd placed what remained of Peter. Angry water drummed against the rough-cut sides of the stone as a frigid wind swooped across the kirk yard.

"Finish your good-byes, William, before too much rain seeps inside," Simon said from the opposite end of the grave.

"I am done. Help me with the lid." William bent down and grasped the stone lid. He would commission a marker for the squire later. With luck, the pain that threatened to choke him would be sealed along with Peter in his grave. The heavy stone grated against William's skin as he and Simon heaved the lid into place.

Simon stepped back from Peter's final resting place and flicked the rain from his brow. "Why do you blame yourself for what happened? Not just to Peter, but to all our Templar brothers?" he asked, studying William from across the top of the tomb.

The rush of a thousand failures washed over William. How could he make Simon understand the emptiness that lingered in every part of his being since their return from the Holy Land?

A gust of wind leapt up to tangle William's long monk's robes around his legs. He'd failed the Bruce. He'd failed his country. He'd failed his fellow Templars. There had to be a reason why all those failures had brought him back to Scotland.

"What's next, William?" Simon asked, coming to stand beside him. "Are you ready to give up? To let de la Roche and men like him have their way?"

Anger took the place of pain. "Of course not."

"Then fight back."

William shook his head. "The Templar Order has been abolished. We would risk everything, if we continued to operate in the open."

"Then we will stay hidden, as we have for years."

William narrowed his gaze on Simon. They had known each other since they were children. Simon's parents had sent him to the monastery to study. William had been there because he'd had nowhere else to go. And they'd become instant friends.

They had gone off together to the Scottish court as young men who were full of themselves and determined to make something out of their lives. And they had. Together, they'd proven their skills as warriors and had joined the Bruce's elite guard. Their lives had been intertwined for years, as they were now that they'd both chosen to return to the monastery after their survival in Spain.

Daily life at the monastery brought order and simplicity back to their world. Or it had, until de la Roche had arrived on Scotland's shores.

William balled his hands. "De la Roche claims Peter told him about Sir John Fraser and his connection to the Spear."

Simon's eyes narrowed. His intense gaze spoke volumes. William had seen the look before on the field of battle, moments before Simon took the enemy down. "Can you—?"

"No need to ask. I ride out at first light." The moment the words left his mouth, a heavy weight slid from his shoulders.

Action. He needed action to move past his failures. He needed the distraction that doing something would bring. Thinking about what had happened was getting him nowhere. The beginnings of a smile tugged at the corners of his lips. Aye, action would be good. He tipped his head back, allowing the rain to pelt against his flesh.

Simon frowned. "De la Roche may know nothing."

"Or everything," William countered, bringing his gaze back to his friend's.

After a final blessing at Peter's graveside, they hurried through the kirk yard to the monastery. "What are the chances of de la Roche getting the Spear?" Simon asked.

"Fairly good, unless we get to Fraser first. De la Roche has enough men to challenge what remains of our forces."

William opened the door at the back of the monastery that led to the refectory. He and Simon hurried inside, out of the driving rain. They made their way across the crowded chamber to the hearth. The monastery's resident monks conversed at long tables over their evening meal. A cheery fire that did not match the emptiness in William's chest glowed in the grate, casting a yellow-gold light across the busy room.

A pool of water started to form at William's feet from his wet robe. With one hand he untied the rope belt at his waist. With his other he jerked the garment over his head to reveal the plain muslin shirt, dark breeches and the scabbard and sword he wore beneath. He hung the dripping robe from a hook near the fire.

Simon followed his example. When they were through, they each scooped a ladle of pottage from the iron kettle that hung before the hearth into a wooden bowl, then took their seats with the others.

William frowned down into his bowl. "The Spear is dangerous in the wrong hands. History has proved that anyone who controls the Spear has the power to conquer his enemy. We need to go to Sir John immediately."

Simon nodded as he chewed a spoonful of lamb thoughtfully. "You can do nothing until the rain lets up."

William pushed back from the table. "I cannot afford to wait either. Perhaps the rain will also slow de la Roche and give me the advantage."

Simon made to stand. "I'll come with you."

William stayed him with a hand to his shoulder. "One of us must stay and protect our brothers. De la Roche could decide to attack here instead of heading for Fraser. We can't risk it."

Simon's expression grew serious. "You're right. We cannot lose anyone else to that madman."

William's hand slid to the hilt of his sword. With a brief nod to Simon, he left the chamber behind. In no time at all, he'd assembled his saddlebag and dressed in his mail as he had so many times before while fighting for the Bruce. He donned a cloak and headed for the stables.

"I hope you're rested, Phantom," he said, saddling the warhorse once more. "We have important work to see to."

Phantom nickered as if in reply.

William swung up into the saddle, finding comfort in the feel of the powerful animal beneath him. At the stable door, he paused. In that moment, the rain eased and the wind stilled, as though the universe heard and understood what was in his heart.

"Scotland cannot afford for me to fail my brothers," William whispered as he put his heels to his horse's side and set off to the north, toward Fraserburgh and the home of Sir John Fraser.

Chapter Two

Siobhan Fraser opened the shuttered window of her father's study and drew in a breath of the morning air. Last night's rain had left the earth fresh and clean. The very air smelled ripe for adventure. Siobhan looked over her shoulder at her father. He sat at his desk, as he did most days, with a sheaf of vellum stacked before him. Pen in hand, he scribbled page after page of gibberish. He called it code. She thought of it as nonsense. Why couldn't he simply write what he wanted to write instead of hiding the message within the context of other words?

"Father," she said, breaking the hushed silence that always hovered over their house. He raised a hand, indicating he'd heard her, but could not answer at the moment. Her father liked silence. Siobhan was starting to hate it.

There had been too much silence in their home as of late. Her father worked day and night on that sheaf of vellum. The more he worked, the less he talked. She turned back to the window, battling the tide of disappointment rising within her. Didn't he see how lonely she was? That she missed the daily discussions she used to have with him before he dove headlong into this current all-important work?

Overhead, clouds sped across the sky, creating a shifting pattern of shadows across the green and purple hills in the distance. Did he not see how much she longed for adventure, and that sitting at the window of their house in an isolated part of the countryside was never going to get her there?

She frowned at the ever-changing clouds in the sky. Did her father have an adventurous bone in his body?

"All right, my dear," her father called from his desk. "What is it you wanted to say?"

She turned to face him. He looked up from the page he'd been writing. He squeezed his eyes shut for a moment, then opened them slowly. Tired brown eyes stared into hers. "You have my attention, Siobhan." His normally strong voice was weak and washed out.

Siobhan felt the stirrings of fear. Her father was never this overwrought or obsessed with his work. Instead of saying what was in her heart she asked, "What's wrong?"

He sighed. "Never could hide much from you."

She angled herself toward him and waited for him to continue.

"I'm feeling some pressure to get this last manuscript completed," he said, looking past her to the open window. "I think it might be time for us to move on, to go back to Edinburgh."

Siobhan hardly dared to breathe. Had she heard him correctly?

He released a tired sigh. "I can see the effect our tedious life in the country has on you. You need to mingle with other young people. 'Tis time for you to marry and start a life of your own."

The breath she'd been holding whooshed out of her lungs. How could he have known her thoughts—not about marriage, but about a change in their situation? Sure, monks had visited occasionally, but since her nurse, Edina MacInnes, had died six years ago, Siobhan had lacked a true companion. "Father, what brought this on?"

"I'm worried about your future." He returned his gaze to her. "What will you do after I'm gone?"

Siobhan shot to her feet, pacing back and forth across his office. She had to think. Why was he talking about relocating now? "What's in Edinburgh?"

"Safety for you."

Her fingers curled, nervously flexing and extending with each step. "I'm safe here with you. I'm just a little bored."

Her father gave her a small smile. "A little?"

"All right, a lot." She mustered a laugh. "I need something to do." She stopped before him. "What can I do?"

Her father pushed back his chair, the sound of wood on wood loud in the quiet house. "You really want to help me?"

"Please."

He gathered up the papers he'd been working on and thrust them into her arms. "Take these to the attic and bind them together in some way. And while you are there, bring me the scroll."

"The scroll?" she repeated in a thick voice. The one he told her never to touch?

He nodded. "You know the one."

Instead of dashing off to do his bidding, she frowned and remained where she stood. "What's wrong, Father?"

He smiled weakly. "All is well, my dear. Perhaps it's time for an old man to share his secrets with his daughter."

Suddenly nervous, she reached for his hand. "Secrets?"

He squeezed her fingers, then pulled out of her grip. "Go get the scroll. Then we will talk."

Something *was* wrong. She left the study, clutching the vellum to her chest. With her free hand, she picked up a candlestick from the table in the hallway and went to the kitchen fire to light it before proceeding up the stairs. As she progressed, she wondered what could have brought this change in her father today? For it was more than her own discontent that had set him on this path.

What secrets could a hard-working, self-exiled man like her father be keeping from the world?

At the top of the stairs, Siobhan set the stack of vellum on a nearby table and held her single candle aloft. She peered around the hazy light of the upstairs chamber. He'd sent her up here to find a scroll. *The scroll*. The one he'd told her all her life to leave alone.

Siobhan's candle illuminated a corner of the room, where she saw a single sheet of vellum tacked to the wall. She moved closer and smiled. Her father had saved the drawing she'd made of Hippolyta, wearing the magic girdle given to the Amazonian queen by her father, Ares. Siobhan had drawn the picture as a child after her own father had told her the story of the golden belt that draped across Hippolyta's hips. Siobhan released a soft sigh. She loved her father's stories of myths and treasures. It was those very stories that made her long for adventures of her own now. Siobhan moved away from the memories of the past and continued to search the chamber. Not finding what she searched for in the dim light, she moved to the chamber's only window and thrust the shutters back. Morning light filtered into the room, catching in its grip swirls of dust as they floated through the air.

For a moment, her attention was caught by the view outside. High rolling hills stood in the distance. Hills she had always longed to explore. In those hills, and beyond in the cities, lay experiences she allowed herself only to dream about at night. With a soft sigh, she turned away. Would they truly leave their old home for Edinburgh soon?

The thought brought with it a frown. What about her father's work? Her gaze moved about the half-lit chamber. Her father's research on ecclesiastical matters filled the space. Books, loose papers like those she'd carried and scrolls were everywhere.

Siobhan's frown deepened as she took in the hundreds of scrolls stacked against the far wall of the chamber. Her father had always told her they were historical documents from the Church. She'd never thought to question why he kept them here instead of in the church vaults. Yet she had always wondered what those documents contained.

Once, as a child, she had slipped into the attic by herself to find out, only to be discovered by her father before she could so much as open one delicate scroll she had lifted from the stack. He'd told her it was best she didn't know what it contained. She would be safer that way.

Siobhan held the candle out before her. Yellow-gold light spilled across the chamber, illuminating a small table in the corner.

After hiding the contents of this attic from her for the last nineteen years, why did he send her to get the scroll today?

The scent of wax mixed with the musty smell of stagnant air as Siobhan stepped up to the table. She set the candlestick down and reached for the forbidden scroll. Its leather casing was embellished with the carving of a rose twining around a Templar cross.

As she started to pull out the scroll, the sound of hoofbeats drifted through the open window. Visitors? Her father hadn't mentioned that any of the monks who regularly came to visit would arrive today. Then again, who else would it be? At least her father wouldn't need her help to entertain them.

She removed the lid of the leather case in her hands and reached for the scroll inside, but the crash of a door stalled her fingers. She heard muffled voices, then a shout. With the leather casing in one hand and the candle in the other, she hastened to the window.

Outside, four men retreated from the front of the house. Three of the men she did not recognize, but the familiar figure of her father stood out. Two men dragged him by the arms across the courtyard to waiting horses.

Siobhan hitched a shaky breath as she bolted for the stairs, but her steps faltered. What if there were others below? Had they come for her father? Had they come for whatever secrets he had been about to tell her?

At the landing halfway down the stairs, she stopped. Though she was wholly unprepared to battle three men, she had to do something to help her father. And before she charged into unknown dangers, she had to keep safe what her father had protected all her life—this very scroll.

With trembling fingers, she slipped the lid back on the leather casing. She then slid the precious document inside a large ceramic water vessel her father had accepted as a gift from one of the monks who had brought it back from the Holy Land. Silently, she crept down the stairs, uncertain of what she might find.

Cool air greeted her. She twisted toward the hallway to see the front door standing open. She paused, listening.

Silence.

The shuffle of her half boots on the floorboards sounded unusually loud as she made her way down the hallway to her father's study.

At the door, she peered inside. No one was there. She moved inside the room, her heart hammering in her chest. Where books had only moments ago lined the dark wood shelves, they were now strewn upon the floor. The chair behind his giant oak desk was pitched to the side.

Why would anyone kidnap her father? He was of no importance.

Siobhan straightened. She had to help him. Careful not to make any sound, she moved to the doorway and strained to listen down the hallway, hearing only the sound of her own thundering heart.

On unsteady legs, she made her way to the front door and stepped outside. A wisp of cool air touched her senses. Morning sunlight spread across the empty courtyard. The gate that separated their home from the rest of the countryside stood open. Siobhan swallowed hard, forcing away fear.

At the bottom of the stairs she grabbed a thick branch that had fallen from a nearby tree during the rainstorm the night before. Her hands tightened around the wood. She hitched her skirts up with her other hand and raced down the path.

At the open gate, she stopped. Her heart lurched in hope that died a moment later. There was no sign of her father or his abductors.

She clutched the branch with white-knuckle force as her heartbeat thundered in her ears. She drew a ragged breath, hoping to slow her racing heart. But even as her breathing slowed, the beat continued. Thump, thump. Thump, thump. Suddenly, a dark shape rose above her. The sound hadn't been her heart. A man on horseback pulled back on his reins, causing the white stallion to rear up.

Her voice went mute, caught in her throat by instant terror. The hooves loomed like raised blades in the morning light. She dropped her branch and braced for the inevitable, but instead of feeling crushing pain when the horse came down, she rose into the air. She came down with a jolt against a leather saddle, which sent her teeth clattering in her head. She twisted toward the stranger. Any words she thought to utter died in her throat as dark eyes bored into hers.

"You could have been killed." His tone was sharp, angry.

The man was irritated with her? He was the one at fault here. "Release me," she demanded in her most severe tone.

His dark eyes narrowed. "Are you always so reckless?"

Siobhan pushed against his arms. Her, reckless? He couldn't be more wrong. "Let me go. I dislike being accosted."

"I *saved* you." The golden-haired man blinked at her in astonishment. He had the look of a man who was used to commanding everyone around him. Well muscled and handsome, he was indeed a change from the older monks who usually came to visit.

Siobhan turned in the stranger's arms. He responded by tightening his grip. She twisted, trying to free herself. "I dislike being saved. Put me down."

To her surprise, he grasped her waist, leaned over and set her firmly upon the ground. "Are you always this disagreeable?" he asked as he swung down from his large white horse. He stared at her, his gaze relentless, assessing.

She tried to look away, but his light brown eyes drew her in even as fear threatened to overwhelm her. Siobhan flinched at the awareness of her own insignificance in the shadow cast by this man. Feeling trapped by the pure energy he exuded, she took a step back.

He caught her arm. Looked into her eyes. His touch was not harsh, but firm.

A large emerald winked at her from the hilt of the long, lethal sword at his side. She stared. She had seen similar swords in her father's drawings. He had never told her much about them, just that they came from foreign lands. She narrowed her eyes at the stranger looming before her.

"I have no time for games, milady," he said savagely. "I came in search of Sir John Fraser." He grasped her arm and started for the house.

"Who are you?" She dug her boot heels into the soil, slowing his progress.

A dark frown cut across his face, making him suddenly seem menacing and dangerous. She jerked out of his grasp and hurried back toward the branch she'd dropped.

"You leave us alone!" As he turned and continued toward the house, she heaved the thick limb straight at his head.

A grunt of pain filled the air. He staggered backward. Surprise widened his eyes as his hand came up to clutch the side of his head. Blood came away on his fingers.

Her skin iced at the angry look in his eyes. He marched toward her. In the next moment, she found herself hauled against his chest. "Enough!" The cutting tone of his voice sent a shiver down her spine.

"Let me go." She sucked in a panicked breath.

His golden eyes held a look of utter scorn. "Don't do that again." He gazed at her for a moment—then abruptly released her. "I am not here to hurt you, but it is imperative I find Sir John. He is in grave danger."

"My father? Why—?"

The sound of hoofbeats coming from the north cut her off. Had her father returned? She strained to see into the distance. She could make out a man atop a black mount. Behind him rode a company of horsemen.

"The day could only want this," the stranger grumbled, dashing the blood away from the side of his head with his hand.

"Do you know them?" Siobhan asked as the leader of the group kicked his horse into a gallop. His troops followed apace.

The stranger held out his hand to her. "If you wish to see tomorrow, come with me."

She remained where she stood.

"Stubborn girl," he muttered as he twisted away. In two long steps he reached his horse and swung up into the saddle. He brought the beast to stand before her, between herself and the advancing men. "Give me your hand." He stretched his fingers out to her.

Siobhan stared at his hand. Her heart thudded painfully in her chest. When she didn't respond, he reached down and grasped her arm, then jerked her up onto his horse, settling her before him.

"Where is your father?" he asked.

"Why should I trust you?" Her voice was raw as she turned to face the stranger behind her.

He cast her a speculative glance, one eyebrow raised in a subtle challenge. "Would you rather trust them?" He inclined his head toward the small army heading their way.

A sigh heralded her capitulation. "Take me back to the house."

"Is your father there?"

She shook her head. "He's been abducted."

"By them?" His brow rose in question.

"I don't know." She set her shoulders, her decision made. "Back to the house. Please?"

"We have no time." He kicked his horse into a gallop, sending them flying down the roadway toward the hills in the distance. Siobhan glanced back over her shoulder at her home. They were being pursued.

"The scroll!"

"Pray your home remains safe."

How could she pray when fear circled endlessly inside her? She latched onto the horse's neck, huddling against the beast while the man behind her drove his horse across the open land.

How could this be happening? Her calm, quiet, orderly

life had eroded beneath her. Her father had been abducted. *Abducted . . . abducted . . . abducted.* She squeezed her eyes shut to block the taunting word from her brain.

A hand curled around her waist, pulling her back against a strong, firm chest. "Are you all right?" His voice was soft, laced with concern.

Her whole world spun out of control. It felt as though her bones had turned to porridge. Her father was gone. Men chased her. And she found herself in the arms of a man she did not know.

What was it just this morning she had longed for? A life of adventure? Siobhan bit her lower lip to keep back a groan. This wasn't how she'd imagined a more exciting day would start—clinging for her life to an absolute stranger, leaving everything she knew and loved behind.

Siobhan drew a shaky breath. It didn't matter what she had longed for; what she'd gotten was life-altering trouble.

Chapter Three

William willed the throbbing in his head to cease as he kicked his horse into a gallop. What the hell was wrong with him? He was a warrior. A Knight Templar. A man who had taken countless enemies down in the course of battle. Humiliation and curiosity mixed as he held Phantom's reins in one hand and securely gripped the girl before him with the other.

He'd let his guard down, and a slip of a girl had whacked him in the head. To draw blood. William frowned. How had he sunk so low in such a short span of time?

Or had he been away from women for so long that he'd begun to underestimate them? The girl in his arms appeared far more poised than he would have expected for someone who had witnessed her father's abduction and was now being forced to flee her home.

The open terrain stretched endlessly before him. Rhythmic hoofbeats sounded from behind. He didn't need to look to know Pierre de la Roche and his men pursued.

William's heartbeat slowed. Calm descended over him. His senses heightened as they always did before a battle. If he and the girl were to find safety, they would have to hide.

He couldn't let her fall into de la Roche's hands. This woman was the last of her family's bloodline. If she died, so would her heritage. William loosened his grip ever so slightly about her waist. He knew what it was like to be the last, to lose everything.

The girl had lost her father today, if William's suspicions were right. De la Roche had abducted Sir John and had no doubt learned by now that the man wouldn't give up his secrets so easily.

Was that why he'd come back? To use Siobhan to make her father talk? William's presence would only be seen as a bonus—gaining de la Roche two prisoners instead of one.

And then there was the Spear, the most compelling reason he had for forcing her to come with him. If she knew its location, she would be hunted by de la Roche until he finally got what he wanted—absolute control over mankind.

William reversed his direction again and again, making it difficult for the men behind to gather speed. He and the girl flew across the peaty soil, heading for the ridge between the two hills. Arrows whizzed past them.

"Stay low," William warned as he forced the girl farther down against his horse's neck, then wrapped himself around her to protect her.

She tensed in his arms. "Those men—" Her words cut short as they headed for a creek bank that offered a more even path.

"I'll keep you safe," he replied tersely.

"I need no empty promises."

Irritation coursed through him. Determined to ignore her response, he scanned the terrain. A sea of purple heather stretched out before them, rising up the sides of the hills and peaks. Their only hope lay in outmaneuvering de la Roche and his men between the jagged peaks.

Amongst the thunder of hoofbeats, they slipped onto the ridge. Now was the time for cleverness, if they were to escape.

"Your name, milady?" William asked. "I at least deserve to know whom I'm protecting."

"Lady Siobhan Fraser."

Lady Siobhan. At the simple sound of her name, an ache moved through him. Names were personal, a connection to another that he hadn't allowed himself to experience with anyone but his Templar brothers for so long. He would love to reach out to her right now and take her hand in his, to feel a connection that went deeper than just words. But that would never happen, he realized with a self-deprecating smile.

Wind crept through the countryside, brushing across his cheeks in soft, cool waves. The chill helped focus his thoughts as he urged his horse not along the long and narrow ridge, but up the steep slope. He slowed their pace as they ascended, grateful that Phantom's steps were steady and strong. Once they'd gained some height, he urged the horse to traverse the peak parallel to the valley below them, looping back to the ridge where they'd started.

They watched from the heights above as de la Roche and his men raced along the narrow ridge. Their pursuers would have to look up and back to catch sight of them now. As the men passed by, William guided his horse back down to the flat terrain, urging the horse into even greater speed as they headed back the way they had come. He would head for the eastern shoreline. They could hide in the seaside cliffs.

As they raced across the landscape, William listened, trying to hear something other than the sound of his own harsh breathing and the rhythm of his horse's hooves. *Nothing.* "We lost them."

"Please stop this horse. I wish to get off."

"Pardon?" Had he heard her correctly?

"Stop this horse," she demanded.

Filled with confusion at her strange request, William stopped at the base of another short, steep hill but did not release his hold on Siobhan. More hills dotted the land behind them. Before them lay an endless expanse of heather-covered moors. A soft breeze caught the loose wisps of the girl's red hair that had escaped her tight plait.

"Where do you plan to go?" he asked, more tersely than he'd intended. The Highlands comprised endless miles of peaks, valleys and moors.

Silence descended as she scanned the landscape. "I must go back. There are important things I must gather."

"The scroll you talked of earlier?"

She nodded.

William frowned. "Is a scroll more important than your life?"

"My father wanted me to protect it. At least I think that was what he wanted." Her eyes snapped to his as though she just realized what she'd said aloud. "Who are you to ask me such a question?"

"I'm a friend. Sir William Keith." He offered her a slight bow. "An associate of your father's."

Her gaze narrowed. "I've never seen you before."

"We are known to each other through the Templar knights."

"The Templars? They're disbanded, gone."

"Nay, we're not gone. Scotland is a haven for many, including your father." He took a huge risk telling her such things. Horrible things happened to those who admitted connections to the Templars. He divulged the secret he and her father shared because something inside him told him he could trust her. She was after all the daughter of Sir John Fraser.

Instead of appreciating his honesty, she scowled. "My

father is no Templar." Her chin came up. "He's a historian for the Church."

"For the Templars."

Siobhan shook her head. "If such were true, my father would have told me."

"Perhaps he wanted to protect you," William offered, softening his tone. "After joining the order, he learned he had a child. He couldn't leave you alone in the world, so the brothers gave him special permission to raise his motherless daughter while still serving a role for the Templars. Very few people are given such a gift."

"My mother did die in childbirth, but my father was with her at the time."

"Or did he just tell you that to make your life more comfortable?"

A look of confusion entered her eyes. "Nay. Why would he lie to me?"

"People do all kinds of things to protect those they love." He thought the explanation sounded reasonable, yet his words didn't have the effect he'd hoped. She turned away, facing forward on the horse, but not before he saw tears spill from beneath her dark lashes.

Suddenly William wished he were deep in the thick of battle, for then he'd know what to do. He had no experience comforting women, especially when he'd caused the upset with his words. William palmed his sword, allowing the hilt to warm beneath his palm.

Robert the Bruce had trusted him with the most sacred of secrets, and this woman's father was part of that secret. William frowned. How could he gain her trust?

William steeled himself to do what must be done, no matter how innocent or frightened she appeared. He needed information about the Spear of Destiny. Her father had known its location. Did that mean she knew the Templar's other secrets as well?

He relaxed his grip on his sword. He pulled her back against his chest. Her body stiffened. A soft sob escaped her. He remained silent, not knowing how else to comfort her. A moment later, she leaned back into his chest. "This day started so well. Where did it go wrong?" she whispered.

William allowed her body to sink back against his. He swallowed hard, trying not to notice the soft brush of her skin against his or the sweet feminine smell that filled his head. God's mercy, it had been years since a woman had been in his arms. He drew in a long breath and let the scent of heather permeate his senses. Had a woman ever felt this soft before?

Something inside him that had been dormant for a very long time sputtered to life. Warmth filled him, then heat. But it was a heat he could never sate. He forced his thoughts back to the present. He needed information about her father to complete his mission.

"We will find him, lass," he said softly.

She turned to face him. "Do you know who did this?" she whispered.

"Aye."

Her green eyes widened. He could see the cold, stark fear reflected there.

"It's someone who wants certain information your father has."

"I have to help him. All his research is back at our home. That would be the best place to start."

He nodded. "I'll take you back and continue to protect you from de la Roche if you, in turn, cooperate with me."

Suspicion narrowed her gaze. "Why? How does this profit you?"

"The Templars need your father." Their gazes met and held. "And you, Lady Siobhan, need me."

She drew a breath, then nodded. "I accept your offer. Take me home, and let's see what secrets the scroll contains."

Pierre de la Roche's company slowed their horses to a stop as they cleared the valley, coming back into the open once more. The landscape stretched for miles with no sign of the Templar or the girl. Anger flared. He needed that girl to make her father talk. The man had shown marked reserve until de la Roche had mentioned heading back for the daughter.

De la Roche clenched his gloved hands as Navarre Valois, his captain, brought his horse alongside de la Roche's. "We were right behind them. How could they disappear into thin air?" the man asked.

"I'll tell you how he slipped away," de la Roche replied caustically. "That blasphemous Templar has been on the run for many years. He's become very adept at secreting himself." His gloved hand snaked out, connecting with the man's cheek and jaw, nearly unseating Navarre from his horse.

"Let that be a lesson to be more careful," de la Roche growled.

The captain rubbed the growing red mark that dominated the left side of his face. "Aye," he mumbled.

Navarre had been with him for years, since long before strands of gray began threading his hair. The man had been competent at one time. Perhaps those days were gone.

De la Roche turned to his troops. All the others remained mounted and kept their distance. A sharp stab of annoyance brought a deep scowl to his face. "I'm gravely disappointed. Will none of you step up to the task at hand? Justice is at stake."

"Let me go after him. I'll find him." Marcus Dumas brought his horse forward from the bunch. The youngest of all of them, his face still held the flush of youth. Similar to the flush that used to mark de la Roche's own cheeks when he'd started his quest for revenge against the Templar Order over twenty-four years ago.

"I believe that you will," said de la Roche. He signaled the young man to come forward and sent Navarre to the rear.

As Marcus came forward, memories swamped de la Roche. He saw himself as a young man, spurned by the preceptor of the Templar Order in France. As he had been an only son and heir to his father's title, the Templars wouldn't accept him amongst their ranks, no matter how much he'd pleaded.

De la Roche cast off the memories with a growl. Those old desires were left buried in the past. The future stretched before him—a future in which he held power over life and death.

He allowed his anger to fester, to swell until he could feel it pulsing through his veins. He'd destroyed hundreds of Templars since they'd been disbanded over two decades ago. He'd slain them, burned them, made examples of what happened to those who fell out of favor with God. And he'd been satisfied with his progress until he'd set his sights on bigger spoils.

The Templar treasure.

Something so precious could not belong to blasphemous swine. De la Roche intended to claim the treasure for his king, while keeping the Spear of Destiny—the Holy Lance—for himself. With the spear, nothing and no one could stop him in his quest for ultimate justice.

He knew the truth about the Spear. *Whosoever possesses*

this Holy Lance and understands the powers it serves, holds in his hands the destiny of the world, for good or evil.

He wanted that power for himself. He wanted to fight battles without the fear of losing, to control men as he had never controlled them before, and to remake the world in a way that suited him. De la Roche's hatred piled atop his anger. The Templar and the girl would not halt his sacred work.

I shall punish them both. De la Roche signaled his men to ride back through the valley. There was nowhere in Scotland the two who defied holy law could hide where he would not find them.

Nowhere.

Chapter Four

As Siobhan and her unwanted protector rounded a bend in the road, the countryside grew quiet. Absent even was the wind. An eerie white mist formed on the ground, and wraithlike fog twined around the low stone walls and thickets of bracken outlining the tenant plots that bordered the road to Bramble House, her home.

Now and again the fading sunlight pierced the broken, scudding clouds, casting a mottled array of golden light and darkened shadows. The strange combination sent a chill down Siobhan's spine.

"Do you see anyone, sir?" Siobhan asked, breaking the silence that had fallen between her and the knight as the horse made steady progress toward her home.

He frowned. "Call me William. And nay, we appear to have left them far behind."

Siobhan heard a soft hissing followed by an unearthly groan. "What was that?"

"I don't know."

She could feel his body tense behind her as they came to the road they had traveled not long ago. The house came into sight. An odd light appeared in the front room's shuttered windows. The light brightened, intensified, until with a flash, flames appeared, licking hungrily at the wood. Within the span of a heartbeat, flames licked the north side of the house, as well as the upper shutters.

Her home was burning!

Siobhan stared in disbelief. "No!" The raw cry tore from her throat. "This can't be happening. I have to save the scroll."

"Why? What's so important about that scroll?"

"It's my father's life's work. Whatever information you need is most likely there. It's all I have left. . . ."

William hesitated a moment more, searching the area. For what? The house was on fire. Who would be lurking near such danger?

A moment later, he kicked his horse into a gallop. He raced up the path. The heat intensified as they approached. Something exploded, spraying chunks of wood and ash outward, allowing the flaming tongues to escape and lick upward over the walls and toward the roof.

Siobhan didn't realize she was sliding from the horse until her feet hit the ground. She ran for the front door, desperate to save the scroll. Her body jerked to a stop.

"Are you mad?" William gripped her arm, pinning her in place.

"Let me go." Siobhan brought her hand up to cover her mouth, shielding it from the smoke.

"Where is it?" he demanded.

"Inside the large clay urn at the turn in the stairs." She coughed.

"Stay here." He released her arm, tore up the front steps, and threw open the door.

Despite the heat, Siobhan shivered. How would he ever make it out alive? How could he expect her to stay outside and wait? She followed him up the steps. Heat and smoke blasted her lungs as she entered the hallway. "William!" Coughing, she fought her way through the smoke to the attic stairs.

"Get out of here," William called from above.

She turned toward the kitchen. Hungry tongues of

fire marched across the wide, wooden table that sat at the far side of the room. With monstrous ferocity, flames devoured the wooden counters and the dried herbs she'd hung in batches against the wall.

A figure surged down the stairs before her. The smoke had grown dense, and Siobhan could only dimly see William's strained face. Then she noticed the leather casing in his hands and felt a profound rush of relief.

"Get out," William said hoarsely as he handed her the scroll and forced her back toward the door.

They burst through the doorway, then stumbled down the stairs. Turning back, Siobhan saw a reddish aura rise from the growing core of heat and flames that spread into the afternoon sky. A heavy rolling mass of choking gray billowed above what used to be her home. A constant roar of flames deadened her ears to any other sound. A dagger whizzed past her head, narrowly missing her. She gasped.

William drew his weapon, angling it at a shadowy figure who emerged from across the courtyard, his sword drawn. "De la Roche thought you may head back here. He left me to tend to you, Templar."

Siobhan's heart hammered in her chest. The stranger charged. William's blade blocked the blow. The sound of steel on steel rang in the air, punctuating the crackle and roar of the flames behind them.

Siobhan had never seen a sword fight before. She'd imagined them in the darkest depths of her dreams. But in those imaginings, there was no blood and no death. Here the threat of both clanged with each sword stroke. William stepped back as his opponent swung his blade in powerful arcs toward William's torso. He didn't attack, but watched, seeming to wait for the moment to strike. The man's blade arced up, and William's blade followed, blocking the strike, then moved in, leaving a slash in the man's sleeve that was soon replaced by a blossom of red that trailed down his sword arm.

Blood. Siobhan hitched a breath and stepped back toward the house, toward the heat and the smoke, not knowing which way safety lay.

She remained there as she watched the macabre dance that stretched out before her as the two men sought to kill each other. The crisp clang of steel echoed loudly, blending with the crackling of the flames.

Another slash from the attacker left a gash in William's forearm. Siobhan gasped. The sound drew the attacker's attention to her. His pale gaze fixed on her face.

With a sinister smile, he lunged toward her.

Siobhan jumped back into a wave of heat. William surged forward. Before she could draw breath, William caught the man with a blow to his back. The man crumpled to the ground at her feet.

A chill rooted her to the spot, despite the inferno at her back. He was dead. She couldn't breathe. The world before her blurred into swirls of orange and red. Blood red. Her knees gave way. Before she tumbled to the ground, William seized her and swung her up into his arms. A few short strides later, he mounted his horse with her in his arms and settled her before him. "This is no time for sentiment." He kicked his horse into a run. The burning shell of what once was her home disappeared in the distance.

Siobhan clutched the scroll, suddenly feeling heavy inside, so weighed down and full of tears. She'd lost everything that had ever mattered to her today—her father, her home, her way of life.

What was there for her now? She clung to the scroll all the harder. Such thoughts would get her nowhere. She might not be the bravest of all, but she was not a quitter. Her father needed her now, more than ever.

As they rode, Siobhan glanced down at the hands that steadily held the horse's reins. They were tanned and scarred. Large and strong, well-shaped and masculine, the hands of a capable warrior. The thought comforted her as she settled back against his chest, heading for who knew where.

They rode in silence for a long time until night began to fall. Finally William brought his horse to a stop along a seaside cliff. "We shall rest here tonight." He dismounted first, then helped her down.

"Where?" Siobhan saw nothing but the great expanse of ocean on one side of her and miles of open land on the other. There were no inns. No houses. No signs of life anywhere.

He ignored her question as he removed the leather satchel from Phantom's saddle and set it on the ground. He lifted the bit from the animal's mouth, then rubbed the horse's neck with a gentle touch, while cooing softly to the beast. She couldn't seem to drag her gaze away from the pair. She was struck by William's gentleness. How many times had she wished that someone would cosset her in that way?

The knight was tall, taller than her father by at least a foot. The seriousness of his expression did nothing to hide his rugged handsomeness. Whether tending his horse or fending off a villain, he moved with a supple strength that exuded confidence. What would it be like to be that brave?

When she realized he had stopped rubbing his horse and instead fixed his gaze on her, Siobhan looked away. In his gaze she had seen intelligence, curiosity and something else she couldn't name. "Are we to sleep beneath the stars along with your horse?" she asked, hoping to turn his attention away from her blatant exploration.

"Phantom will not be staying." The words had barely

been spoken before he patted the horse's rump, sending him racing off along the cliff.

Siobhan gasped. "How will we ever outdistance those men without a horse?" Suddenly the events of the day seemed to catch up with her. Siobhan swayed on her feet.

In a heartbeat, he stood beside her, supporting her. "Trust me."

"But the horse . . ."

"Phantom is well trained. We have used this ploy many times before. If de la Roche's men are anywhere near, the horse will lead them away from our hideout. Then, when dawn approaches, he knows to make his way back to me."

The white horse vanished into the hazy darkness. Siobhan shivered as a slight breeze moved in off the ocean.

"Come," he said, guiding her to the saddlebag. He secured the load over his arm, then held his hand out for the scroll she carried. "Allow me. The next part of our journey could be a bit dangerous."

Siobhan held tight to the scroll. "I'll manage," she said, not willing to sacrifice the one small piece of her old life she still retained.

"As you wish." He turned toward the cliff and the almost obscured path that headed down into nothingness.

The climb proved far more difficult than Siobhan had anticipated. The rutted, narrow path slanted steeply down and sometimes disappeared altogether. Clinging desperately to the scroll for fear that it would fall into the churning waves below them, Siobhan picked her way down the treacherous trail. When the large opening in the shale cliff came into view, she felt as though they'd been hiking down the cliff face forever. A pale moon pierced the darkness with silver light, creating an unearthly landscape of dark shapes rising from a luminous haze.

At the cave's opening, William held out his hand to

assist her through the last few steps and onto the solid ledge. "Are you well, milady?" he asked.

She nodded breathlessly as she stepped into the cool moisture of the cave.

"Stay here while I take a look inside." He disappeared into the darkness.

The moonlight illuminated only the smallest portion of what appeared to be a rather large opening in the cliff face. She could see shadowy walls, with their slight glimmer of moisture, only a few yards back.

When William reappeared, she asked, "How far back does it go?"

"Only a few hundred yards. It'll be drafty and wet, but at least we are safe here for tonight." He set his satchel down near the wall and dug inside. A moment later he pulled out a light-colored cloak and wrapped it around her shoulders.

Warmth enveloped her. "My thanks," she said. "But what about you?"

"I'm fine," he said, turning from her.

In the light of the moon, the pale woolen cloth nearly glowed. But it was the bloodred cross sewn onto the fabric at the side of the cloak that riveted her attention. A Templar's cloak.

Her gaze shot to his. "Yours?"

He nodded as he settled himself on the ground next to the opening.

"How long have you been . . . ?" She hesitated, not quite certain how to phrase what she wanted to know.

"Hiding?" he provided for her.

She nodded.

"It feels like a lifetime, but in reality it's been only four years for me."

Sorrow lingered beneath his words. "Do you miss your home?"

He averted his gaze, hiding any emotion the darkness might not conceal. "I never truly had a home. All my life I've lived by my sword. It shelters me, feeds me and protects me."

"It sounds very lonely," she said, casting a glance at his profile in the darkness of the cave.

"It gives me what I need."

Siobhan hesitated to ask more because of the dour tone of his voice. She'd touched on something that he didn't want to discuss. As her eyes adjusted to the pale moonlight, Siobhan looked around the small cave. Nothing but bare, damp rock surrounded them. The soft surge and retreat of the waves sounded below. She crossed her arms over her chest, hugging the scroll close to her, trying to ward off the chill of the night.

"We can't risk a fire," he said, as though he sensed the shudder that raced through her just then. "Come, sit beside me."

She sat, leaning back against the shale wall. With hesitant fingers, she brushed the smooth surface of the leather case on her lap.

"What's on the scroll?" he asked, his tone even now.

"I'm not certain."

Despite the darkness she could see his puzzled frown. "You risked your life for that scroll, and you do not even know what it contains?"

She frowned down at the leather that protected the contents inside. "My father sent me to retrieve this moments before he was abducted." She turned toward William. In the half light his face was a study of dark planes and angles. "I can't help wondering if he knew something would happen to him today." She bit down on her lip as she fingered the container's cap. "This is all I have left." She didn't expect him to understand.

"Open it," he said softly with no accusation in his

tone. Did he understand? Or was he anxious for her to reveal the scroll's secrets for another reason?

Could she trust him? William had saved her life today. . . . Her own curiosity forced doubts about William's interest aside.

She forgot about the cold. She forgot about the tragedy of the day. She forgot about everything as carefully, almost afraid to breathe, she opened the case and gently shook out the papyrus scroll inside. She unrolled it. Straining her eyes in the dim light, she stared down at line after line of her father's dense writing. Even if she'd been able to see it clearly, she doubted she could identify the words he'd hidden in the strange cipher. She angled the paper toward the cave's opening, trying to catch what light she could. Dark shapes appeared. A map? She sighed. "It's too dark. I can't make anything out."

"Then any discoveries will have to wait until first light." He shifted beside her and, with a rasp of sound, drew his sword. He set the weapon across his lap, his hand on the hilt. "Just in case," he said as he settled back against the wall. "You had best sleep. Who knows what challenges tomorrow will bring?"

She knew he was probably right. She rolled the scroll and placed it back in its case, then held the treasure close to her chest, protecting what she had left of her life with her father.

She tried to block the sound of the surf, but the further darkness only made her more aware of her surroundings—especially the man sitting next to her, a sword gripped in his hands. "Why did you come to see my father today? Did you know de la Roche would come as well?"

He shifted, turning toward her in the darkness. His face was cast in complete darkness now. And for a moment she wondered if he'd planned that, secluding himself in darkness. "Nay. 'Tis mere coincidence that de la

Roche appeared when he did, although there were those of us who suspected he would show himself sooner or later."

A gust of cool wind touched Siobhan's cheeks. She pulled the cape he'd given her closer around herself. "Those of us?" she prompted.

She could feel his gaze upon her. "The Templars. Your father has information we desperately needed."

"And now that he's gone . . . ?"

"I am hoping you have that information. Or that the scroll we saved from the fire contains something we can use to find what it is I need."

Siobhan's hands tightened on her father's work. A surge of hope moved through her. Today's events had taught her one thing: she needed this man's help to rescue her father from de la Roche's clutches. Could the scroll help her secure his aid?

"What do you need?" she asked, trying to temper her growing excitement. This man was still a stranger. His motives were unproved.

"The Holy Lance. It's the one piece of the Templar treasure de la Roche wants above all the rest. Your father was the treasure's guardian."

A shiver rippled across her nape. Her father had told her stories of many legendary treasures over the years, but she'd had no idea he was so intimately connected to them.

"My father called it the Longinus Spear. . . ." Her voice trailed off in wonder. She shifted, trying to see his face in the darkness. If only she could see his eyes. Then she'd know whether he was being honest or not. "How do you think I can help you?"

"It's how we can help each other, Lady Siobhan."

"Please, just call me Siobhan. No one ever refers to me as anything more."

"Siobhan. Help me locate the Spear, and I'll help you find your father and get you both to safety."

She knew nothing about this man, except that he had saved her from de la Roche earlier and that he had gone back into her burning home to rescue the scroll without fear for his own life. Were those things enough to trust him with her father's life? His deepest secrets?

"Do we have an agreement?" he asked, his voice deep, expectant.

She nodded. Then, realizing he could not see her any better in the dark than she could see him, she said, "Aye."

"Then you had best try to get some sleep, because tomorrow will be another difficult day if I know de la Roche."

Instantly, her mood sobered at the reminder of the dangers outside of their dark cave, no doubt the reason he'd drawn his sword. "Will you be able to sleep?" she asked.

"Nay."

Siobhan released a soft sigh. She doubted she'd find sleep this night either. Her sleeplessness wouldn't stem from the ever-present danger, even though she knew she should be more fearful of discovery than she was. Instead, her mind filled with a million possibilities of what secrets the scroll might reveal.

She shifted her gaze to what little she could make out of William. Did her father truly have something to do with the Knights Templar?

Coded text . . . Drawings . . .

What could her father be involved in?

Chapter Five

Neither William nor Siobhan slept during the night. At one point, William was tempted to call his horse and continue their journey. Yet he knew that without light, travel near the ragged edges of the seaside cliffs would be far too dangerous. The rough terrain notwithstanding, de la Roche and his men could be anywhere.

Yet the hours of darkness had been well spent. Even without sleep, resting his exhausted body had cleared his head. He needed that focus to keep them alive.

With the first light of dawn, he took his cloak from her shoulders and repacked it in his saddlebag. It would do neither of them any good to be caught wearing the mark of a heretic. He gathered his saddlebag, and in silence they headed up the path. After checking that the way was clear, William helped Siobhan over the ledge, to more solid ground.

William whistled for his horse, but his gaze remained on Siobhan and the leather casing in her hands. "Aren't you going to open it?"

Something that had been dead inside him for many years stirred when her eyes met his. A man could lose himself in their green depths.

"Suddenly, I'm frightened," she said quietly, breaking into his thoughts. "Last night in the darkness I ran through so many possibilities about what the scroll would reveal. Yet now I almost fear what could be written there."

Honesty. It had been a long while since he'd been exposed to such openness outside of the Brotherhood. The fact that such things still existed in the world, even from one source, lightened his soul.

"What's the worst thing that could happen if you open it?" he asked.

She frowned. "Pardon?"

He took a step closer. "'Tis a game I play with myself when I'm frightened. If you imagine the worst thing that could happen, then whatever is truly revealed will never be as bad as that."

She opened her mouth to speak, but he silenced her with his hand. Siobhan tensed.

A sound. Hoofbeats.

The tension left his body when a splash of white appeared in the distance. Phantom. "What's the worst that could happen?" he repeated.

"That I won't understand what is in the scroll my father wanted me to protect."

He nodded. "If so, you're no better off but no worse either. Open it."

She hesitated only a moment. Slowly she unfastened the lid and shook out the papyrus inside. She carefully unrolled the document. Her brow furrowed as she studied the scribblings. After several moments, she still hadn't said a word.

"Is something amiss?" Tension flooded his body. His hand moved to his sword. He forced his fingers to relax. The scroll was no threat to them.

"I had hoped to find some meaning, but it's indecipherable. My father always made his notations in code." She turned the scroll toward him.

"Templars are famous for their coding."

She nodded. Her look of desolation tore at his insides. He knew the kind of hopelessness she must be feeling.

He'd experienced such himself. Instead of the cliff's edge and the ocean, William saw a battlefield, soaked red with blood. The blood of his brothers, defeated, undone.

Pain shot through his body as William clung to his sword. He dragged himself through the carnage, searching the jumbled mass of shredded and broken bodies—some Saracen, many more Scottish—for his brethren.

Ten of them, bonded in service to their king, each bearing a similar sword . . . How many survived? He wouldn't die, he couldn't. Not until he knew if others yet lived. They might be defeated, but there was still more that they might do, given time to perform the deeds.

William staggered through the dead, slipped on the blood-soaked turf, in a desperate search. He'd thought then, at that moment, of the worst that could happen—that he would be alone—when he saw a familiar sword glinting in the distance.

He was not alone.

William gritted his teeth and pressed on, blinded, eyes burning, throat clogged by the smoke rolling across the fields. But he could still recognize his kinsman, his brother. For they had the same passion, the same fierce determination, the same oaths sworn and held to their country and their king.

Kenneth Moir, his longtime friend and mentor from the monastery, was sprawled on the ground but alive. The same hope that tightened William's chest reflected in the older man's eyes. That Kenneth lived was a great testimony to his strength and determination.

William reached Kenneth's side and helped him to his feet. They clung to each other amidst the carnage and death. Kenneth's flesh was torn, his bones shattered, blood seeping from a gaping slash in his chest. And yet he lived.

They both had lived.

Forcing the memory away, William said, "I may know someone who can help." He lifted Siobhan onto his horse, then mounted behind her. With a flick of the reins, he sent them racing across the open land, to the west. The monastery was their only hope.

He gave a short, bitter laugh. "It seems entirely appropriate that we'll have to see the Reaper in order to begin our quest."

At William's odd words, Siobhan tensed. Her heart was pounding so hard, she was certain he could hear it. She wanted to ask him what he meant, but the seriousness of his expression warned her otherwise.

She had only been in his presence a short time, but already she knew he didn't like to have his motives questioned. Besides, Siobhan thought as she clutched the scroll to her chest, she needed his help to decipher the code. If she could find the treasure before de la Roche, she could use the Spear of Destiny to ransom her father's life.

Siobhan looked back at the man behind her. His expression was intent, his brow furrowed as he concentrated on the open ground. She became acutely aware of the arms that circled her, of the strength of his hands guiding his horse with exquisite care. She noted the way the muscles of his thighs bunched and relaxed with each stride of the horse beneath him.

She looked up to find him staring at her. Slowly, he brought one finger up to trace the outline of her jaw. "You shouldn't look at me like that," he said hoarsely.

A primal shudder went through her as her senses heightened. She could smell him—sandalwood mixed with the scents of smoke and sweat.

His gaze had moved to her lips when suddenly a shadow darkened his face. He made an incoherent sound, flicked his gaze away and kicked the horse into a faster gait.

As they flew over the land, uneasiness surged through Siobhan. Was it fear she experienced or something more? She knew so little about him. Yet she instinctively felt at ease in his presence. But did her intuition tell her all she needed to know?

He slowed the horse, then came to a stop as they reached a line of rowan trees. Siobhan drew breath to ask him why, when he held up his hand, silencing her.

He tilted his head as though straining to hear something from the trees before them. A moment later he dismounted and drew his sword. He looked up at her. "Keep riding to the south. Not more than a league away you will come upon Crosswick Priory. At the iron gates, ring the bell and ask for Brother Kenneth, the abbot there. Tell him William Keith has sent you into his protection. He will understand."

She didn't move. "Why? What's wrong?" she whispered.

"We're being followed." His gaze moved back to the trees. "De la Roche and his men."

A flash of unnatural brown appeared among the trees. "What about you?"

He lifted his sword, poised for battle. "I stand a better chance of defeating them without you near to worry about."

"There are too many."

"The worst that can happen is that I die."

"I cannot leave you—"

"Go!" The knight slapped the rump of his horse, sending Siobhan speeding away.

She tried to pull back on the reins, tried to stop the animal's charge away from his master. The horse continued, regardless of her efforts. A cry of despair wrenched from her lips. She didn't want to leave him. She feared what de la Roche would do to William—a Templar—if he was captured.

William. Yesterday he was but a stranger. Today her life seemed intimately entwined with his.

She twisted in the saddle, looking back over her shoulder. Agony tore at her heart as a line of men in brown tunics advanced on William. She murmured a quick prayer for his safety as she abandoned the man who would risk his life for her, again.

The horse sped across the open territory as though it knew where it headed. Siobhan held tight to the saddle horn, giving up all hope of steering the beast. It seemed like forever before a stone building appeared in the distance, then grew ever closer.

At the iron gates of the monastery, the horse lurched to a stop. "Good boy, Phantom," Siobhan breathed, grateful the ride had come to an end. She moved to dismount, then paused as she realized how far away the ground suddenly seemed.

She used one arm to steady herself and she clutched her father's scroll with the other, then twisted onto her stomach and slid down the horse's side.

When her feet hit the ground, she raced to the gate and reached for the bell. A peal of sound cut through the air. She was about to pull the rope once more when a robed man appeared. His face was cast in shadow by a dark hood. He paused behind the closed gates. "What may I do for you?" he asked in a low, gravelly voice, as though he were not used to talking.

Had she interrupted this man's vow of silence? "I'm sorry to intrude, but I was sent here by William Keith."

"Brother William?" The man slid his hood back, exposing his face. His skin was tan, as though he spent much of his days in the sun. It wasn't his skin but his eyes that made her stiffen. Black eyes—the color of obsidian—probed hers with an intensity that frightened her.

Her heart raced. "He needs help."

The man stepped forward and opened the gate.

"Where is he?" the monk asked when he spotted William's horse.

"I don't know," Siobhan answered. "We were attacked. He forced me to flee." She searched inside the gates. "Is there anyone here who we can send to help him?"

"Aye." His voice held a grim note. "But we would never reach him in time."

"Should we not try?" She felt as if someone had kicked her in the stomach and knocked the breath out of her.

His brow arched. "You care about William?"

"Of course, I care." She balled her fists at her sides. "He's in trouble." She paused before adding, "Because of me. I will not let him die."

The man's gaze narrowed. "Brother William is the best fighter I've ever known. I'd be more worried about the others, if I were you." The man stepped back and waved her inside the gates. When she entered the small courtyard, he closed and locked the gates behind her. "I'll send Brother Amos for William's horse."

"You'll send no one to aid him?" Siobhan pleaded.

He turned his dark gaze on her once more. "Brother William has the grace of God on his side."

Siobhan flinched. "He's a monk?"

The abbot nodded. "A warrior monk."

She frowned, not understanding. "Is he a man of war or a man of peace?"

"Sometimes it takes war to ensure peace." Brother Kenneth waved her inside the monastery, then led Siobhan to a chamber down the corridor. At the door, he paused for her to precede him. "I shall send one of the brothers up with a meal shortly." He handed her the lantern. "This should make you more comfortable."

Siobhan offered her thanks and accepted the light. As she entered the small chamber, she wondered if anything would make her comfortable ever again. Too anxious to sit on the small chair in the corner, she paced the windowless room. The air in the chamber was cool, but the lantern cast ample illumination around the small monk's cell, making the wood flooring and stark stone walls appear warm.

This was a room meant for silent contemplation. A place to listen to one's inner voice. It was that inner voice that troubled Siobhan now. William needed her. He would die without help. And yet what could she do? She could not fight. She didn't know anyone she could call upon for assistance.

Because she'd let her father's life become more important than her own. She had always wanted a life filled with excitement, exploring new places and experiencing exotic things. But she'd set her own desires aside to support her father while he finished yet one more bit of research, wrote his ciphers in one more document.

She paused in her pacing and dropped her gaze to the scroll in her hands. Supporting him was her duty as a daughter. Wasn't it?

In the hush of the room, a slow prickle of understanding came over her. Was there a reason she could not be a good daughter and still get something out of this life for herself? Be something more than what she'd allowed herself to be over the course of her nineteen years?

Siobhan moved to the simple cot in the corner and sat down. She set the leather casing containing the scroll on the woolen blanket beside her. Something had to change, because she hated the feeling of absolute powerlessness that swelled inside her now.

Last night she'd lain awake worrying about de la Roche finding them. And as if that hadn't terrified her enough, a growing anxiety had taken root inside her that she might never understand the importance of what her father had entrusted her with. Siobhan looked at the scroll but didn't touch it.

She'd always believed that things in her life had happened for a reason. It was how she'd explained her mother's untimely death. It was how she'd justified the time she spent in isolation with her father. It was that thought that comforted her now. Her father's abduction and William's appearance in her life were not just random acts, but parts of a bigger whole.

The hush of the room pressed in upon her. But that larger purpose did not include sitting back and watching others. Siobhan stood. It was time for her to take charge of her life. She scooped up the scroll's leather case and slid it beneath the ropes and the thin heather ticking that made up her bed before heading for the door.

She clenched her fists, remembering yesterday when she had defended herself against William with a hefty branch. Perhaps that skill would help her save him now. With a purposeful stride, she moved down the corridor, back toward the door.

She was no great warrior. She was inadequate to the task ahead. But she would never abandon those who needed her help. William would not suffer alone.

Chapter Six

With Siobhan en route to the monastery, William concentrated on the battle ahead. He gripped his sword firmly in his hands and prepared for the onslaught. Four men attacked without so much as a shout of challenge.

William stayed upright as his sword sank home in the bowels of one warrior, then in the chest of another. Both dropped to the ground, replaced by two more. A horse and rider bore down on him, the morning light at the rider's back. The horse might not kill him instantly, but it most certainly could cripple him long enough for the other warriors nearby to do the deed.

Dodging the beast, William threw himself aside, rolled and came up with his sword at the ready. De la Roche roared at his foiled attempt. "I'll have your head, Templar. One way or another," he goaded.

He brought his horse around for another charge as William continued to defend himself against the half-dozen foot soldiers who advanced upon him. An arrow shot at close range pierced his mail, but William did not register pain. He twisted to the left and drove his weapon into the back of one man, then took the arm off another.

William jerked the arrow from his shoulder and tossed it aside. He grasped one of the men's fallen swords in his left hand, now fully armed against the enemy.

More men. More swords. More arrows. More horses.

How many of them could there be? Too many, his brain registered, as his body started to falter. Judging by the red seeping through his chain mail, they'd wounded him several times. He still didn't feel the pain, but he knew his body wouldn't hold up long.

His arms grew heavy. He braced for more, found depths of strength deep inside and continued to fight.

De la Roche came at him again, his horse's eyes bulging, nostrils flaring. William advanced on the horse as he had during other battles, mounted on his own steed. He stumbled, but he kept pushing himself forward.

Frightened by the flash of steel a hairsbreadth from its eyes, the horse reared, sending de la Roche to the ground.

William mustered all his strength and charged, forcing the men back, forcing de la Roche back. But that one burst of energy cost him. He stumbled again and hit the ground with one knee. His borrowed sword fell to the ground. His arm went numb. His chest heaved. His own sword wobbled in his grip. He held tight. Losing his sword meant losing his life.

De la Roche grinned. "You've fought well, but now it's time to die."

Suddenly a volley of arrows pierced the doublet of the Frenchman, and cries of anguish filled the air.

William staggered to his feet and stumbled away from the next volley. Hoofbeats sounded behind him. Friend or foe? He braced himself for more. Holding his weapon high, he turned to see a horse and rider bearing down upon him.

William's chest tightened at the sight of Simon heading toward him. And then he saw the others and went weak with hope and excitement. The air's cold dampness suddenly seeped into his bones, and pain sizzled along his nerves, but he barely let the sensations register. All he could think about was maybe, sweet Mary, maybe there was hope to survive.

Simon rode straight for him. "Take my arm, you fool."

William reached out and felt himself being hoisted into the saddle behind his Templar brother.

Arrows continued to rain down on de la Roche's men as Simon guided the horse away. "Where's your horse?" Simon asked with a hint of irritation.

"I sent Phantom away with the girl. She's at the monastery." William gasped as pain rushed over him, no longer willing to stay buried inside. Battle was like that. It had a way of disguising the pain until the danger was gone. Then, when one's body relaxed and felt safe once more, pain flowed over one's being with bitter intensity.

"Hold tight," Simon said as he kicked the horse into a gallop.

"How did . . . you know . . . I needed help?" William forced out the words between waves of agony.

"We still have friends in this land. Friends who would lay down their lives to preserve our cause." They crested a hill. At the top stood several men on horseback, each bearing a longbow and quiver. Crofters, and men he knew as former Templars. His brethren.

William could only nod at the men as he and Simon rode by. *We have friends who will help us.* The thought comforted him as he clung to the saddle, trying to keep the pain at bay.

They remained silent during the rest of the journey. At the monastery, Simon dismounted. William slid from the horse's back. He hit the ground, then stumbled as pain seared him.

Simon frowned. "Just how bad are your injuries?"

"I've been through worse."

Simon's gaze lingered on the red that covered his tunic.

"I know you have." Simon gripped William's arm and placed it over his own shoulders, disregarding the look William sent his way. "I'm amazed you can even stand."

William didn't comment. He allowed Simon to support him as they approached the gates. Simon pulled the rope attached to the bell.

Before the peal of the bell had fully formed, the gates flew aside and two robed men rushed forward, grasping William by the arms, bearing his weight.

"Tempting death again, are you, Guardian?" the Reaper asked as he hauled William inside the gates of the monastery, addressing him by his Brotherhood name.

Resolved to help William in whatever way she could, Siobhan left the tiny monk's cell and stepped into the corridor, only to come face-to-face with three men. Two faded from her view as she concentrated on the man between them.

William.

"You survived," she breathed.

"I can walk on my own." William stiffened and pulled away from the others. He staggered a half step forward before the men beside him once again draped his arms over their shoulders. William reluctantly relaxed against them.

"This way," said one of the men holding William upright. Siobhan flattened against the stone wall as they walked past her and to a small room down a long hallway from her own.

Siobhan followed, pausing at the door to see Brother Kenneth pull back the covers of a serviceable cot against the wall. The others laid William's large body down upon the ticking.

"He's badly hurt," one of the new men stated. "Is there anyone here who can attend him?"

"The apothecary is a day's ride away, and Brother John is visiting his dying father in Aberdeen. There's no one," Brother Kenneth said with a frown. "Looks like it's up to us."

Siobhan stepped into the chamber. She took a deep breath before she spoke with a calm that belied the maelstrom of fear and doubt that raced through her. "I can help."

Four pairs of eyes turned to her.

"Spare yourself, Siobhan. These men have seen the wounds of battle before." Pain reflected in the depths of William's sherry-colored eyes.

"Brother William, don't argue with the woman. If she can heal you, let her," said Brother Bernard from next to William's side. He removed William's sword and sheath and his tunic, then unlaced the pieces of mail covering his torso and set them on the floor.

William scowled.

Siobhan ignored him and strode to the cot. "Yes, you are fearsome," she said with a wry smile. "But you can't intimidate me." She knelt beside William. From the amount of blood she could see through the links of his mail, she marveled he survived.

Simon removed William's hauberk. Gathering her nerve to continue, Siobhan turned to Brother Kenneth. Thank goodness her father had allowed her to read anything in his library and had possessed a multitude of books on the healing arts. "I'll need some ale to help dull the pain, as well as hot water, salve, a needle and thread, and strips of clean linen, if you have them."

"We do." He turned and left the room.

Siobhan turned back to William just as Simon removed the quilted aketon from William's chest. She gasped. A multitude of scars and wounds crisscrossed his skin, some fresh, with ragged red edges, some whitened with age.

"A warrior's life is harsh," he said, watching her closely. For what? Revulsion? Fear?

She straightened her shoulders. He would see no weakness in her. "You need not apologize. We all have scars, William. Some of us wear them on the outside, others on the inside."

He raised an eyebrow. "And your scars? Are they inside or out?"

"We aren't discussing my scars. Yours are the only ones of interest at this moment."

William's eyes pinned her in place. She had a sudden terrifying feeling that he could see inside her, see the very scars she talked about.

He reached for her hand. His fingers curled around hers, held fast. "Siobhan," he said softly. "It's not weakness to be afraid. Someone else can treat my wounds."

She ran her tongue along her lower lip and swallowed hard, then slowly lifted her chin. "Nay, I can do this. Please, let me help you."

He nodded and released her hand.

Mustering all her inner resources, she searched his torso for the deepest cuts.

Brother Kenneth returned a moment later with a mug of ale. He and Simon assisted William to sit up and helped him drink. The tangy scent of the strong spirit lingered in the chamber.

While they helped William lie back down, Siobhan tore the cloth Brother Kenneth had brought into tourniquets. Some of the strips she folded, and when the men moved back from William's body, she set the folded linen atop the worst of his wounds before she tied strips of fabric around his arm, his upper chest, his shoulder. With a sigh, she sat back. That would help forestall the worst of the bleeding while she sewed each wound.

Brother Bernard patted Siobhan's shoulder. "We will

leave William in your care, my dear. Brother Patrick will be just outside the door should you need anything. Brother Simon, might I have a word?"

Brother Simon hesitated. "I think I should stay—"

"I'll be fine," William reassured his friend, his voice steady and calm as the effects of the ale set in.

Simon's gaze lingered on Siobhan for a moment before he turned and left the room. A shiver coursed through her. Did the man not trust her with his friend? She pushed the thought away, forcing herself to focus on the task at hand. Siobhan picked up the needle, wishing she had spent more time at her embroidery frame. The needle took only a moment to thread. She ran the metal through the hot flame before she set to work sewing the worst of his wounds.

The room suddenly seemed too warm, the air too thick, as she tugged from one side of his rent flesh to the other. Bent so close to him, she could perceive the tightening of his muscles, the increased rhythm of his breathing. As she sewed his shoulder, she turned toward him, realizing how close his face was. How close his lips were.

He looked at her intently through dark lashes, as if to read her thoughts by studying her features. She drew a sharp breath, suddenly aware that she was breathing too fast, as though she'd been running. It wasn't fear that moved through her now, but something else.

Siobhan sat back, forcing her attention on the wound on his chest. Her stitches were even and steady. Silence stretched between them, broken only by the gentle duet of their breathing.

She stared at him, and her breath caught. In that moment she saw past the blood and grime still covering his face to the true handsomeness there. Golden hair framed his face, a face that held no brutality and menace, but determination.

It was the kind of face a woman couldn't help but stare at in awe and with desire. Before she could think about what she did, she brushed a lock of hair from his eyes. Her hand strayed to the strong, straight line of his cheekbone and down to the cleft of his chin. "I'm so sorry to bring you pain," she whispered.

A faint smile came to his lips and a curious light filled his eyes. He brought his hand up to cup her cheek. "I hardly felt a thing." He let her go with a slight caress along her jawline.

Siobhan curled her fingers against the light flutter that took flight in her stomach. To be the focus of such a look was not something she was used to. She returned his smile with a nervous one of her own. "That's stretching the truth, even for a monk."

The light faded from his eyes. "Monks are not without sin. We have failings, just as everyone else. Besides, I am a lay monk."

"What is that?"

"A monk who gives more of his time to manual labor, or in the case of the Templars, to battle. We spend our lives in the service of the Lord."

"I see." She hesitated, still a bit disconcerted by the rapid change in his mood. "If I offended you a moment ago, I am sorry."

"I need out of this bed," he said changing the subject. Slowly, he sat up. Siobhan moved to assist him, but he waved her away. He reached for his quilted aketon, then pulled his hand back at the sight of his own blood.

"Might I help?" Siobhan asked.

"The robe," he said, a bit breathless, pointing to the brown homespun monk's cassock hanging from a hook on the wall. Attempting to sit so soon was taking its toll.

Siobhan brought the robe to him.

With a grunt, he settled the fabric over his head and

blocked his broad, well-muscled chest from her sight. "Where is the scroll?" he asked with a frown.

"Safely hidden. I assumed that in the monastery it would be less of a risk to leave it unguarded."

His eyes hardened. "Assume no such thing." His voice grew tight. "Trust no one with that scroll. No one."

Siobhan took two steps back, toward the door. Her breath caught as his features chilled. He was tired, she reminded herself. Wounded. If he sounded a bit harsh, it was to be expected.

Yet now that he was tended to, she wanted to check on the scroll. She had hidden it well, hadn't she? She twisted for the door and raced down the hall, startling Brother Patrick, who sat outside the doorway. She entered the tiny chamber she'd been taken to previously and dived for the bed. Only when her hands grasped the leather casing did she release her pent-up breath.

She sank onto the heather ticking. A shudder went through her. She'd always known the scroll was important. Why hadn't she pushed her father for answers long ago about what it revealed?

She shook her head, clearing away her regrets. Such emotions served no purpose. She didn't have her father to help her understand. But she had the scroll.

And William. The thought brought a flutter to her chest. She frowned and gripped the casing all the harder. This was not the time to worry about such strange reactions. Siobhan straightened. She would have to focus more diligently.

She had done harder things in her life than resist the temptation of Sir William Keith. She pursed her lips. Hadn't she? How many years had she lived in absolute isolation with her father? That had been far more difficult than resisting the temptation of a chaste knight.

With a sigh of frustration, she forced her attention back to the scroll. The man was a monk, for Heaven's sake.

William left his sickroom and gingerly made his way to the chapel. A need to pray that he had not felt in a long while grew inside, fueling his unsteady steps. He pushed open the heavy wood door and entered the sanctuary. Empty. He was grateful to have the sacred place to himself.

He bent clumsily to his knee, crossed himself, then stood and proceeded to the altar, where he knelt once more. He drew a deep breath, letting the silence of the chamber sink into him. He willed the peace he usually felt in this room to sink inside him. It did not.

Perhaps nothing could help him. Or perhaps the new feelings he'd had since meeting Siobhan were tearing him away from the path he had once followed.

William closed his eyes and bowed his head, again willing that peace to find him as it had four years ago, when he'd taken his vows. At the time he knew he was making the right choice—to dedicate himself to the Templars, to God.

Upon his return from Teba, filled with pain, sorrow, remorse, he'd come back to the chapel desperate for understanding. He'd been spared in that horrible battle. To this day he wondered why. Why had God protected him when he'd allowed so many others to die? His life was no more important than those of the others. Probably less.

He had no blood relatives, at least no one who cared whether he lived or died. He had only his Templar brothers. All the others had mothers, fathers, siblings who'd mourned their loss when William had returned their bodies for burial. That fact had made the pain of his failure to keep his brothers safe that much worse. Not one soul would have missed him, yet he'd survived.

For what purpose?

He opened his eyes and sought out the crucifix that hung suspended above the altar. "Why?" he whispered. "And why tempt me now with desires I know are at odds with the vows I've given you? My vows are all I have left to cling to. My service to you is all I have left."

He let his words die away into silence, and he prayed once again for that peace to fill him. The only thoughts that filled his mind were of Siobhan, the woman who needed his protection.

A calm came over him. Was that why he'd been saved? Had he been spared—not just from the battle at Teba, but from his uncle's slaughter as well—for some greater purpose?

William paused, let the thought circle inside him. No great awareness came over him, no dawning moment. He frowned. Why did holy guidance have to be so obscure? At this moment he would prefer booming voices or raining fire—even a burning bush.

With a sigh, he staggered to his feet. He'd have to trust that God would show him the way.

After a final prayer for insight, William turned and left the chapel. He found himself drifting down the corridor of the monk's dormitory to the room where light spilled from the doorway. Brother Kenneth had given Siobhan William's old chamber. Leaning against the stone wall for support, he stood in the doorway.

Siobhan sat atop the bed, an oil lamp burning brightly at her side. Deep in thought, she stared down at her father's scroll. Emotion stirred inside him at the sight of the scroll and—if he was honest with himself—the woman who held it.

Lost to her thoughts, she hadn't noticed him. He

studied her, curious about the woman who had so easily changed her father's dreams. Her father had abandoned everything he'd worked so hard to achieve once he'd learned his daughter was headed for the orphan home. Was there something special about this particular girl?

William pressed his lips together. Was she different from other women? The lamplight turned her red hair a burnished gold as it cascaded over her shoulders. Something inside him stirred to life. He tamped the emotion down with an acknowledgment that her pale skin, red-gold hair and delicate frame gave her an ethereal presence.

And regardless of her slight stature, she had challenged him with the swing of a branch. The corner of his mouth rose in a half smile. Perhaps she was a bit unusual, he'd give her that, but unusual enough to change the course of one's life purpose? He doubted it.

The room itself brought back dark memories of his past. As a young boy, he'd once had a warm and loving home with his mother and father at Stonehyve Castle. Then his uncle Alasdair had murdered his parents in their bed. William had only escaped with the help of his aging nurse, who'd smuggled him out of the keep and into the courtyard and had hidden him in a pile of hay.

Too terrified to fight his uncle's warriors, he'd stayed huddled inside the dank and musty hay as the sounds of battle raged around him. Men and women of his clan had lain dead, warriors undone by deceit, women who had tried to defend their homes, their families, slain by another bearing the same clan name. When William had climbed free of his prison of hay, even his nurse lay dead for trying to keep him safe.

William shivered, remembering the metallic scent of blood, the spatters of flesh, of bone, of sweat that had covered the ground. He had crept out of hiding, almost praying for a blade to strike him down so that he could join his clansmen in the afterlife instead of slinking away to carry on without them.

On unsteady legs, he had stumbled to the gate and slipped into the night. Every breath had set his lungs afire as his world collapsed in upon itself. He would die apart from his people.

He didn't know how far he'd walked or how many days had passed when he collapsed at the edge of a tree grove. He'd lain there, praying for death to claim him, when Brother Kenneth had come along and taken him back to the monastery.

"I'm here with you," the man he'd named the Reaper had said. "You'll not be alone in this, I promise, on my honor as a Scot, and as a Templar."

The Reaper had nursed him back to life and filled his spirit with hope. At the monastery he'd learned writing, reading, mathematics and how to fight with a sword. The monks had become his family. But they could never replace everything he'd lost.

William had accompanied Brother Kenneth on the sacred mission to the Holy Land. Then it had been William's turn to be the rescuer, pulling the half-dead Reaper from the battlefield and helping him get home safely.

William forced his thoughts back to the present, back to the woman who studied her father's scroll. Determination shone in her finely sculpted face. Compassion pulsed through him. She knew what it was like to lose everything, just as he had.

He cleared his throat, signaling his presence.

Startled, Siobhan looked up.

"What are you searching for?" he asked, stepping into the room.

"Trying to make some sense of all this," she said with a touch of frustration.

William gingerly sat down beside her on the bed.

"Are you well enough to walk about?" she asked with a slight frown.

"A few cuts can't keep us from our goal."

"Cuts?" Her eyes widened. "Our goal?"

"Nothing has changed." He reached over, his fingers lingering atop her soft skin. Their eyes met and held. There was something in her eyes that hadn't been there before. It sent an icy shiver through him. He might say nothing had changed, but something subtle had shifted between them. "We will find the Holy Lance before de la Roche. Your father will be rescued. Fear not."

"I believe you," she whispered, her gaze never leaving his.

The reflection of the lamplight shimmered in her eyes. The warmth of the light and the beauty of her face mixed to extraordinary effect. William drew a breath and released it slowly, feeling every one of the new wounds in his flesh.

"Look at this." She settled the open scroll in his hands. "Do you recognize this symbol?" She pointed to a small sketch at the far-left-hand corner of the papyrus.

He turned his attention to the symbol. "It's the head of the Spear."

She nodded. "And this? Do you know what this is?" She pointed to a drawing of two craggy peaks rising above three others.

"The Cairngorm Mountains," he replied. "The highest peaks in Britain. Stark, bleak, and dangerous territory."

"The kind of place that might naturally protect a treasure of this significance?" she asked.

"Only one way to find out." He stood.

She blinked. "Right now? Shouldn't we let your body heal some before we—"

He put a finger to her lips, then drew her by the hands to a standing position. This close he could smell a hint of heather coming from her hair. He swallowed and took a small step back. "We are going to see Brother Kenneth. He understands the Templar coding system, and if we are lucky, he'll be able to tell us all that we'll need to know before we set off for parts unknown."

He turned back to the cot and lifted the finely woven tartan that served as a covering. Grasping the fabric between his hands, he ripped off a long piece. He took the scroll from her, returned it to its protective casing, then concealed it within the folds of the wool. "'Tis best to keep the scroll hidden. Besides you and me, only Simon and Brother Kenneth should know it exists."

Siobhan nibbled nervously at her lower lip. "You think the treasure is there, in the Cairngorms?"

He grinned. "Let's find out."

She gave him a bemused smile. "You're excited about this?"

"For the first time in a long while I feel . . . alive and ready for something new."

Her smile broadened. "Is that what I'm feeling in the pit of my stomach?"

Her face was alight with laughter, and he found himself caught and held by the sight. He wanted to reach out and touch her cheek, to share that joy, to immerse himself in it.

To do so would be playing with fire. He needed to keep his distance, to stay objective. His life had one purpose now, and that had nothing to do with personal fulfillment. He couldn't take the loss of one more person he cared about. He'd had more than enough loss in his life already. Anything more would devour him whole.

He wouldn't dwell on that. He couldn't. He clenched his fist and turned away without touching her face. "Come. Brother Kenneth will be in the refectory about now. He'll have the answers we need."

Chapter Seven

At the door of the refectory, Siobhan paused, forcing William to do the same. "What if Brother Kenneth cannot decipher the code?" Siobhan asked, suddenly filled with doubts.

William's face was pale, but determination shone in his eyes. "Let the man attempt to read the symbols before you start worrying about the future." He opened the door, then stood back for her to enter.

Siobhan frowned into the semidarkness. He was right. She need not borrow trouble. They already had enough with de la Roche and his troops at their heels.

With a nod, she stepped into the chamber. The savory scents of roasted mutton and onions filled her senses. A bright, cheerful fire illuminated the room, revealing several long tables with benches neatly tucked beneath them. Clean, fresh rushes covered the floor. At the far end of the chamber, Brother Kenneth sat with another man dressed in a monk's robes. The two were bent over a sheaf of papers. At their approach, both men straightened. Brother Kenneth shuffled the papers to the side, then pressed them into the younger monk's hands. With a quick bow to Kenneth and to Simon, who was on the opposite side of the room, the monk excused himself and brushed past them without a word in his haste for the door.

William tensed beside her as he watched the man

leave. Brother Kenneth's voice boomed. "Good evening, milady." The older monk turned to William with a frown. "Are you well enough to be walking about?"

"I'm quite recovered." After another swift glance at the door, William guided Siobhan to sit beside Brother Kenneth.

At his touch, her stomach tensed. She found a place on the bench and clutched the tartan-covered scroll in her lap in an effort to settle whatever suddenly ailed her. William sat across the table from her.

Simon came to join them. "You look improved," he said, seating himself next to Siobhan.

"Brother Kenneth, we need your help," William said.

The old monk studied the three of them, his face unreadable. "If it takes three of you to ask me, then it must be serious."

"Deadly serious." William cast a glance about the room, as though ensuring that only the four of them remained. He nodded to Siobhan. She placed the tartan cloth upon the wooden table, then unwrapped the leather casing. An unnatural stillness fell between them as she removed the scroll and spread it upon the table.

Brother Kenneth sat back, his gaze moving between the scroll and William. "What are you all involved in?" He shook his head. "This is Brother John's handwriting, his code. . . ."

His words trailed off as his gaze came to rest on Siobhan. He searched her face, his expression dark. "You are his daughter."

A chill chased up her arms at the mention of her father as Brother John. "I am."

He drew a sharp breath. "De la Roche is after the scroll. That's why he attacked you, Brother William and Lady Siobhan."

William nodded. "De la Roche is after all the Templars

who hide in this country." William paused before continuing, his expression grave. "He also wants the Holy Lance."

Brother Kenneth paled. He leaned closer to the scroll. His mouth moved, but at first, no sound came forth. Finally he said, "The Spear of Destiny? Oh, Heaven help us all."

Siobhan didn't understand the man's words or his fear. "What's wrong?"

Brother Kenneth shook his head. "This is no ordinary spear that de la Roche wants. The Spear descends from the lineage of Adam, forged from a curious metal that came down from the heavens in a flash of bright light. The heavenly metal gives the Spear unique powers that can be used for either good or evil."

"Did my father ever use the Spear?" she asked cautiously.

The old monk patted the back of her hand where it rested beside the scroll. "Be assured, milady, your father's role with the Spear was only as its protector."

A wave of relief washed over her. She still could hardly believe her isolated, introverted father was connected with this band of warrior monks. Had she truly been that blind to the things happening around her? Or had her father just been exceptionally clever at concealing his activities?

Siobhan turned to Brother Kenneth, studying his features. A sense of familiarity came over her. "Did you come to our house to meet with my father in the past?"

The old monk returned her gaze with a soft smile. "When you were a young girl, aye. But it has been many years, and you are much changed from that time. 'Tis why I didn't recognize you at first glance."

Siobhan straightened and stared at the scroll. At one corner, there was a drawing of an older man draped in robes with a crown of leaves circling his head, holding a long spear toward the sky. Her father had drawn all these sketches for a purpose, and he had entrusted them to her. She pointed to the string of letters below the drawing. "What does this say?"

Brother Kenneth leaned toward the scroll. He tapped his finger against the line of letters. "Your father's usual code was something along the lines of every second letter, then the seventh, every third letter, then the seventh, every fourth letter, then the seventh, over and over again. Let us see what happens when we use that method."

Slowly he read, 'Whosoever possesses this Holy Lance and understands the powers it serves, holds in his hands the destiny of the world for good or evil.'

"My father would have wanted the Lance to be used for good," Siobhan said.

"Agreed," Simon and William said at the same time.

Siobhan shifted her gaze to the center of the scroll, which looked like a map. "Did my father leave directions for us to find the Holy Lance?"

Brother Kenneth frowned as he studied the text. "'The mother cradles the Spear of Humanity.'"

"And over here." Siobhan indicated the light text that appeared more like the ripples in a river than actual words.

The old monk startled. "How did you see that, milady?"

She shrugged. "All of a sudden it just stood out."

The monk narrowed his gaze and pulled the single tallow candle on the table closer to the scroll. After a slight pause, he read, "'Only with faith and might can one leap the divide to part a mother's tears.'"

Siobhan frowned. "What does it all mean?"

"A riddle," William said.

Simon's gaze darkened. "Why could it not have read, 'Go here and you'll find the Spear'?"

William raised an eyebrow. "When has anything to do with the Templars ever been simple and straightforward?"

"Never," Simon replied, without a hint of humor.

"How do we decipher the meaning?"

William leaned back and grimaced, pained by his wounds. "We go to the Mother's Cradle and figure it out."

"Where is that?" Siobhan asked.

William's gaze narrowed thoughtfully. "There is a cave in the Cairngorms known as the Mother's Cradle. Seems like as good a place as any to start our search."

"What if we are wrong?"

"Then we will know it when we find nothing there," William said without expression.

"My father—"

"De la Roche will not kill him," William interrupted. "He needs your father to find the Spear."

The thought did little to comfort her.

"We'll leave at first light." William stood, grimacing as he did.

Siobhan stood as well, noting the lines of tension around William's mouth and eyes. When had she become so familiar with the expressions on his face? "Are you well enough to travel?"

"We must get to the Spear before de la Roche does. So, aye, I am well enough. Besides, I've no wish to see the monks here endangered by de la Roche." William reached down and curled the scroll up. He placed it in its case, then handed it back to Siobhan. "We leave in the morning."

Simon stayed seated along with the older monk. "You two find your beds. We will make certain you have all the provisions you need by morning."

William nodded. He offered Siobhan his arm. "Come, milady." He guided her out the door and down the long hallway.

Siobhan glanced at the man beside her. "Do you really think we have a chance of finding the treasure in the Cairngorms?"

"We'll find it."

"How can you be so sure?"

"Because I have to find it."

"To save my father."

He didn't answer.

She stopped walking and turned toward him. "Why are you helping me? The real reason."

His features hardened. He looked off in the distance, refusing to meet her gaze. "I've pledged to you my sword and my life until your father is safe."

The look on his face told her she would get no further explanation. She didn't understand why, but the realization hurt her. When she'd first accepted his help, she had done so because she'd had no other choice. She still had little choice but to accept what he offered.

But somehow she had hoped for more.

"I accept your sword, but I will never ask you to give your life for mine. The wounds you suffered today will be your last on my account."

She strode off alone to her monk's cell. Inside the room, she dropped down onto the simple cot, setting the scroll between herself and the wall, then stared at the ceiling.

A soft knock sounded on her door.

"Siobhan?" William called softly through the wooden barrier.

"Go away," she groaned, not wanting to continue any conversation with him whereby she would end up with even more doubts.

The door opened. William stepped inside. His gaze traveled from her tousled hair to the flowing linen of her plain, homespun gown to her half boots. Instead of irritation in his sherry-colored eyes, she saw a fleeting moment of heat. She was suddenly acutely aware of the confined space. How alone they were.

She sat up, smoothing her skirts down over her legs. "I'd like to be alone."

"You're not responsible for my injuries or my pain," he said in a soft voice. He came forward, then sat on the bed beside her. "That is no burden I wish you to carry."

She closed her eyes, trying to shut out not the pain of his injuries, but her own loss. It had been easy to forget about the fire and her father while she'd been worried about William. Now that he was safe, her pain returned tenfold. "So much has happened," she admitted, opening her eyes. His hand rested by her leg.

"Aye." As though sensing her gaze upon him, he laced his fingers through hers, his grip strong, warm, excruciatingly intimate.

"Why did they burn the house?" she asked. "They had already taken my father."

"I—don't know."

"They wanted me to know they could hurt me, too— take everything away from me unless they got what they wanted."

His hand tightened on hers. "No one can take away the things that are truly important, Siobhan."

He understood. She could see it in his expression, feel it in his touch. He knew what it was like to lose everything.

"Tomorrow we head for the Cairngorms. And we *will* find the Spear."

She swallowed, feeling fragile, vulnerable. "Everything is happening so fast."

"Change usually does." The pain they'd shared a moment ago shifted, took on a different tenor as his touch softened. He leisurely rubbed his thumb back and forth across her sensitive flesh. Her pulse accelerated.

She looked up at him, unable to pull her gaze away from those rich amber-colored eyes. She could feel her heart beat faster, her skin warming as the blood quickened in her veins. "It scares me."

He leaned closer. "I'll protect you."

She swallowed. Who would protect her from him?

His lips were mere inches from hers. She could see the pulse drumming in his temple and watched the feathery curve of his dark lashes as they came down to hide his eyes. She caught the faint scent of sandalwood.

She willed herself to breathe slowly, to think of something to say that would end this tension between them.

The warmth of his breath caressed her throat. She began to tremble. The man was a monk, a man of the cloth. What did all of that truly mean? The way he looked at her, touched her ... she could almost imagine he cared. But could he? Could he go beyond a look and a touch?

Could she?

Siobhan pulled her hand out of his grasp and brought her fingers to her cheeks to hide the flush she could feel burning there. "I'm safe enough here tonight," she breathed.

He stood, his lowered lids still veiling his eyes. "Aye, you are safe within these walls." When he lifted his gaze to hers, his eyes were cool. All evidence of what they'd shared had vanished.

How did he do it? He'd been as aroused as she only moments ago. She had seen the flare of his irises and noted the sudden shift in his breathing. Now he acted as cool as though he'd never touched her. She released a pent-up breath and was grateful for the distance between them. It gave her time to gather her composure. As her heartbeat almost returned to normal, she reached for the scroll.

"Will you sleep tonight?"

She shrugged. How could she sleep, knowing he slept

nearby? "I'm going to study the scroll for a while, see if anything looks familiar to me."

He nodded, turned, then closed the door behind him.

She hadn't lied. She was frightened. But suddenly she wasn't sure what scared her more, the thought of de la Roche finding them or of William's continued presence by her side. Siobhan stared at the door.

What had passed between them had only been a momentary madness, best forgotten by them both. The man was celibate. Nothing could ever come of her desires.

William had evidently succeeded in forgetting his momentary passion. She must, too.

Lucius Carr hid in the shadows of the hallway outside Lady Siobhan's chamber. He pressed himself to the wall, trying to disappear into the darkness, as Brother William left the chamber to go into his own across the hall.

As William closed his chamber door, Lucius released his breath. He hadn't been detected, but he'd heard everything he needed to know. The Spear had to be in the Cairngorms. Why else would they go to those desolate mountains?

Lucius's heart pounded in his chest, and his skin prickled with a cold sweat. Could he do it? Could he betray his Templar brother? Would his need for revenge justify such deceit?

An explosion of rage and loss consumed him as it had the moment he'd seen Peter's charred body. He closed his eyes and tried to control the shudders that wracked his body. He would never get that vision out of his mind— Peter strapped to the stake, flames at his feet.

Thinking about Peter was unbearable. His throat clamped tight. He missed his brother.

All his life he'd tried so hard to be what Peter had wanted him to be. His brother set high ideals for the two of them—that they would go away together and fight for the causes of justice and freedom. They'd become Templars together and had dedicated themselves to their new lives.

They had helped to keep English invaders from crossing the Scottish border. They'd helped keep order amongst the clans, all while they waited for that big moment when they could change the face of the world together. But they would never get that chance. Not together anyway. Peter's death had changed all that.

Lucius couldn't think about Peter without thinking about de la Roche, who had robbed them of their dreams. And for that, the man deserved whatever ill came his way.

No one could rob a man of his dreams and walk away unscathed. Nay, de la Roche had to pay for what he'd done to Peter.

Lucius opened his eyes. The shaking was easing now. Thoughts of revenge kept the pain and the guilt at bay. He had no choice but to proceed. No matter what that made him, no matter whom he hurt.

Peter's death demanded justice.

William could feel a familiar frustration welling up inside him. He moved restlessly around his small monk's chamber, from the door to the tiny casement window, and peered out into the garden beyond. His hands clenched the wood of the sill as he gazed out blindly. He had thought this would be easier. He had thought he could remain remote and untouched, to manipulate events to his liking, to further his own goals without being affected.

Yet the past two days he'd been with Siobhan had been harder than he would have imagined. The heat of her presence touched him in places he had thought had grown too cold for embers to glow anew. When he looked upon her he felt . . . moved, concerned, guilty?

He had no reason to feel guilty. He might not have been completely open with her about why he needed the Spear, but he would do everything he'd promised. He would help her find her father. He would fight de la Roche's men. He would make certain she and her father were safe before he . . . left them, taking the Spear with him.

His grip tightened on the windowsill as he remembered the feel of Siobhan's hand in his. Something about her touch moved him, excited him. He could feel himself hardening at the thought.

He pushed away from the window, strode across the tiny monk's cell and jerked open the door. Stewing in his chamber was no help at all. He had to keep himself busy, find something to occupy his mind and think only about what he would do once he found the Spear.

Chapter Eight

Siobhan stepped from the monastery into the gated courtyard that separated her from the rest of Scotland. Early morning light cast the world around her in hues of pink and gold. A soft breeze brushed her cheeks, her arms. She shivered. Today she would leave the safety of the monastery with William, and the next phase of their adventure would begin.

An odd mixture of fear and excitement swelled inside her. She gazed out at the open land before her and straightened her back, facing her future.

There was nothing for her anywhere but out there. The Cairngorms would be the start of her new life. Despite her resolve, she shivered again.

A blanket of warmth enveloped her.

"This should keep you warm," the rich tones of William's voice sounded from behind her. He smoothed the thick, luxurious animal pelt across her shoulders. The cloak fell to her calves, cocooning her in welcome heat.

"My thanks." She turned and met his gaze. Cool composure tightened his features, calm and in control. Disappointment joined her other emotions. No hint of whatever it was that had passed between them last night seemed to remain with him this morn.

Why should it? To him, their adventure was all about duty. His duty to the Templars. His duty to keep her safe. She had to remember that. "Are you well enough to travel?" she asked, needing to redirect her thoughts.

"I'm quite recovered."

She didn't believe him, but did not argue the point.

"Do you have the scroll?" he asked.

She'd used a small piece of the tartan he'd given her to sew a hidden pocket inside her gown. "Yes, it's concealed here." She patted the slight bump, feeling the protective leather beneath her fingers.

At her acknowledgment, he guided her to the courtyard where he placed her on Phantom's back. The massive white beast remained steady as William mounted behind her.

"We're only taking one horse?"

"Phantom is strong enough to carry us both," he said, stroking the animal's thick neck. "Besides, another horse would be unpredictable." William spurred the horse toward the gates where Brother Kenneth stood waiting.

The old monk's expression softened when he saw them. "I'm saddened by your departure. William's been away too long, and, my dear, it's been a pleasure to see what a fine woman you've become."

Siobhan's cheeks heated. "It was kind of you to offer us shelter," she said in earnest.

A smile lit the old monk's face and caused laugh lines to fan out around his eyes. "You may always find shelter here. Remember that." He reached up and took Siobhan's hand in his own larger one. She experienced an overwhelming sense of well-being. All her earlier fear melted away. "I offer you my blessing as you both go forward toward your destiny." He released her hand and opened the iron gates.

"Guard yourselves well," William warned as they started through the threshold. "De la Roche is capable of anything."

Brother Kenneth nodded. "Simon is here. He's all the advantage we need against such a foe. And I still know how to wield a sword with the best of you. God be with you both," Brother Kenneth said before closing the heavy gate behind them.

The cool breeze stirred again. Siobhan turned her face into it and could feel the tingle of misty droplets against her cheeks.

William's arm tightened around her waist. "It seems we are in for some weather."

"A little rain never hurt anyone," Siobhan replied.

He chuckled and pulled her back against the solid wall of his chest. She caught the scent of sandalwood and musk—earthy, male—a scent that she would always associate with him. "We'll be riding in the open this morning and most of the afternoon, so keep alert to anything suspicious."

Siobhan nodded and willed herself to concentrate on the scenery before her and not on the entirely unavailable male who held her close. She focused her awareness on the terrain they crossed.

They traveled in silence for some time until chilling winds swept in from the north, bringing with them a rolling mass of black clouds that snuffed out the rosy glow of the sun along the eastern horizon. Droplets began to fall, first in a light sprinkling that washed the dust from the air and brought with it the sweet scent of rain. Then, without warning, a torrential downpour marched across the open land.

"We'll have to find shelter before we are soaked." William kicked Phantom into a gallop. The ground sped past. Siobhan's grip tightened on the horse's mane as she adjusted to the new rhythm.

The ends of her hair escaped her tight plait to whip behind her, until the rain plastered the heavy mass about her shoulders. A smile came to her lips. She'd experienced rainstorms before, but never outdoors with no shelter in sight. Siobhan tipped her head up to the sky. Large raindrops pelted her face and ran down her neck. Laughter bubbled up in her throat. "Oh my heavens!" She found herself laughing.

At an answering laugh from behind her, she twisted around. William's eyes glowed with the same exhilaration. The blood pounded in her veins. Her senses heightened. The weight of her wet cloak pressed her garments against her flesh. The rhythm of the horse moved through her in time with her breathing, the very beat of her heart.

The world seemed to stop as William stared down at her. She was suddenly aware of the warmth of his body as it pressed against hers, his gaze intent on her lips.

If he were to lean forward, their lips would touch. . . .

With an effort, she tore her gaze from his and turned around. She swallowed to ease the tightness in her throat. It didn't help. She'd wanted him to kiss her.

A chaste monk. What was wrong with her? Did she not respect his vows? What of her own chastity? Was she ready to toss that aside all for the feel of William's lips upon hers?

Siobhan forced back a groan and closed her eyes. Once again she turned her face up to the rain, hoping it would wash away the lust cascading through her. What was it about this man that turned her senses inside out?

She drew a deep breath and released it slowly. What was she going to do if every time he looked at her she felt these overwhelming sensations? What possessed her to act without reserve? She never had before. Or was that the heart of the matter? She had little if any experience in such things. She'd been raised by a father who had never remarried. When she was young, her nurse had never taught her about the happenings between a man and a woman. And the nurse had died before Siobhan had come into her womanhood.

Siobhan released a soft sigh. She wondered what her mother would advise. Should she do what she always did—hide from her feelings, close herself off? Or should she embrace her emotions, whether they were returned or not? Were the emotions that threw her off balance even real, or were they a result of the desperate situation she and William found themselves in?

Behind her, William sat perfectly still. She could feel the tension in his body radiate into her own. Siobhan held herself taut, trying not to touch any part of his body, as they raced through the storm.

They needed shelter.

He needed distance from the woman in his arms. Her complete joy in the downpour they found themselves in had taken him by surprise. Most of the women he'd known while at the Scottish court would never have taken such delight in the discomfort the rain usually brought.

Instead of shying away from the rain, Siobhan had embraced it. Her face had brightened and her musical laughter filled the air. Desire for her tightened every muscle in his body. The slashing rain continued to pelt them as William guided his horse toward the trees. He sucked in a deep breath. His body burned with needful heat. But it was a heat he could never sate.

There could never be anything between them. He had taken vows of piety, poverty, obedience and chastity. His future was with the Templar Brotherhood. His life belonged in the service of God. Yet even as the thought formed, his heart protested. The Church had granted permission for her father to leave the Order to pursue a secular life.

A different life. What would it be like to have a different

life? To have someone who cared about him . . . for him?
To have a home he could return to each night? To have a
woman who would bear his children?

A family. Love. William tightened his hands on the
reins. He had never let himself think about such things
before. Warring left little time for fantasy.

But it was fantasy that filled his senses now. If he
leaned forward ever so slightly, he could catch the scent
of heather in her hair. His groin jerked in response.
He'd been with women while at the Bruce's court, before
he'd taken his vows. He'd experienced passion, pleasure . . .
but nothing like the temptation Siobhan held for him.
What would it be like to indulge in her sweetness, experience her passion? Just once?

He set his jaw. Love, or even affection, had no place in
a warrior's life. Too many things could steal that love
away. Then he'd be alone once more, having failed yet
again to protect those he loved.

Nay. He was better off without such things.

The pelting rain slowed to a steady shower as they
came to the forest surrounding the Cairngorms. Phantom gratefully dashed beneath the boughs of the rowans,
heading deeper into the forest. Under the cover of the
trees, the light shifted from gray to silver, and the rain
slowed to a drizzle.

"We need to find somewhere protected from the rain
and yet still defensible should de la Roche surprise us,"
William said, forcing his thoughts away from his body's
cravings.

"We got lucky today, didn't we?"

He frowned. "What do you mean?"

"That de la Roche and his men were nowhere in
sight."

"Luck." He paused, feeling more in control of himself
again. "I'd like to believe in such a thing, but I've been a

warrior too long. We must stay alert and prepare for anything." He stopped the horse when they came to a rocky area in the side of the mountain. They continued up a rutted path for some time until they reached a gaping hole in the hillside.

William stopped and slid from Phantom's back. "Stay here. I'm going to take a look." He disappeared inside the cave.

He returned a moment later. "Empty." He reached for her waist and swung her down from the horse's back. "Our new home, yet another cave, for the night."

"I'm starting to think you like sleeping in caves." She smiled up at him.

"Better than in the open during a Scottish rain."

She stepped inside the cave, out of the rain. "It's dry. That's a blessing in itself."

William guided Phantom inside the cave. He unfastened the saddlebag, then leaned it against the wall of the cave. It took only moments to find and light a tallow candle. He placed it into the lantern he pulled from his bag.

The golden glow illuminated the front part of the cave, revealing a ceiling that rose some thirty feet above their heads. The interior didn't feel cool or drafty. Compared to the storm outside, it felt almost cozy in their dry little space. He held the lantern up to illuminate the large boulders at the back of the cave, sending eerie shadows to creep up the walls.

"Take off your cloak and set it against the boulders to dry. It will do you no good to sit about in wet clothes." He set the lamp in the center of the cave and removed his own cloak.

He watched as she unfastened her cloak, slipped it from her shoulders, then plucked the scroll from its protected pocket with a smile. "Safe and dry."

Her motions brought his attention to the front of her

gown, where her cloak had failed to protect her from the driving rain. The wet fabric was molded to her breasts, her hips, her thighs, revealing a curvy feminine shape.

William forced himself to look away. She had no idea of the erotic picture she presented as she settled on the ground near the lantern and withdrew the scroll.

"The scroll is dry as well." She set the papyrus on the dry earth, her finger outlining the drawing of what they'd decided were the Cairngorms. "Where do we go from here?"

William squatted beside her and peered down at the map. With his index finger he tapped the V between the two tallest mountain peaks. "First we must make our way here."

He traced a complex series of dashes and markings near the middle of the peak on the left. "This is where we'll find the Mother's Cradle. If it has been used as a storehouse by the Templars, no doubt it will be well concealed. Finding it would be next to impossible without this map."

A shadow of worry darkened her brow. Siobhan leaned closer to examine the drawing. "What if we can't find it?"

"We will." He set his jaw. Nothing would get in the way of his safeguarding the treasure and keeping the Spear out of de la Roche's hands.

Chapter Nine

Hidden deep in the bowels of a Scottish castle, de la Roche stared down at his prisoner. Sir John Fraser kept his face remote. Showing any kind of fear would give his captor an advantage. At least de la Roche hadn't found Siobhan, or the man wouldn't have returned here to torture him again. Sir John took slight comfort in that knowledge.

"Where is the Spear?" De la Roche twisted the thumbscrews until a soft crunching sound filled the dark underground chamber where Sir John lay strapped to a table by the ankles, waist, shoulders and wrists. Despite his determination to remain unaffected by the torture, a gasp escaped his throat. A sharp stab of intense pain tore through his thumb, before a blessed numbness took hold.

The Frenchman's assistant, Claude Lemar, smiled down at Sir John in the torchlight. The man was dressed in a mud-colored monk's robe. His face was long and lean, with pockmarks dotting his cheeks. His lips were pouty like those of a sullen boy as his light eyes gazed at his subject. "Shall we move on to your other thumb?"

"Kill me now." Sir John struggled to keep the fear from his voice. He had to stay in control. He didn't fear dying, but the torture was wearing him down. "I'll never tell you anything."

De la Roche frowned. "Every moment of every day

will be filled with slow agony until I get what I want." He reached for the torch and held it close to Sir John's shackled bare feet. The stench of burning flesh filled the small chamber.

Sir John clenched his jaw, fighting the red-hot pain as it seared his heels. Sweat broke out on his forehead. He tried to control his breathing, but only succeeded in sucking in short, sharp breaths as agony rocked him.

"My men were forced to retreat." De la Roche's dark eyes glittered with a strange illumination cast upon his face by the torch. "We lost Keith and your daughter."

Sir John sucked in a relieved breath at the news he already suspected.

De la Roche's eyes narrowed. He ran the torch up to Sir John's toes. "We'll find them again. My spies are scouring the countryside now." His voice was seductively gentle. "When we find them, they will suffer most horribly. Lemar will see to that."

Beside him, Lemar grinned.

Fear shot through Sir John. What would they do to his daughter if they caught her? He struggled against his bonds. "Leave Siobhan alone." He hadn't realized he'd spoken aloud until he saw both men smile.

"Tell me what I want to know and I might spare her." De la Roche's voice grew gentler, almost tender. The torch against Sir John's skin vanished. Stinging pain rippled across his feet as the cool air from the chamber replaced the heat.

Sir John closed his eyes, willing the pain away. He'd known this day was coming, that someone someday would come after him and the Templar treasure. He should have sent Siobhan away to a nunnery years ago. When he'd approached her about the idea, she'd insisted on staying with him. And he'd relented because of his love for his only child. In hindsight, he should have pressed her to go, no matter how much he would have missed her. He should have insisted—for her own protection.

All he could do for his daughter now was pray. Pray that she could keep herself safe. Pray that she wouldn't try to follow him.

No one could save him from this madman. De la Roche might be ruthless, but he was no match for Sir John's own resolve. No amount of torture could pry the secrets of the treasure from him. And no force under Heaven would ever make him reveal that his daughter had the ability to find that treasure if she remembered the clues he'd given her all through her life. If the time ever came, she would remember. The treasure would find a new guardian. All would be well.

Sir John opened his eyes.

De la Roche gazed down at him, his pale eyes filled with anger. "Perhaps you need more persuasion." All the gentleness vanished. "Lemar, see if the rack doesn't loosen his tongue."

Morning light pierced the opening of the cave, breaking Siobhan's fitful slumber. Regretfully, she opened her eyes. It seemed only moments ago that she'd finally fallen asleep. The dawning rays stretched across the rocky floor with increasing brightness. Siobhan sat up and looked beside her. William was gone.

Coming fully awake, she stood and wrapped her cloak about her shoulders, then headed outside. The rain had stopped. Blue sky stretched overhead, dotted with fluffy white clouds.

Siobhan drew in a breath of the rain-soaked earth as she looked out upon the Cairngorms. The twittering of birds sounded all about her as she took in nature's beauty. Beneath her feet the rich, red soil sported leathery green ferns and lacy, small-leafed shrubs.

Tall evergreens pushed toward the sky, and hearty rowan trees filled the space in between. The leaves of a tree off to her left rustled. Her heart raced. Instinctively, she darted back into the cave.

"Siobhan?" William's voice called out to her.

She stepped forward once more to see him striding toward her. In one hand he clutched a silver fish by the jaw. His other arm curled around several tree branches. He raised the fish in salute. "To break our fast." He laid the fish on a rock near the cave's opening and dropped the wood to the ground. "It won't be long before we eat, once I set a fire."

"Can we risk a fire?" she asked, kneeling beside the salmon. Her stomach gurgled at the thought of a hot meal.

"I hiked to a vantage point earlier. There are no signs of de la Roche anywhere. It appears that we lost him."

"For now," she said in a low tone.

William must have heard her, because he stopped in the process of arranging the wood into a stack. "You're right. He will come for us again, so prepare yourself."

She pulled her cloak tighter about her shoulders. How did one prepare for a battle between life and death? She shuddered.

He stood, then strode into the cave, returning a moment later with his saddlebag. From the bag he withdrew a flint stone and a bit of wool. It only took a moment for him to catch the dry kindling with a spark. He bent toward the tiny flickering flame and with his breath coaxed it to life. Some minutes later, once the coals had turned red, he set the salmon on top. A rich, fragrant aroma filled the air while they waited for the fish to cook.

Siobhan moved away from the fire and slowly moved about their little campsite, exploring the spiky ferns and underbrush that she'd never seen up close. But even the beauty that surrounded her couldn't disguise the reality of their situation. They were in desperate trouble, thanks to de la Roche and his men.

"Can I ask you a question?" She returned to the roaring fire and knelt beside William.

"Anything."

"We would have a better chance at survival if there were two of us fighting de la Roche's men, wouldn't we?"

He turned toward her. "Two of us?"

"Teach me to use a sword."

His brow knitted. "Women shouldn't have to fight in the battles of men."

"From what I've seen so far, it doesn't appear de la Roche is concerned about my gender." She moved to the fire. "If I'm to die, I'd rather do it trying to defend myself than unprepared and filled with fear."

William scoffed. "With any luck, neither of us will be dying today. But your point is taken." He nodded. "I'll teach you later this evening, when we stop for the night." He reached into his saddlebag and withdrew two wooden bowls. Drawing a dagger from his boot, he deftly cut a wedge of the fish and placed it in the bowl. He handed the steaming pink meat to her. "As soon as we've eaten, we will begin our climb."

As he cooked their meal, she noticed once again the sword at his side. "Does your sword have a name?" she asked, breaking the silence that had settled between them.

"Nay. Should it?" he asked with a frown.

"Some warriors name their swords. My father told me tales of Beowulf and his sword Naegling, then there was Arthur's Excalibur and Lancelot's Arondight, as well as Constantine's Joyeuse." She shrugged. "I just wondered if you had named yours, being that it came from the Bruce."

He shook his head. "I don't believe any Templars

named their swords. Perhaps we should have," he said with a slight smile.

They finished their meal quickly and wrapped the remains of the fish in a spare length of cloth from his bag for their evening meal. William put out the fire, careful to bury the embers with dirt before dousing them with water.

In short order, he had packed his saddlebag and they were ready to proceed. As they left the cave behind, she noticed Phantom was nowhere in sight. "Where's your horse?"

"I sent him back to the monastery earlier this morning. The climb would be far too dangerous for him. Besides, his hoofprints retreating from the mountains will also serve us well if anyone tries to track us."

Siobhan followed William's example as he picked his way up the ledge of rocks that formed their cave and onto a narrow trail no doubt formed by the deer that frequented the forest.

They spent the better part of the morning in silence as Siobhan concentrated on the breathtaking scenery around her and tried not to be distracted by the man in front of her. As they reached a particularly jagged patch of rocks, William turned to her and offered his hand. After they successfully reached the top of the ridge, he suggested they take a short break. He sat atop one of the large boulders and motioned for her to sit beside him.

Seated, she tipped her face up and let the slight wind dry the pearls of moisture from her forehead and neck.

"Here." He offered her a bladder of water.

She was grateful for the cool liquid that slid across her tongue. After a few more minutes of rest, she asked, "How did the Templar treasure end up here in Scotland?"

He offered her a slight smile. "That is a long and sordid tale."

She looked down at the distance they had covered so far today, then glanced up at the height they had yet to go. A lot of the mountain still remained before them. "It appears we have plenty of time."

He laughed. "Too true." His expression grew more serious. "Are you ready to continue? If you are, I'll tell you what I can as we climb."

"Aye."

He stood and offered her a hand, pulling her easily to her feet. "How much do you know about the Templars?" he asked as they began to hike up the mountainside once more. This time they forged their own trail.

"I know what most people know. How they began as protectors of pilgrims to the Holy Land," she said, falling into an easy stride beside him. "I've heard tales about their bravery in the Crusades and of their chivalry. And I remember my father talking about King Philip IV of France needing financing for his wars. When he asked the Templars for money, they refused him."

"That's where the trouble started for the Templars and when the treasure left France," William explained. "When King Philip was refused, he then tried to get the pope to excommunicate the Templars, because we answer only to the Church."

"The Templars were very powerful," Siobhan admitted as she kept pace with William.

"Aye, they were. But the French king had the power to murder Pope Boniface VIII and his successor, Benedict XI, when neither would do as the king wanted. The next pope, Clement V, was brought into power with the help of the king."

William turned to face her as they continued to hike. "Two days before the Templars were arrested in France under orders from the new pope, eighteen ships left the port of La Rochelle in the middle of the night, sailing for Scotland with the treasure and as many men as possible."

The features of his face softened. "It was your father who met those ships and instructed the men aboard where to take the treasure."

A chill chased across Siobhan's neck. "That was when my father was still a Templar." She frowned. "He must have been very important to be in charge of hiding something so precious."

"Aye, he was." William's voice was gentle.

"Why was he not arrested with all the other Templars?" Siobhan asked.

"Because Scotland was at war with England in October of 1307, and in the chaos, the papal bulls dissolving the Templar Order were never proclaimed in Scotland. So the Order was never dissolved. As a result, Scotland became a sanctuary for Templars. Robert the Bruce, being excommunicated himself, welcomed skilled warriors with open arms. Others, such as Archbishop Lamberton of Saint Andrews, gave the Knights Templar his protection. Archbishop Lamberton always believed in the Templar cause. He risked much to support us, and he has been a good friend to me."

"If the Templars are protected here by the Crown and the Church, then why are you so secretive? Cannot the monks at the monastery admit who they are and live in peace?"

"With agents of the French Crown like de la Roche combing the country for them, there is no hope of that."

Siobhan nodded her understanding. "Then why risk your life by staying in the Order?"

He offered her a pained smile. "Because it was divine intervention that led me to the Templar Order. They took me in when I needed them. My brothers have been constant companions as we fought to protect the faithful, then later our king and country."

His explanation was simple, yet she realized there must be so much more that he hadn't said. She longed to question him further about the things he'd passed over. Why did the Order take him in? Where was his family? How had he earned the right to protect the king himself?

"Those men back at the monastery, they are your family?"

"Aye."

She reached over and patted his arm, wanting to console him, but not knowing exactly what to say.

William stared down at his arm where her hand touched him. He cleared his throat and averted his gaze. "Come, let us pick up the pace a bit. We have much ground to cover before dusk.

His stride lengthened, and Siobhan had to push herself to match it. At this rate, she wouldn't be able to talk, as her heart thumped in her chest at the extra effort. Is that what he wanted? To stop her pointed questions?

She frowned. They would have to rest eventually. Then she would ask more about his life. For she still was not certain why he was helping her. What would he gain, besides having the treasure for himself?

She might have lived for years in isolation with her father, but she was wise in some things. William would have to earn her trust before she led him to the Templar treasure.

Chapter Ten

"How do we know we're heading in the right direction?" Siobhan asked between halting breaths as she kept pace with William.

It was the first time she had spoken in quite a while. For a moment William felt guilty that he'd pushed her so hard. "Let's rest." He stopped and turned to face her.

She nodded breathlessly as she wiped the sweat from her forehead and neck with the back of her hand. She scanned the area, then headed toward a fallen log a few paces away. "I'm going to sit for a—"

The sound of wood snapping echoed through the forest. Her words fell away. She screamed as she plunged from sight.

William's heart jumped to his throat. "Siobhan?" He whipped the saddlebag from his back and lunged to where she had vanished. A huge hole gaped in the ground. "Siobhan?" he called into the dark pit.

Nothing.

A thrill of fear pulsed through him. His gaze tripped over the snapped branches that jutted out from around the pit. He'd seen similar traps before, built by his fellow Templars. She had wondered how they'd know if they were on the right track. This trap proved they were. If she wasn't dead or injured, he would delight in telling her so.

William found little comfort in the thought as he sped

back to his saddlebag and grabbed a long rope. Quickly, he tied one end to a nearby tree and tested to make certain the line was secure. Climbing would be easier without his mail, but he didn't want to waste valuable time taking it off. He stepped to the edge of the pit and leapt into nothingness.

He hit the side of the pit. Pain radiated through his injured body. He bit back a groan. Siobhan needed him. Rock. A good sign. It would be harder with a rock bottom to line the pit with sharpened stakes, as was usual in this type of trap. "Siobhan?"

William's voice echoed all around him. His feet slid down the rock walls of the pit and the rope slid through his fingers in his haste. His palms burned. He quickened his pace. He had to reach her.

He strained to see in the darkness. A dark mass appeared off to his right. It had to be Siobhan. A heartbeat later, his feet touched the ground. Smooth, even ground devoid of stakes. He released his pent-up breath and raced to her side.

She lay facedown, unmoving. Carefully, he reached around her and placed his hand above her lips. Warm air brushed the back of his hand. She breathed.

"Siobhan?" No answer. Slowly, he rolled her onto her back. He had to get her out of there to assess what damage had been done.

Praying he didn't do her any further harm, he lifted her in his arms and draped her slight body over his shoulder. He grasped the rope and climbed, bracing his feet against the wall, and began to half walk, half pull the two of them toward the light.

They would survive this trap. His fingers were bleeding, he noticed vaguely as he left blotches of red on the rope. His arms trembled. His shoulders ached. Then the pain was gone, numb with strain and weariness.

He could see daylight ahead.

Sweat stung his eyes, but he remained riveted on the light ahead. He put one hand over the other until finally he reached the edge of the pit and pulled them both over the top.

He carefully set Siobhan on the ground, then collapsed beside her, panting. He stayed there a moment before pulling himself up and crouching beside her. He rolled her over. A bright red gash marred the side of her forehead. Blood flowed from the wound across her delicate temple and onto her cheek.

William reached beneath his mail, and with one mighty jerk ripped a section of linen from the shirt he wore beneath his padding. He quickly folded the fabric and pressed it firmly against her wound. "Siobhan?" he called softly. "Please open your eyes."

She groaned. Her eyes fluttered. They snapped open and fixed on his face. Fear and confusion darkened her gaze.

"Do you remember what happened?" he asked. *Please let her be well.*

She studied his face. Her brow knitted, then cleared. "I fell," she said, her voice thready and weak.

"You've cut your head. Does anything else hurt? Your legs? Arms?"

She started to shake her head, then groaned. "My head feels like it's going to explode."

He bent over her. "Might I have your permission to check your limbs for further damage?"

"As you wish."

Carefully, he lifted each of her arms and worked her shoulders, elbows and wrists. Apart from a few scrapes, she appeared unharmed. Methodically, he searched her gown for rips or telltale splotches of blood. When he found none, he moved on to her legs.

He brushed the hem of her gown up her calves and brought his big hands down on her slender legs. His callused hand stroked her flesh, searching for injury, yet as he touched her his body awakened.

She gazed at him as if caught in a spell, her pulse fluttering wildly in the hollow of her throat.

Her skin was as velvet soft as it looked, and warm, so warm, despite her recent suffering. He could feel the hot pounding of her pulse against his fingertips. And it gave him a moment's satisfaction to know his touch affected her as well. When he'd finished examining one leg, he slipped his hands up the other.

A shudder trembled through her. Her gaze flew to his face. Wild color flooded her cheeks. His palm moved up her calf and onto her thigh, then back down again. "You appear to be unharmed."

"But not unaffected," she breathed.

He instantly released her.

"I'm sorry," she said.

He startled. "For what? Falling into a well-hidden pit?" He moved to a sitting position, then cradled her head in his lap, continuing to apply pressure to her wound. With his other hand, he reached up and gently stroked the hair from her forehead. "There is nothing to apologize for. In fact, you answered your own question about us being on the right track."

Her eyes widened in her pale, drawn face. "What do you mean?"

"That trap was set by the Templars. It proves we're exactly where we need to be."

Her hand drifted to the folds of her skirt. "The scroll appears to have survived my fall as well." She attempted to sit up. "We should continue."

He pressed her back into his lap. She looked as delicate as the most fragile of blossoms. Why could it not have been he who'd discovered the trap? He was used to the abuses of war, whereas she had no such experience. He would have to be far more careful to protect her from danger. He offered her a reassuring smile. "We'll make camp here for the night."

"In the open?"

She had suffered enough. "The sky is clear. There will be no rain tonight." He wouldn't move her until he was certain she was perfectly capable of continuing their journey. "I've spent many a night in the open with the stars as my blanket."

Her body relaxed back into his. "Thank you," she said, her eyes fluttering closed. "I admit I'm quite weary all of a sudden."

"Siobhan." His voice was sharp.

Her eyes flicked open.

"You must stay awake, at least for a time." Once again he brushed the hair from her brow and across her temple. So soft. So incredibly soft. "It's been my experience with soldiers who've had head wounds that if they fall asleep too quickly after the injury, they don't wake up. I need you to stay with me until we're certain you're well."

She smiled. "It'll take more than a pit to put me under, Sir Knight."

A pang of tenderness stirred within him. It did his heart good to hear her make light of the circumstances. He'd been in far too many situations of late that had gone desperately wrong. He gazed out at the forest surrounding them.

Off to his right a bush rustled. His muscles locked with tension as he stared at the place. He caught a glimpse of brown. A deer? Or had someone else besides de la Roche followed them up the mountain?

At Siobhan's soft gasp, his gaze returned to her face.

"Too much pressure," Siobhan said. Her hand came up to his, releasing the bandage he'd pressed a little too firmly against her skin. "I think this has stopped bleeding."

He allowed her to remove the compress. After noting that the bleeding had indeed stopped, his gaze shot back to the bush. All was silent now. He scanned the area. Had the motion truly been an animal of some sort? How would he keep them safe without moving Siobhan?

He spotted a wall of rock farther back from the pit. "Stay here." He shifted from beneath Siobhan, resting her head upon the forest floor while he stood, then gathered the saddlebag from where he'd dropped it. He moved between the pit and the wall and laid down his cloak before returning to her side and helping her up. "Come, rest here between the pit and the wall." The open pit and the solid wall would serve as protection. That left only his right and left to guard as the night approached.

He drew his dagger from his boot and extended the grip toward her. "I think you were right to ask me to teach you how to defend yourself."

She accepted the weapon. "You want to teach me now?"

"Nay, but I must leave you for a moment. I won't go far. I need to gather wood for a fire." His gaze dropped to the dagger in her hand. "This is just in case."

Before she could question him further, he turned and headed for the bush. He would not rest easy until he made certain the area was clear.

He crept through the dense foliage, searching the ground for footprints, anything that might reveal whether he'd seen man or beast. He halted as the proof he sought lay before him. Two boot prints were clearly discernable in the dirt.

Not an animal. A single male pursued them.

William's hand moved to the hilt of his sword. His gaze pierced the surrounding area that was bathed in the dappled light of the late afternoon sun. Nothing stirred. But he'd been warned. And once he'd been warned, no one got the best of William Keith.

Chapter Eleven

"Siobhan."

Siobhan snapped her eyes open to see William standing over her. "You must stay awake, at least for a short while."

She let the words run through her as he sat down on the fur cloak beside her. With an effort she opened her eyes and focused on the trees in the distance. The distinct leaves shifted, blurred as her eyelids grew heavy once more. She knew she should keep her eyes open, but suddenly they seemed so heavy.

"Siobhan," his voice crept into her thoughts. "You have to try." He scooted closer until his thigh rested against her own.

Silence hovered between them, but it wasn't a silence filled with tension. It felt companionable, soft, relaxed. Without thinking, she leaned her head on his shoulder. He leaned closer, providing more support. Gradually, Siobhan relaxed and became aware of the coolness that laced the late evening air, the sound of the birds twittering endlessly overhead, the scent of loamy soil beneath them that still held a slight dampness from the rain. The warmth of William's body enveloped hers. Heat radiated between them, prickling her flesh. She forced herself to think about something other than the feel of his leg and the firmness of his muscular thigh.

For the first time she wondered if it could be true . . . if the Templar treasure existed. "William?"

"Aye," he shifted his head to glance down into her face.

"Have you ever seen the treasure?"

He shook his head lightly. "But that doesn't mean it doesn't exist," he said, as though reading her thoughts. "It is said to contain legendary pieces of every culture, ancient to modern, along with many holy relics."

Siobhan frowned. "Why aren't others besides de la Roche after it?"

"Its location has always been a well-guarded secret. Many people no longer believe the stories."

Her father had been part of that secret. The thought still met with much disbelief. "If someone were eager enough to discover that secret, then nothing would stop them."

William shrugged, jostling her head slightly. "Perhaps that's why your father sought to keep the two of you hidden from the world for so long."

She brought her fingers to her throbbing temple. "It worked for a while, until de la Roche came along."

William offered her a soft smile. "Does your head still pain you?"

Siobhan nestled deeper against his shoulder, feeling more relaxed as darkness started to fall. "It's getting better."

"Then close your eyes and let sleep come. I'll stay awake and make certain you are safe."

His hand drifted to the hilt of his sword. He didn't draw the weapon this time, but left it sheathed. Siobhan took that as a sign that the danger to them was not as imminent as it had been last night. Perhaps if she closed her eyes for just a moment . . . A short reprieve was all she

needed, and then she would keep William company for
what remained of the night.

William sighed in his sleep and turned on his side, spoon-
ing against Siobhan's warm body. The delicate fragrance
of heather surrounded her, despite the overwhelming scent
of smoke that had permeated their skin and clothes.

He tightened his arms around her body and slid a leg
gently atop hers. He wanted to be nearer. He was protecting her, he told himself. Even with the two of them
fully clothed, he could feel the heat of her body as it
pressed against his chest. He nuzzled his cheek against
the silken strands of her hair.

A soft sound came from Siobhan. She rolled over, still
asleep, to press her body against his. Her breasts met his
chest each time he drew a breath. Each innocent brush
sent a shock of awareness through him.

She sighed. He froze, almost afraid she would awaken
and end the serenity of the moment. Instead, she nestled deeper into his embrace and released another contented sigh.

Her face was turned up to his, and their lips were no
more than a fingertip apart. Her calm, even breath teased
his face, his lips. He stared down at the long, thick eye-
lashes that fanned her pale cheeks. He had the sudden
urge to shift his body ever so slightly so that his lips would
come into contact with hers.

It took all his willpower to hold himself in check as
he remained still, afraid to move forward or back. He'd
never in his life experienced the tumultuous emotions
that churned inside his chest, his loins, his heart: exhilaration, fear, desire and guilt, all mixed with an overwhelming sense of rightness.

They had been together for three nights. It felt more

like a lifetime. Siobhan knew more about him than he'd let anyone but Simon and Kenneth know—his goals, his desires, what events had shaped him into the person he'd become. He found it easy to talk with her. In her presence, he felt no pressure to be anything other than who he was.

On impulse, he reached out and smoothed a lock of her red hair away from her cheek. She sighed. Her eyelids fluttered. William's hand froze and his heartbeat stuttered. What would happen right now if she opened her eyes and found him staring at her? Would that comfort between them vanish? He swallowed roughly. He didn't want to find out. He slammed his eyes shut and pretended to be asleep.

Siobhan awakened slowly, not quite ready to let go of the peacefulness that wrapped itself around her. After last night's sleeplessness, it felt wonderful to be so comfortable, warm and secure.

She stretched. Suddenly, she became aware of the leg atop hers. She opened her eyes and stared straight into William's sleeping face. She stilled, afraid to move or even breathe, lest she bring her lips into contact with his. The gentle whirring of his breath fanned her face. And after a moment, she found herself relaxing once again.

She studied the man before her. He looked so peaceful in his slumber. He'd been as exhausted as she when they'd been forced to stop here because of her fall. Yet now, after some sleep, William looked refreshed and ready to go forward.

Siobhan drew a soft breath and allowed the sensations of the moment to wash over her. William's hand was threaded in her hair and rested at the side of her face. His leg was thrown casually over her thigh—warm, masculine, possessive. Truth be told, she didn't object to the sensations at all. It brought her much contentment, as she'd always imagined a lover's embrace would feel.

She smiled, but that smile faded a moment later. How would William react if he awoke to discover the two of them entwined like this? Would he object? Would he feel a similar contentment? Or would he pull away, wondering how their intimate entanglement had come about?

She wasn't certain she could handle seeing the cool aloofness return to his eyes when she'd enjoyed this moment so much. Saving herself from another rejection, she slowly, deliberately, eased out of his embrace. She had almost succeeded in extricating his hand from her hair when his eyes popped open.

"Good morning, Siobhan," he said, his voice thick.

"Good morning," she replied. Her heart beat wildly in her chest. They stared at each other for a long moment.

"Ready to start the day?" he asked, shielding his gaze from her now.

"Yes," she replied breathlessly, despite her efforts to hide her feelings from him.

William scooted backward until his body no longer touched hers. The cool morning air rushed in to replace the heat that had wrapped itself around them. "I'll warm up the remaining fish." He sat up and shoved his feet into his boots, then thrust his sword into the scabbard at his side. "We can break our fast and be on our way."

He turned away.

Siobhan sat up, grateful that her head no longer pained her. She drew a long, deep breath of the fresh morning air. They were back to the status quo. Despite the riot of emotions that careened inside her and the desire she had seen ever so briefly in William's eyes, they would go on as though nothing had transpired.

She stood. If he wanted to pretend nothing had happened, then she could, too. She was made of sterner stuff than even she had ever imagined.

Chapter Twelve

William and Siobhan hiked up the mountain at a steady pace. Silence had fallen between them as they concentrated on their surroundings. Yet as they climbed, William kept asking himself what he was so afraid of.

Tension that hadn't been there while they'd slept hung heavy in the morning air. He'd hurried them out of camp after they'd finished their meal, telling Siobhan it was because he wanted to take full advantage of the daylight. He knew it was more than that.

He needed to keep busy. Clinging to a mountainside for balance and support meant there was little time to think about or give in to the desire to wrap his arms around her once more. Her softness beckoned like the light of a candle to a lost and lonely moth.

Was he lost and lonely? He was starting to think so.

They continued to hike through the day, until finally, as the late afternoon cast long shadows, William slowed his pace. He turned to Siobhan. "Let's stop here and rest. We need to decide whether to go on or start looking for a camp for the night."

Siobhan nodded and came forward to rest against a large boulder that sat off to the left near a copse of trees. She dabbed at her temples and neck with the back of her hand.

He reached inside his saddlebag for the bladder of water he kept there and offered it to her.

"My thanks," she said. She took a long drink.

"My apologies, Siobhan, for pushing you so hard today. But we cannot afford to stop until I know we're safe."

"What do you mean? I thought we'd left de la Roche far behind."

"We did, but last night I found tracks in the woods."

She frowned and handed the water back to him. "Why didn't you tell me?"

He took a drink before he answered. "I didn't want to worry you."

"We are partners in this, William." Her hand moved to the place in her gown where she'd hidden the scroll. "For better or worse. I deserve to know the dangers."

He nodded. "Agreed."

She hesitated a moment before she continued, as though trying to decide if she should press him on the matter. "Are we still being followed?"

"I don't know for certain. But it is only one man. If we stay alert, we'll be fine. But we must be cautious. A lot is at stake."

A flicker of worry brightened her eyes. "Perhaps we should keep going."

He returned the bladder to his saddlebag and set it on the ground at her feet. "We will, but just to be safe, why don't you rest here a moment. I'll be right back."

"Where are you going?"

"To see that we are not being followed."

Siobhan watched as William left her to double back to where they had just hiked. He'd said no one was following them. Had something happened to change his mind? For a moment she considered following him, then changed her mind. She was tired and would welcome a rest, no matter how short.

Despite her attempt to relax, the thought of unknown danger kept her on edge. Siobhan wandered to the edge of the trees and picked up a thick tree branch from the ground. She carried the makeshift weapon back to the boulder and set it at her feet next to William's saddlebag.

Now at least she could defend herself if the need should arise. Her thoughts settled as she leaned back, and the one thing she'd tried not to think about since leaving the monastery entered her mind. Her father. What was happening to him? William suggested that de la Roche wouldn't kill him until he had the Spear. But did that mean he might harm him, torture him as she'd heard other Templars had been tortured after their arrests in France? Siobhan shivered and rubbed her arms in an effort to settle the goose-flesh that pebbled her skin. Her father was strong. She had to believe he'd be well while she and William searched for the one thing that would truly save him. Only the Spear could set him free.

Still trying to find a way to settle her mind, Siobhan dusted off her skirt. Pieces of her hair had tugged free of her tight plait. She brushed her fingers along the edges only to find a leaf here and a twig there. No doubt she'd acquired the extra decorations in yesterday's fall. How had she missed ridding herself of them prior to now? She hurriedly picked out the debris and tossed it to the ground. Dust darkened her skirt and no doubt other parts of her person that she couldn't see. She brushed herself off as best she could.

Siobhan closed her eyes and tipped her face up to the late afternoon sun. The heat was a welcome sensation upon her cheeks. Despite her dire thoughts only moments ago, an unexpected bubble of laughter rose inside her. She let it form, expand, break free in a bright musical sound.

Before she'd met William she had rarely laughed. She

still did not understand why she felt so different today from other days gone by. Yesterday she'd fallen into a pit. Today she was covered with sweat. She'd dipped into reserves of strength and energy to keep up with William as they hiked up a mountain. She'd never felt more unattractive or more covered with grime. Truly it was nothing to laugh about. And yet, she'd never had more fun.

A light breeze picked up and tossed the loose ends of her plait against her cheeks. She opened her eyes. Since they'd left the burned shell of her house behind, she'd felt different, changed in some way. All her life she'd waited for the day when things would be different for her and her father, for a day when she'd be set free to explore the world around her. That day was now, and for the first time in her life she was no longer afraid of what lay ahead.

"Siobhan?"

She startled at William's voice. Running her fingers once more down the fabric of her dusty gown, she smiled up at him.

He smiled in return. "Whoever was tracking us is gone."

"He probably couldn't keep up with your pace."

His smile broadened. "It was necessary. We can slow down now that I know we are safe." He offered her his hand.

"We're not stopping here?"

He shook his head. "Until we find a suitable shelter, we must keep going." William's fingers curled around hers and squeezed gently. "Just a little farther."

At the warm, reassuring contact, a tingle moved through her. She forced her mind away from the sensation.

He released her hand and headed back up the mountainside. "You're a quiet one," William remarked.

"Seems you're of a similar nature. Or perhaps we've

both been alone so long that neither finds conversation a must."

He made a face. "Do you really believe that?"

She cast him a sideways glance. "Nay. It's more a case of being out of practice."

A smile came to his lips again. "Living in the monastery was quite the opposite. Conversations abound. The monks love nothing better than to discuss theology, politics, even what herbs are growing in the garden and how they should be used, at all hours outside the chapel."

"It sounds rather pleasant." She looked up at him quizzically. "Why did you leave the monastery?"

"Two reasons. Brother Kenneth encouraged me to go experience life outside its walls. And once he planted that seed, duty called." His smile faded. "As I matured and mastered the use of my sword, I had a difficult time ignoring the discussions about Scotland's abuses at the hands of the English." He shrugged. "One day Simon and I had heard our fill. We left the monastery that day, along with Brother Kenneth, fired by purpose, and headed to Edinburgh, where we met up with other men who shared our desire to liberate our country."

They came to a steep slope, forcing their conversation to end as William first navigated the incline, then turned to offer Siobhan his hand until they were back on even ground.

"That's when you became a warrior."

He nodded, matching his steps to hers. "Brother Kenneth remained a steady influence over us as he continued our training in Edinburgh. He remained dedicated to the Templars, while Simon and I—" His words broke off. "Simon and I were there to learn all about what life had to offer. We were so young and filled with ourselves." He sighed. "Fortunately for us, God granted us the skill to see us through as we followed the Bruce to northern

England for his invasion. We helped launch raids on Yorkshire and others. That's where our military skill and brazenness drew the Bruce's notice. We became part of his elite guard."

William's hand drifted to the hilt of his sword. "Ten of us accepted the call as the Scottish Templars, the Bruce's own warriors. For our devotion, the king gave us these swords, each bearing an emerald to remind us of our home-land."

"I thought I recognized the sword from a drawing my father made. There were ten of you. Where are all of you now?"

Instantly his expression shuttered. He didn't reply at once, and for a moment she thought he wouldn't answer. "Dead. Except Simon, myself and two others."

"I'm so sorry."

"It's the price a warrior pays."

William stopped midstride.

"What?"

"Listen," he said.

Siobhan strained to hear whatever had alerted him. A low, deep hiss came to her. "Wind?"

"I cannot be certain, but we should proceed cau-tiously." He drew his sword and moved ahead of her on the path.

The hissing came again. Louder, deeper. A shiver moved through her. She'd never heard the like before.

They set a steady yet cautious pace as they continued to climb. The ground beneath their feet became rocky and uneven, slowing their progress. Finally they came to a rock outcropping and the hiss suddenly became a roar.

William stopped.

Fine white mist danced in the air, wetting Siobhan's neck and face. "What is it?" she asked when they stopped.

"I recognize the sound now," he said as he reached for

Siobhan's arm. He helped her forward until they stood on the edge of a crevasse that plunged over two hundred feet down. To their left, water surged forth from a hole in the rock face, cascading in a long, glistening stream toward the jagged rocks below. "A waterfall."

Siobhan stared in awe at the pulsing display of water. She'd never seen anything like it before. "It's beautiful."

He frowned. "That may be true, but nature's beauty has cut us off with nowhere to go."

The edge of the mountain plummeted before them—a fissure in the earth's crust formed by time and God's divine hand.

"Could we hike around it?" Siobhan asked, trying to see what lay beyond the glittering, writhing water.

"It would take less time for us to find a way across the crevasse."

"A way across?" Siobhan gasped. "It must be twenty feet from side to side."

"We either find a way across, or turn around."

"I refuse to give up."

He grinned. "Then we go forward."

"How?"

His gaze shifted to the area around them. His grin became a smile. "We'll build a bridge." He tossed down his saddlebag, and from within, he withdrew a long length of rope. "Come, help me."

They spent the next forty minutes collecting hearty saplings that had fallen in the nearby woods. William dragged the four largest alongside the crevasse, and they began lashing the logs together with his rope.

When they had finished, their makeshift bridge stretched twenty-five feet long and a foot and a half wide. "How do we get it across the crevasse?" Siobhan asked.

"I have an idea. Pray it works." William tied a length of rope to one of the end logs. A moment later, he stood and walked the length of the bridge to the other side, stopping before a tall tree with one branch that jutted out over the open fissure. He tossed the rope up and over the tree limb, grasped the end that dangled down, then pulled. Slowly, one side of the wooden bridge rose into the air while the other side remained on the ground.

"Is there anything I can do to help?" Siobhan asked.

"Pray that the bridge lands where it is supposed to. We are only going to get one chance at this. If I miss . . ."

She didn't need him to finish his sentence for her to understand that if he missed, the bridge would tumble into the crevasse. "I have every faith."

He released the rope.

Siobhan held her breath. The bridge fell, leaned to the right slightly, then slammed into place against the opposite side of the fissure. "It worked."

They both hurried to the edge of the crevasse and, with a sense of relief, gazed at the wood bridge they had created.

"Who goes first?" Siobhan asked as the dust settled on the opposite side.

"You're lighter. You should go first."

Siobhan nodded, took a deep breath and slipped off the solid earth onto the wooden bridge.

The other side of the crevasse danced before her eyes as her dizziness from when she'd hit her head in the pit returned. Siobhan tensed, fighting the sensation. She fixed her gaze on the rocks at the opposite side. She had to keep her concentration and not give into weakness. She took a step, then another.

A third of the way there. She was dimly aware of William's encouraging words as she continued. One step, another. She looked down. Water writhed below her in an unending, serpentine chain.

Her stomach dropped. She swayed.

"Don't you dare fall." William's words broke through her panic. "Keep your eyes on the rocks ahead."

It wasn't his words that pushed her forward, but the intensity in his voice that steeled her resolve. She kept moving. She'd reached the two-thirds mark.

"You're almost there."

Her legs trembled as she pushed herself to continue. When she reached the other side, she sagged to the ground with relief. A glance to the other side of the crevasse told her that William had started across.

His progress was steady and even. He held his hands out at his sides, balancing himself as he came. Halfway across, an ominous crack sounded—the sound of breaking wood.

Panic screamed through Siobhan. The wood they had carefully bound together sagged, snapped. William surged forward, almost at a run now. The wood bent downward, threatening to slide into the crevasse on both sides.

"Hurry!" Siobhan surged to her feet. William dived for the sheer edge of the crevasse. The logs fell away. His big body thudded against the rock. His fingers dug at the ground. His breath came in ragged spurts.

"Give me your hands!" Siobhan grasped him and pulled back with all her might. Terror wormed icy tentacles through her body. She wouldn't lose him. She couldn't lose him.

A thunderous crash sounded as the bridge hit the rocks. Siobhan gritted her teeth and pulled all the harder.

Slowly, William inched forward. Silence surrounded them now, thick and oppressive. Beads of perspiration snaked down her temples. Fear clogged her throat.

"Nay!" Siobhan released her breath in a sharp, angry rush. They'd come too far to give up now. She pulled with all her strength. His body jerked forward. His shoulders cleared the edge of the rock. He used his feet to propel himself up over the ledge until they both collapsed upon the ground panting, trembling.

"I thought you—" Siobhan buried her face against his chest. Her teeth were chattering.

"Me, too." He pulled her close.

His chest was firm and strong, and she could feel his strength as she lay against him.

After a long moment, she pulled back. Breathless, she gazed into William's face. His lips touched hers, and shock trembled through her body. A feeble protest shivered free on a sigh, but she couldn't summon the wit or the will to make it convincing. Her senses centered on the feather-light pressure of his mouth, on the teasing, taunting appeal of his tongue as it sampled, tasted.

Her arms tightened around his shoulders. His lips slanted more forcefully against hers, and his tongue slid possessively into the heated depths of her mouth. Her stomach turned to molten heat that slipped downward on each silky, probing caress.

Her fingers spread across the woolen thickness of his tunic and inched higher and higher until her arms encircled his neck. She pressed eagerly into his embrace, thrilling in the feel of his arms as they enfolded her.

Her body melted against his. She wanted to move with him, to quench the tension that curled tauter, tighter in her belly.

He ended the kiss suddenly, breaking away with an abruptness that brought a cry of surprised disappointment from her lips.

His face was a shadow, but she sensed a shared feeling of surprise. As if he hadn't expected the rush of pleasure she could feel thundering through his chest.

"I shouldn't have done that." His words were light and casual, yet he held her away from his body as if he didn't trust any further contact.

Siobhan felt her cheeks flush. What had just happened? It was as if William had cast a spell over her, had enveloped her so that she couldn't think or move or even breathe.

Her lips still burned where he'd touched her. It had been a simple kiss, but that one touch threatened to turn her whole world upside down.

Chapter Thirteen

William struggled to breathe. *A taste of heaven.* That's what her kisses were. He forced himself to pull back, to sit up and put some distance between him and temptation. What would it be like to lose himself in her?

He clenched his jaw. He would never know.

Siobhan's cheeks flushed scarlet. "Forgive me," she whispered.

"There is nothing to forgive," he said as he scrambled to his feet. "I think it best if we both just forget this ever happened."

The color faded from her face. She stood, looking away from him. "Are we safe here from whoever is following us?"

He nodded. "They would have to cross the crevasse as we did, or hike around to cross above the waterfall. Even if he does manage, we'll have had a long head start."

"Then if you'll excuse me . . ." She strode past him.

"Where are you going?" he asked, stunned by the sudden shift in her mood.

"I'd like to spend some time alone." Siobhan stalked across the rocky ground, heading for the base of the waterfall.

He watched her go, the pain of rejection tightening in his chest. He dashed his fingers through his hair and turned away. It was idiotic to feel hurt. He didn't even know her, not really. And perhaps some time apart would help him keep perspective.

He had taken vows, and one of those was of celibacy. He had to keep that at the front of his mind every time she tempted him. . . .

Yet the more he tried to justify why he should not feel the pain of rejection, the more the sensation swamped him. He did know her, for she was very much like himself— independent, isolated and terrified of making herself vulnerable.

William moved to where he'd dropped his saddlebag. He hoisted it over his shoulder. While she had her time alone, he would hunt for their supper. If he stayed busy, he could keep from thinking of her . . . of how good her lips felt against his, of her soft skin. He'd known from the moment he saw her that there could be nothing between them, but something had drawn them together despite his attempts to stay neutral.

Despite it all, something had developed between them.

They had joined forces to escape de la Roche, successfully translated her father's cryptic notes, taken their meals side by side, argued the benefits and drawbacks of going after the Spear. They'd hiked through the hillsides of Scotland and made it through treacherous moments, helping each other. These past few days they had shared a joint purpose that had forged the tentative bonds of friendship.

Friends. The word had a precious quality to it. William turned to look once again in the direction Siobhan had gone. One didn't abandon one's friends. He had to go after her and apologize. For what? Kissing her?

He sighed. Nay, he had wanted to kiss her in that moment more than he wanted to draw breath. He wanted to kiss her still. But he couldn't bend to his own desires again. It would be unfair to them both, to their friendship.

Feeling more in control of himself and his thoughts, he hurried down the path toward the waterfall. Suddenly, fresh fish seemed a very tempting supper. His steps were light as he stepped across the thick moss that grew alongside the pool at the base of the waterfall. Lush, green foliage surrounded the embankment. Birds flitted overhead and settled in the boughs of the nearby trees, their song lending tranquility to the scene. Squirrels skittered from branch to branch in an endless search for food.

William paused. The sunbeams were bolder and broader here, exaggerating the brilliant greens of the leaves and ferns, silvering the surface of the water and glistening like pearls around Siobhan's naked torso.

His body hardened at the unexpected sight. He stood absolutely still. His gaze drifted to the shoreline, to where her cloak and gown lay along with a shift of fine white linen, two woolen socks and her half boots. He hitched a breath as his gaze moved back to the woman in the water. She'd twisted toward the mist the falls generated. Long strands of red hair curled down her back, dripping against skin that gleamed like freshly sculpted marble.

She reached up and combed her fingers through her hair to remove a bright shower of excess droplets onto the water's surface. She released a long, refreshed sigh that was part satisfaction, part ecstasy.

He must have made a sound low in his throat because she suddenly twisted toward him, her hands coming up to cover her exposed breasts an instant before she dipped below the water's surface.

For a moment they stared at each other without further sound or movement. Her eyes commanded most of his attention as she stared at him with a mixture of betrayal and wide-eyed innocence. "What are you doing here?"

He blinked. "I came to fish." His voice sounded raw to his own ears. "What are you doing?"

"I wanted to wash off the dust." The look in her eyes shifted to annoyance. "Please turn around," she commanded.

He pivoted and dropped his gaze to the moss beneath his feet. He heard soft splashes of water behind him, then the whisper of fabric as she dressed. All the heat they had just shared during their one kiss returned tenfold. The weight of his mail suddenly became stifling.

With urgency that had more to do with his thoughts of Siobhan than the heat of his body, William unfastened his cloak, then his scabbard, and tossed them to the ground. His tunic, mail hauberk and quilted aketon followed, until he stood on the shoreline in only his braies.

"What are you doing?" Siobhan gasped as she looked up to see William disrobing. As she fastened the last hook on her gown, he raced past her and dived into the misty water with barely a splash.

She waited breathlessly for him to reappear above the water's surface. Several heartbeats passed before he jutted upward, like a fish jumping for bugs. The sound of his laughter rippled across her as she watched him glide through the water.

He stopped by the shore, close to her feet. "Refreshing," he breathed, as he perched half in, half out of the water.

Her earlier anger had vanished along with the dust that had covered her body. "You, sir, have a very curious way of fishing," she said a bit more tartly than she intended.

He simply smiled at her. The blond hair at William's temples glistened with tiny beads of moisture. She watched as droplets fell on his broad shoulders. The slash on his shoulder had healed—she could no longer see the stitches. No doubt he had removed them himself. In another week the mark would be nothing but a thin white line cutting through his tanned flesh. With his tunic and chain mail removed, Siobhan saw the hard, sinuous muscles in his arms and across the breadth of his chest.

With another laugh, he pushed himself backward, sending ripples of water up against the shore as he crashed back into the pool. He swam to the base of the waterfall and ducked his head into the spray before returning once again to the nearby shore, where he reached up to an overhanging tree branch and snapped off a limb. He stripped the bark back and worked the end into a point with a small dagger he had withdrawn from the waist of his braies, before he headed back to the falls.

She tried to look away, but found she could not. He possessed deadly grace and the power of a lynx, and Siobhan was just as keenly aware of the danger as if she were sitting in the open, and his prey. He thrust the stick down, then jerked it back. A fat silver trout writhed at the end of the stick.

He moved to the rocks and, taking the fish in both his hands, looked into the trout's eyes. He said something she couldn't hear, then brought the fish's head down against a rock. The trout lay still.

A moment later he returned to the shore and set the fish gently down upon the moss. "I told you I meant to fish for our supper."

"So you did." She drew a sharp breath when she realized he meant to dress. She looked away as he pulled his aketon on over his wet skin. Nervously, she set to plaiting her hair. She needed something to distract her from the man who had stolen all her focus from the moment they had met.

"All clear," he announced a moment later. He was near enough that she could smell the sunshine and sweet water on his skin. She looked up to see beads of water glittering in his hair, dropping onto the dark fabric of his tunic and dampening it so that it clung to his broad shoulders in darker patches. Her dizziness returned, though not from the wound at her temple. She steadied herself with a slow, deep breath.

"Come, *ma chérie*." He offered her his hand. Siobhan felt the heat of his eyes appraising her. "From the water I saw the perfect spot for us to make camp tonight."

Ma chérie. The endearment echoed softly in her ears. She took two steps forward and accepted his outstretched hand. "We don't have to keep moving?"

"For tonight, we are safe in this little oasis." His fingers closed tightly around her smaller ones. He bent to retrieve his saddlebag, their cloaks and the fish, then led her along the water's edge to a glen covered in a thick blanket of moss. At the back of the clearing, a wall of rock stretched several feet overhead. The clearing was outlined by row after row of bracken. The area was perfect, warm and protected and surrounded by nature's beauty.

"It's beautiful," she breathed. "This setting reminds me of the stories my father told me about Avalon, King Arthur and his knights." A smile came to her lips. "Avalon would have been a paradise such as this."

"Your father told you many stories?"

"Oh, yes, all the time. About King Herod and Odysseus and Hippolyta, and so many others. I loved listening to his stories. They made me long for adventures . . . like the one we are having now."

A shadow of pain passed through his eyes, only to vanish a moment later. He released her fingers and handed her both of their cloaks. "Arrange these next to the rock wall while I gather wood for a fire."

He remained oddly silent as he set about making a fire. Had she said something to upset him? "William?"

"Please, Siobhan, let the matter rest."

Silence fell between them. It didn't take long before a fire blazed in their encampment. As the sun faded against the western horizon, the warmth of the flames kept them comfortable. Tendrils of smoke curled in the air. The savory scent of roasted fish filled the air, and the sound of the wood as it popped and crackled brought a sense of peacefulness.

Siobhan sat on her own cloak and pulled William's over the top of her. They would have to sleep side by side tonight to stay warm. The thought sent flutters through her stomach.

William stood by the fire, slicing thick, juicy portions of the trout he'd caught into two bowls. When he finished, he turned toward her and offered her a bowl, his expression once again clear. "What did you say to this fish before you—?"

"Killed it?" he finished her sentence for her and shrugged. "I thanked it for its life, and bid it to rest in peace."

That wasn't what she'd expected a warrior to say. "Is it easy for you to kill?"

He came to sit beside her on top of the cloaks. "Killing is never easy, whether man or beast." Something in his manner shifted, became more mournful. He gazed blindly at the flames. Despite the fact that she wore the bandage about her head, it was he who looked broken in that moment.

She reached for his hand, folding her fingers around his larger ones. To her surprise he didn't pull away. Instead, the tension left his body. He leaned against the stone at his back.

She longed to understand more about who William was, and why he'd been so sad moments before. "I am sorry for my outburst earlier," she said between bites of fish. "I don't truly want to be alone."

"We have that in common." He chewed thoughtfully.

She eyed him curiously. "Why are you alone? Where's your family?"

He set his bowl aside. "Dead a score of years and more." His brow creased, as though weighing how much to tell her. "They were murdered by my uncle on the night I fled Stonehyve Castle forever."

"Stonehyve? That's not far from here."

His jaw tightened. "I know."

"You were a lad when you left. Have you had contact with your uncle since?"

"Nay. He and his men were certain I died the night of my uncle's assault. I've never disproved that notion."

"Have you ever wondered what it would be like to go back? To challenge your uncle as an adult?"

"I have no wish to risk the lives of others to take back something I let go of long ago. Nothing will ever bring my parents back to me."

She knew that feeling all too well. "I used to pray for my mother's return, especially when things were difficult between my father and me." The pain of yet another parent lost tightened her chest. She forced herself to take a slow, even breath. Her father was still alive. He had to be. They would find him.

When she felt more in control of her emotions, she continued. "Eventually, I accepted that she was gone. When I was old enough, I started to take over the household duties. My father was always so cautious about our servants. He didn't trust easily. Now I can understand why."

"He had much treasure to protect—a young daughter and countless artifacts from all over the world."

Siobhan could not stop the smile that came to her lips. There was something infinitely pleasurable about being compared to the treasures of the world. "You are kind to say so."

"'Tis not kindness. Only truth." He released her hand and stood. "Treasure needs protecting." He smiled down at her. "Would you like to learn how to protect yourself with a sword?"

"Very much." She set her bowl aside.

He helped her to her feet, drew his sword and handed it to her.

She accepted the weapon. Instantly, the tip dipped toward the ground.

"You will never win a battle fighting your opponent's boots. Lift the weapon higher, toward the body's core."

Siobhan tightened her grip and brought the tip up toward William's waist. The weight of the weapon tugged at her arms, but she strained to do as he'd asked.

He frowned. "We'll need to find you a small sword or perhaps a rapier as soon as possible. Meanwhile . . ." He moved behind her, pulling her against his chest. His hands came out to wrap around hers where they rested on the hilt.

"Better?" he asked.

"Aye." Her voice hitched.

Moving her arms for her, he lifted the sword and then brought her arms down in a slow, controlled movement. "Feel the motion. Make the sword an extension of your arm. Extend your stroke all the way out to the tip of the blade. Let the sword do the work."

She swallowed at the feel of his hard body against the softness of her own.

"I'll move you through the basic motions. Guard. Slice. Thrust. Upward cut. Downward cut. Parry. Keep the balance of your weight on the balls of your feet."

She listened as he moved, took each movement into herself, feeling as though they were dancing, not fighting.

"That's it. Let your body flow." He leaned more intimately against her. Her heart beat harder. "Get in close.

Stay inside." Then he changed his motions, moving in tight irregular steps. "Confuse your opponent. Focus. Stay balanced."

Siobhan followed his every movement. The two of them flowed together as the sword came up, then down, blocking their imaginary opponent. Behind her, she could feel his breath against her ear—short, sharp bursts that changed with the intensity of their swordplay. His body brushed against hers, then retreated. She tried to concentrate on the sword in her hand.

The long, hard muscles of his body pressed against her back, and the heat of him enveloped her. She swayed back against him, overwhelmed by her own desire. This slow, torturous seduction meant nothing to him. If it did, how could he continue to stand, when her own legs felt as though they would dissolve beneath her?

She gazed at him over her shoulder. "No more. Please."

"Does your head pain you?" His movements ceased. "Forgive me. I lost myself."

"Aye." She lied. An aching emptiness swamped her as he moved away. She clenched her teeth, fighting her yearning to pull him back. *Lost.* She was the one who felt lost without him.

Chapter Fourteen

A primitive jolt of desire rocked William as he gazed down at Siobhan. *Sweet Mary*, he groaned silently. The blood pounded in his veins and quickened in his loins to a point he had never experienced before. He'd lost himself, all right. He'd lost himself body and soul in the feel of her body next to his.

Firelight flickered across her red hair and gilded the softness of her alabaster skin. When had the sun vanished from the sky? He hadn't noticed light or dark, nothing but the woman who stood not two paces from him.

He wanted to reach out to her, to shatter the tension between them and end this madness. Surely, once he tasted her, his senses would return to normal. Then they could move forward with their journey.

His thoughts stopped him. *You're a monk. And you have other responsibilities.* William clenched his jaw, fighting desire. He had dedicated himself to something other than the concerns of mortal men.

He felt *very* mortal at the moment, and vulnerable to the desires of men. Suddenly, the question he usually asked himself in times of great fear sprung forward in his mind. *What's the worst that can happen?*

William clung to the question like a lifeline. The worst might be that he'd want more than a sampling of what Siobhan had to offer. The worst might be that he'd be forced to recant his vows, to leave the Templars, to take up a secular life. Or worse yet, that God might turn his back on him.

Never had he been so tempted to turn away from his vows or from God than in this moment. He took a step closer, reminding himself that God would forgive his failings. He forgave all men their imperfections. William swallowed roughly as he stepped closer. Her delicate fragrance filled his senses. Forbidden or not, he wanted her.

"Siobhan," he whispered her name. He could feel the warmth of her against his chest, yet they did not touch. He lifted the end of her damp plait where it hung across her shoulder and curled it around his finger. Slowly, slowly, he increased the pull. Not hurting her, simply drawing her forward until her hips touched his.

He toyed with the single strand of hair at the end of her plait that she'd used to hold the whole tight. His thumb brushed the end backward and forward until it gave under his gentle caress.

He could not stop the low groan when the ends of her hair came free. He worked the plait apart, higher and higher. "You should let your hair go free." He kept his manner light, but he couldn't hide the desire that deepened his tone.

A shiver moved through her as he continued. With each fraction of an inch that he moved up the length of her hair, unplaiting it, he drew her closer. Her breasts brushed his chest. He brought the fall of her hair up to his mouth. He brushed the silken texture against his lips.

He let it fall back against her neck and followed it down, pressing the softest of kisses to her hair and the flesh of her shoulder beneath. Her skin was exquisitely soft, and he lingered there, unable to pull away.

She shuddered at the contact. "William, we should not," she whispered.

"I know." His body pulsed and ached as he shifted his gaze from her to the pool beyond them. Mist crept across the moonlit waters and a whisper of a gentle breeze chased through the silver-backed leaves overhead. "Everything in my head says nay, but you here in my arms feels right." His voice was shaking, and shivers ran down his limbs.

She pulled him closer.

He buried his face in her hair and drew in the soft scent of heather that lingered there. He felt the curve of her body against his. His body filled with longing, with the need not just to take her, but to possess her as his own.

She wanted that, too. He could feel it in the beat of her heart against his chest, the ripening of her breasts where they pressed against him.

Being near her without possessing her was pure hell. The emotions that drove them to this moment, the force of their passion, was a gift given freely by the Maker above. They had every right to explore that gift. He was only a man, and man was flawed. He knew his sins. He knew what his judgment would be. And he found he didn't care what it cost him.

He wanted to lose himself, to put an end to his self-imposed isolation with the woman in his arms. He had always been alone, had wanted to be alone, until she came along. He held her tighter. "Tell me if you want to stop," he breathed as the flame inside him burned ever brighter. He would use that fire within to incite her, to please her, and would make a world where only he and Siobhan existed as they became one flesh.

Siobhan felt William's body tighten, stir against her. He bade her to tell him to stop. His lips found her neck, the sensitive curve of her shoulder, the base of her throat.

She longed to say "Stop" as each whisper of sensation

shivered across her flesh. She longed to stop as he trailed his fingers over her arms and down her thighs, gently caressing the hidden flesh beneath. She meant to stop him as he traced lines of hot delight down her chin, across the rise of her breast, then back to her lips, devouring her in a deep and passionate kiss.

So much was at stake—her heart, her virginity, her future. But even those things didn't pull her back. She didn't want to stop him. She couldn't stop herself. On a groan of capitulation, she leaned into his kiss.

His fingers found the ties of her gown and worked them loose until her dress fell to her ankles and she stood before him in only the thinnest layer of linen.

Despite her state of undress, she had never been warmer. The heat came from within in unquenchable waves of desire. *Desire.* That's what had taken possession of her senses and heralded her course down this darkened path.

She reached for his tunic. Her fingers stalled on the laces at the front.

He stared down at her, the line of his cheeks hollow with tension. "Yes?" he asked, the word guttural.

"Aye." She could barely answer past the thickness in her throat. Her fingers worked the lacings of his tunic. When she reached his mail, she fumbled with the ties.

"Allow me." His fingers quickly unfastened his scabbard and sword, then tossed them down. His mail, aketon, breeches and boots followed. "Take off your shift," he said in ragged tones. "I don't trust myself not to tear it from you."

His words delighted and terrified. She stared at him uncertainly. He looked fierce, almost tormented.

"Hurry." He stripped off his braies and tossed them to the ground, his gaze never leaving her face. "No second thoughts?" He stood naked before her. Starkly, boldly aroused. "I couldn't take it if you had regrets now."

She stared at the man before her. Thick blond hair covered his chest. She followed the V downward, across his flat abdomen, to the wounds that laced his torso, particularly a dark purple wound in his side, to the thick nest of hair surrounding his rampant arousal. Siobhan swallowed and moistened her lips. She should have had reservations about what was to come, but she didn't. It felt right being here with William like this—completely and utterly right. "No second thoughts."

He reached for her, pulling her tight against his bare flesh. Her naked breasts pressed against the coarse hair of his chest. The sensation was strangely seductive against the smoothness of her flesh.

He held her close and pressed a gentle kiss above the wound at her brow. "Does it pain you much?"

"Nothing pains me at the moment."

With a chuckle, he bent to kiss her neck as he slid his left hand down her abdomen to the thatch of curls surrounding her womanhood. His lips moved farther down, to the top of her breast, to her nipple. With his tongue, he circled her breast in smaller and smaller circles until he laved her nipple in warmth.

Just when she had started to adjust to the new sensation, his hand moved lower still. Slowly, he rubbed back and forth against the juncture of her thighs, igniting a strange burning need.

Siobhan gasped and tangled her fingers in his hair. She swayed helplessly as sensation after bewildering sensation tore through her.

She brought her hands down to caress the corded muscle of his arms, his back, clinging to him as though he were the only solid thing in her world. He was all iron muscles and brawny power. And in this moment, he was hers.

The thought made her bold as she allowed her fingers to explore the hard planes of his chest, his abdomen and farther down, until she came to his sex. Boldly, she ran two fingers along its length. He released a guttural sound as his manhood pulsed in response.

He pulled her down to the soft bed of moss along the shoreline. Siobhan was vaguely conscious of the heady scent of earth, of the moonlight edging William's golden hair with silver as he rose above her.

"What a treasure you are." He pressed her back against the earth and spread her thighs, his palms running feverishly up and down her flesh, feeling every nuance and texture of her. His forefinger and middle fingers touched her, probed her, sank deep.

She cried out. The muscles of her stomach clenched, convulsed, as his fingers began a slow rhythm. Her heart was pounding so hard she couldn't get her breath. Her hands clutched his shoulders, careful not to press against his healing wound.

She could hear the harsh sound of his breathing above her as the rhythm of his stroking changed, becoming faster, steadier, stronger. A coil of sensation tightened inside her, growing in intensity, as he plunged into the depths and texture of her very core.

Heat poured through her in a pure stream of desire. She gasped, arched against his fingers as shivers of pleasure pulsed through her. She cried out as wave after wave rippled through her body. His fingers left her as he gripped her thighs and moved between her legs.

She drew a sharp breath, wanting more, but not quite knowing what it was she longed for.

"Hold steady," he said as though reading her thoughts. "This might hurt just a bit." His arousal nudged against the center of her womanhood. He lunged forward.

Her entire body tensed as his presence in her body sent waves of pain through her. White-hot pain. She gasped.

"It's done," he said, covering her lips with the softest

kiss, a warm caress meant to heal. The caress did just that. The pain eased. She became aware of something more. Fullness. She lifted her hips, trying to take more of him.

A shudder went through him as he gazed down at her, his eyes shimmering with pure, primal pleasure. He drew all the way out and slowly entered her again. She could feel the soft prickle of the hair around his sex against her own. The muscles of her stomach clenched. "Don't stop."

"Never entered my mind." His voice sounded like a low growl. He drew back and plunged deep, thrusting and thrusting again.

She arched up, meeting each thrust, pulling him deeper inside her. He responded with even more urgency, more desperation. As though he wanted to make them one with every thrust.

His rhythm was wild, hard, driven by hunger and passion. Her head thrashed back and forth in the moss as she attempted to keep from crying out with the intensity of the raw emotion shuddering through every muscle and nerve of her body. He was trembling, too, she realized dimly, his breathing harsh, his chest moving in and out as though he were running.

He cried out and threw back his head, his strong neck arching, his body going rigid as a shiver passed through him and into her as deep as life itself.

She held him tight as her own pleasure exploded in a fiery release that left her stunned and weak.

He collapsed on top of her, his big body not heavy, only comforting, as he nestled his head in the crook of her neck. He lay against her, still intimately entwined with her, his flesh hot, his breathing heavy.

A shudder ran through her. What had just happened between them? She had never experienced anything so powerful, so all-consuming before in her life.

William's breathing gradually steadied, slowed. "I lost control." His voice was still ragged, uneven.

"We both lost control," she said, looking up at him.

The tension had left his face. He looked relaxed, content. "It's been so long since I let myself even dare—" He cut his own words off as he rolled to his side, ending their intimate contact. His hands moved to her breasts, cupping them gently in his hands as though he weren't ready to release her altogether.

She wasn't ready for the magic of the night to end either. Everything since they'd come to the waterfall had been perfect. A dream. Past experience told her that dreams had to end eventually.

But not right now. She longed to see the smile in William's eyes once more. "Do you trust me?" she asked sitting up.

"Aye." He sat up as well.

She extended her hand. "Prove it."

William laughed, the sound deep and lusty, as he put his hand in hers.

Siobhan stood, pulling him up beside her. She watched in fascination as a slight dimple appeared in William's left cheek. In the glow of the fire, his eyes sparkled and color tinged his face, drawing attention to the glossy thickness of his hair and the roguish shadow of stubble on his jaw, which accentuated the cleft in his chin. "What did you have in mind?"

She smiled. With a jerk on his hand, she tugged him into the water. The two of them fell backward with a splash into the liquid coolness. Mingled cries of delight and surprise filled the night air.

"You minx." William roared with laughter. "See if I trust you again."

He swam up behind her and pulled her to his chest.

Despite the coolness of the water, warmth enveloped her. He kissed the top of her shoulder. In the next instant, he lifted her slightly and tossed her into the deeper water. With a squeal, she swam back to him and dunked his head. They splashed and frolicked back and forth as carefree as children, until William held up his hands in a sign of surrender. "You win, *ma chère*," he laughed, heading for the shore. "Let us rest and regain our strength for tomorrow's climb." At their campsite, he picked up her cloak, then held it out to her as she rose from the water.

"My thanks," she said as he enfolded her in the soft warmth of the fur.

"Dress by the fire to avoid a chill." He motioned her forward. "I'll join you in a moment." He picked up his discarded clothes and slipped into the shrubs nearby.

The sound of the falls rushing toward the rocks below filled the quiet of the night. The sound comforted her as she slipped her shift over her head and fastened her simple gown over that. She'd just finished with the lacings and ties when a rustling sounded off to her right, the opposite direction from which William had vanished into the woods. "William," she called softly, expecting him to reappear.

A squat, dark figure emerged from the bushes.

"Who are you?" Siobhan asked, searching about for something to protect herself with.

"My compliments, milady. You are indeed a force of nature to take down a man as devout as our Brother William."

Her cheeks flamed at his unspoken implication. "Reveal yourself." She bent and grasped a long branch from the fire, sending a shimmer of sparks and smoke into the air. Flames at the opposite end illuminated the stranger's face.

She recognized him. "You are a brother from the monastery. The one I saw conversing with Brother Kenneth the day I arrived."

"So I am." He came forward, and it was then she saw the crossbow he clutched in his hands.

"Brother Lucius." A reclothed William leapt from the shrubs, his sword drawn. He thrust her behind him, standing between her and the crossbow. He leveled his weapon at the man in monk's garb. "What do you want?"

"Isn't it obvious?" He glanced around their campsite with a frown. "I had hoped you'd already retrieved what it is I want."

William's muscles tensed. "The Spear?"

The man gave a jerky nod. "I must have it."

"Why? You took an oath to protect and preserve the Templar artifacts."

"As I recall, you took an oath as well." The man's gaze moved beyond William to Siobhan. "Sometimes need overcomes our past commitments."

"I was a warrior before I took the cloth. I am a warrior still." William's body coiled, prepared to strike. "I have no desire to harm a fellow Templar, Lucius. But I shall if you force this issue."

The monk's eyes widened. His grip tightened on the crossbow. "I can kill you before you ever reach me."

"Are you sure about that?"

Lucius's fingers shook on the crossbow. He moistened his lips. "Don't test me."

"What do you want with the Spear?" William's voice was harsh.

"I want revenge. The Spear will ensure that I get it."

"Killing de la Roche will not bring Peter back to you."

"Killing that villain will save others from dying as Peter did." Lucius's voice was raw. "Do you want to burn like all the other heretics he's captured?"

"Nay," William said. "But if we keep the Spear from him, de la Roche is just a man. Men can be taken down."

The monk straightened. "I'll be the one to send de la Roche to his grave."

"You can't handle the Spear's power."

For a moment, an expression of unease crossed Brother Lucius's face at the certainty of William's tone. "I'll take my chances. With the Spear I have some hope at revenge against de la Roche and his men. Without the weapon, my fate will be the same as my brother's—tied to a stake and burned as a heretic."

"You might be dead regardless." William lunged.

Chapter Fifteen

William struck not with his sword, but with all the force in his body. Brother Lucius flew backward. The crossbow fired toward the sky before the man and his weapon fell to the ground with a thump. Brother Lucius rolled and leapt to his feet, searching the hazy darkness for his weapon.

With his booted foot, William sent the crossbow into the ferns beyond them. "Go back to the monastery."

"I want the girl."

William startled. "Why?"

"She can read the scroll that shows the way to the treasure."

"Who told you about the scroll?" William tightened his grip on his sword.

"Word carries fast around the monastery. To have my revenge, I must have her."

"Revenge is no worthy master." William took two steps toward Brother Lucius, threatening to strike him again. "Praying for Peter's soul will help him more than spilling more blood."

The monk edged backward. "I am done praying. I want to fight."

"Then fight for a cause worthy of your sacrifice." William frowned at the monk he thought he knew. "I miss Peter as well, but this isn't the way to grieve him."

"What do you know of my grief?" Anger flared in

Brother Lucius's gaze. "You want the Spear for your-self."

"Nay," William said quickly. "The Spear must be pro-tected, not used. That's why I'm here."

Brother Lucius looked to Siobhan. She stood back from the two of them, silhouetted by the light of the fire. "Is that her purpose as well? Or does she want some-thing more?"

Brother Lucius tried to twist Siobhan's reasons for finding the Spear into something more sinister. But Wil-liam knew her motives. He sent her a soft smile. Her fa-ther's life depended on their success.

She smiled in return.

Brother Lucius bolted for the bushes. In a rustle of leaves, he vanished into the foliage. William's body coiled, prepared to chase him.

"Let him go," Siobhan said softly.

William's gaze darted to her, and he relaxed. "He'll only follow us."

"What would you do? Capture him and tie him to a tree? Sentence him to a slow and painful death? You might as well kill him now." She folded her arms. "At least we know who was following us. We are warned, and we can take precautions."

"You're right. Brother Lucius on his own is no great threat." But the young monk's presence raised a thought William hadn't considered. Once they found the Spear, how would they keep it away from those who would use it for ill purposes? Finding it would be easy next to that Herculean feat.

William sheathed his sword. He crossed to the fire and took Siobhan's cold fingers in his own. "Come, sit. Let's warm up. Brother Lucius likely won't come back tonight."

She nodded and followed him down to sit on his cloak

by the fire. Siobhan moved close, nestling into the circle of his arms. William pulled her cloak around their shoulders, warding off the chill of the night.

"Why did Brother Lucius threaten you with being burned at the stake?"

William looked down at her head resting on his shoulder and gave her a small smile that did not quite reach his eyes. He took a deep breath. "All Templars await the fate of heretics until we are cleared by our accusers."

"That's horrible." Siobhan pulled away from him. William watched her dark eyes cloud with concern.

"That's what de la Roche's purpose is in Scotland, to cleanse the world of heretics. The Spear is only a secondary purpose."

"Have you known . . . Have any of your brothers died at his hands?" she asked.

"While Simon and myself and others were away from Scotland, aye." He reached out and ran a finger down the softness of her cheek. "The man will be stopped."

She took his hand and held it in both of her own. "The Spear will help you stop him."

William looked down at her fingers, so slender and delicate, clasped around his large palm. "Tempting as it may be, I'll not use the Spear for such purposes."

"Yet your sense of loss is just as great as Brother Lucius's."

He startled. "How can you know that?"

She looked up at him. "I'm not blind. Anyone who looks at you, William, can see that you carry a great burden of pain. Is it your family that grieves you so?"

"I lost them so long ago, they are but a distant memory to me."

Her brow furrowed. "Then for whom do you suffer?"

Could she see so clearly into his heart? Did he truly carry so much of his grief in the lines of his face? William remained silent, and she let that silence fall between them in a soothing, comfortable way without judgment or expectation. He drew a deep breath and released it slowly. Could he tell her his greatest failure? Admit his weakness and still remain whole?

He searched for a way to begin. "I told you about being one of the Bruce's guardsmen. What I didn't tell you is the nightmare that took the lives of six of those knights."

He waited, giving Siobhan a chance to speak, but she simply watched him with concern in her eyes, waiting for the words yet to come.

"When King Robert the Bruce died, he bid the ten of us to remove his heart from his chest, embalm it and return it to Jerusalem for burial in the Church of the Holy Sepulchre. It had long been his dream to go on Crusade, but the wars here kept him close to Scottish shores. So we made the journey for him. We got as far as Teba, Spain, before all hell rose to meet us."

William stared off into the distance as the memories surged forward in his mind. He drifted back to the terrain of the Iberian Peninsula.

Forty thousand Moors advanced upon their army of a hundred. Spanish forces had yet to engage. There was no time to consider why they waited. Like a wave of rolling thunder, the black-clad Saracens swept across the dry terrain, impervious to the sun's punishing rays.

Flanked on both sides by his brethren, William Keith ignored the heat, focusing on his own breathing and that of his horse. Phantom's muscles bunched and quivered beneath his legs. William reached forward and stroked the animal's neck. "Hold steady, Phantom. Wait until they're upon us."

A deathly moan of sorrow seemed to hang in the air until a war cry shattered the stillness. William dug his spurs into Phantom's side, charging into the fray. Like white foam on the tide's crest, the white-coated knights broke across the enemy, a small wave of destruction on an endless, turbaned sea.

A horse bore down upon William with alarming speed. The dark-cloaked rider on the animal's back was poised to kill. They came together. William ducked, leaving the air between them filled with the whistling sound of Saracen steel.

There was no speech exchanged, no sound at all, save for the screech and clangor of steel and mutual grunts of exertion each time the two warriors clashed. Time slowed even as the day died, leaving William the ability to see each move before it was made and counter each mortal blow until he took the man down with a cut to the knees.

Carnage surrounded them. In less than an hour, Christian troops had been shredded by the Moors' hooked swords, burned by their flaming arrows and trampled by their cavalry.

William pierced the heart of a man, but not before the man put an arrow into Phantom's side. The horse's legs buckled, and the two of them slammed to the ground. William hit the rocky desert floor hard. The hot, arid air robbed him of breath, and for a moment the battlefield swam before his eyes.

He rolled from the saddle, grateful to see that his horse yet lived, and came to his feet. A Saracen charged toward him on foot, battering William's broadsword in an attempt to take him down.

He was losing ground, being pressed. Despair began to swamp him. He had only begun to live this life he'd been given. He was not ready to die. Not yet. William advanced, forcing the enemy back. He had the advantage now. His chest heaved, his muscles ached as he delivered a lethal blow to the man's neck.

Before he could catch his breath, another Moor appeared, then another. With a thrust of his sword he took them down one after the other. He twisted left to find two more. Over and over he slashed his way forward, back to his brethren.

Red Sinclair stood up in his saddle as he and his horse surged forward into the tide of unending black. Walter the

Small pursued, covering his flank. Robert followed, protecting them both with lethal swipes of his blade.

Blood turned the desert floor into a bog. And the blood continued to flow. Men William knew, men who had followed the ten Templars into this battle, lay dead around him. Others lay dying, praying, crying, moaning as they were shredded by a relentless foe. As the Saracens set fire to the tents, the smell of death mingled with sweat and the acrid scent of smoke.

Black Douglas charged forward into the worst of the fighting. He held the small silver casket containing the Bruce's heart high into the air. He screamed a terrifying battle cry and flung the casket into the melee as a beacon of protection.

William watched the heart's protective casket arc, then fall. It hit the red, rocky ground in the same instant that a sword pierced deep into his side. The impact of the cold steel slicing through muscle and tissue took what breath remained in his lungs.

There was no pain, only a curious sensation as the sword pulled free. It was smeared with blood—his blood—glinting red in the sunlight. The heat pounded his flesh as relentlessly as the enemy's weapon. He raised his sword to counter, but the weapon fell free of his numb grasp. He dropped to his knees, no longer able to stand.

William hitched a sharp breath as a chill swept over him. How could he be so cold in this inferno? He collapsed against the soil, his gaze still on the silver vessel containing the king's heart. The casket lay on the ground not ten feet from him. The Bruce's heart was supposed to protect them. But how could a heart, even his heart, defy an unholy force?

William dug his bare fingers into the rocky soil. Slowly he edged forward, toward the relic he'd sworn to protect. He clenched his fists in the soil as a wave of pain consumed him.

Rivulets of sweat formed beneath his heavy mail, even as a chill half deadened his limbs. Still he inched forward, grim determination spurring him on.

Another wave of a hundred turbaned Moors bore down upon him. His hand moved instinctively to his side to grasp his sword, but he came up empty. His weapon was gone.

From somewhere nearby, Sir James Douglas yelled a battle cry: "We will follow you or die!"

The words did not halt the enemy as they rushed over Sir James, Sir Walter Logan and William. Their horses' hooves barely missed William's head, his body. The talisman had failed. The heart had not protected them as the Bruce had claimed it would.

William watched the Moors kick the casket out of their way, intent on victory.

Like a force of fury, they slammed into him, shredding his clothes, lacerating his flesh. Pain rippled up and down his nerves and through his mind as he lay upon the ground. His arms ached, his body grew numb, blood seeped from countless wounds as the forces moved on, leaving him for dead.

The thunder of battle and the anguished cries of the fallen faded. Stillness hung in the air, broken only by the rasp of his breath. Of the ten knights who had formed the Brotherhood of the Scottish Templars, how many had fallen among the hundreds dead? Would any of them survive to carry the king's heart home to Scotland now that their quest had failed?

With what remained of his stamina, William pulled himself closer to the precious vessel now nestled in the lifeless arms of Walter the Small. What Black Douglas had thrown into the fray, Walter now protected in death. William crawled toward Walter and the casket, his mind finding energy his body didn't know he possessed.

He would survive to take the heart back to Scotland. He drew a painful, wheezing breath. He would survive, somehow—he had to.

William startled when he realized he'd told Siobhan the whole tale. He expected to see blatant rejection staring back at him for what he had failed to do.

Instead, she leaned forward and brushed his lips softly with her own. "You've suffered so much at the hands of others." Her voice remained steady, strong and filled with understanding. "The secrets of your heart are safe with me."

He didn't know what to say or how to react. The cold ache of failure that he had kept buried deep inside suddenly didn't seem so cold or so desperate any longer.

He'd shared his darkest secret with the woman tucked once again in the folds of his arms. Hope surged. "What have I ever done to deserve you?" William smiled against the softness of her hair. "Tomorrow we will find the Spear, Siobhan. Tomorrow, life begins anew."

Chapter Sixteen

Siobhan stood at the water's edge the next morning. The wind blew across the hills, cold and sharp. It scattered the mist that had gathered across the water and around the glen. Gray clouds hung overhead, threatening rain.

She pulled up her hood as the wind caught the length of her cloak and her skirts beneath. The garments snapped and fluttered like banners. Despite the strength of the wind, it felt good to draw a breath of the cool, crisp air. The process cleared her senses and helped her see things as they were.

In the stark reality of day, she felt no shame, yet she had to wonder what had possessed her last night. Was it the serenity of the glen, the charged emotions of surviving the dangers of their journey so far, or was it the danger itself that had thrown them into each other's arms? Without any hesitation she had given herself over to William. Doing so, she had always been told, was wrong. Yet it hadn't felt that way. Being in William's embrace and merging with his body had felt as natural as the breath she drew now.

Miss Edina MacInnes, her nurse from days gone by, had warned her that sacrificing her virginity to any but her husband would cost her dearly, indeed. Had William not sacrificed as much as she had in that moment by turning against his vows? A flush crept into her cheeks at the thought that sacrificing her maidenhead probably meant less to her than violating his vows had to him.

So where did that leave them? They would continue on to the treasure, of course. But what about the two of them?

Last night had been magical. Perfect. She craved more of the same. Siobhan brought her fingers to her lips, remembering the honeyed taste of his kisses, the warmth of his body pressed against her own, the passion that had ignited and burned beyond their control.

But it was more than just her desire for William.

She wanted to know more about him. She wanted to understand what brought the haunted look into his eyes when he thought she wasn't aware of him. He'd told her about his journey to the Holy Land and all that he had suffered there. Was there more he still held back?

He was clearly of importance in the Templar Order, yet he often stood apart from the other monks. He'd talked of his family's brutal murder, yet he had no desire for revenge against his uncle. Each time they talked, or whenever she studied him, she discovered a new facet that intrigued her.

Slowly he had begun to reveal himself, and she wanted to discover who he truly was beneath his protective armor. Would he be as vulnerable as she often felt herself? She frowned down at the sparkling blue-green waters at her feet. Perhaps that is what had drawn them together last night: that deep down they were the same, two people struggling to find a place in the world.

"There you are," William said, and Siobhan turned to see him striding toward her, his hair and cloak tossed by the wind.

Without hesitation, he drew her into his arms and held her tightly.

She closed her eyes and leaned into him, pretending for a moment that they belonged that way, looking out over the waters of the pool on a spring morning, that they lived in a time of peace and prosperity. Birds called softly in the distance and the scent of grass and wild-flowers tickled her nose. If only there were no de la Roche, no Spear to find, no threat to their lives or to the life of her father . . .

"Are you ready to go?" William asked, as if he'd heard her thoughts.

Siobhan's eyes flew open. Her daydream vanished. Her father needed them to continue. "Aye." Her own questions could wait. They would have time to discuss whatever future lay before them as the journey progressed.

He offered her his hand. She gripped it tightly, without fear or reservation, as he led her from their encampment.

The Spear awaited.

As they climbed the steep slope beyond the waterfall, Siobhan kept looking into the foliage on both sides of the path.

"Are you looking for Lucius?" William asked with raised brow.

"He's still out there," she whispered. "I can feel it."

"You're right." William inclined his head to the left side of the trail.

She came to a stop.

William kept up their pace. "Keep moving, and keep talking."

She hurried to catch up. *Keep talking about what?* Her former nurse would have advised her to discuss the weather—always a topic of interest, given Scotland's var-ied climate. "The sky is growing darker, and the wind is picking up. I dare say we shall see rain before the night is through. I'm quite certain this path will turn to mire, if there is any rainfall at all. But the waterfall below," she said, trying to inject a bit of wistfulness into her voice, "will no doubt be lovelier than ever with—"

William was gone.

She drew a quick breath and kept on walking. "The view from the top of this hill will be quite spectacular, I'm sure. Even if it's raining, might we—?"

A cry of pain echoed across the hillside, followed by a male voice sputtering expletives in Gaelic. Then silence. Siobhan stopped, waiting for William to reappear. He re-emerged from the foliage after a short time, sheathing his sword as he strode toward her.

"What happened?" Siobhan asked.

William tossed her a satisfied smile. "Our friend will not be any more trouble to us."

"You can't leave me here. Come back and untie me," a male voice called from the foliage where William had reappeared.

Siobhan hurried along after William. "Will he be all right?" she asked, pursing her lips with concern. She didn't want the man to meddle in their affairs, but she didn't want him hurt either.

"Trust me." William met her gaze. "I left him food and water and enough slack to get it. It'll only be a day or so until we send someone from the monastery to get him. He'll be just fine, I promise."

She didn't have much time to linger over thoughts of Lucius's fate as the ferns and shrubs thinned, then vanished, and the path they followed became a steep and rocky slope. "Stay close," William advised as he continued upward. Siobhan grasped at brush to keep her balance while clambering over boulders.

The wind calmed as they continued, but the sky grew darker and the heavy air pressed in around them. *If only the rain holds off a while longer,* Siobhan thought as she picked her way across the rocks.

When they came to an area that flattened out, William stopped. He offered Siobhan his hand, pulling her up over yet another boulder that obstructed their path. "How's your head?" he asked. It was the first time they had spoken since they'd encountered the rocky terrain.

"Better today." She nodded breathlessly, grateful for the small respite. "How much farther?"

"I'm not certain. Let's take another look at the scroll." His breathing was steady now.

Siobhan removed the container from her pocket and set it carefully upon a nearby rock. She settled on the ground beside it.

"We must be getting close." William sat opposite her and waited for her to open the scroll. She unwound the papyrus, careful to make sure it did not fly away in the breeze. The paper looked stark, pale, eerie in the darkening afternoon light.

Siobhan concentrated on the sketch William had said represented the Mother's Cradle high in the Cairngorm Mountains. A smattering of dark dots littered the base of the cave. She twisted the scroll toward him. "Could these be the rocks we're climbing over?"

"Could be." As he studied the drawing, she looked at it from the opposite side.

She drew a sharp breath as something she hadn't seen before appeared on the upside-down page. "From this angle, the whole drawing looks like a cave."

William moved to kneel beside her.

"It's a bit like looking at cloud formations and seeing something in the odd angles and depths. But if you look at it just right, you can definitely see a cave."

Siobhan stared at the drawing that had not made any sense when they had viewed it in the monastery. But upside down, random marks formed into images before her eyes. The same smattering of dark shapes lined the bottom of the page, along with two vertical lines crossed by a horizontal line.

"Look here," William said pointing to a long, flowing line that split in the middle. The words that had looked like gibberish before now looked the same as those on the bottom of the page that Brother Kenneth had translated as "mother's tears."

Siobhan inhaled sharply as she stared down at the drawing. "Could that line be a hidden waterfall inside yet another cave? Could the treasure be hidden there, behind the falling water?" She paused. "An underground waterfall?"

William sat back, staring not at the scroll but off in the distance. "We'll know soon, because I do believe that is the Mother's Cradle up and off to the left."

Siobhan looked to where a dark shape yawned in the hillside. She frowned. "It's just a shadow." She squinted and glanced down at the scroll, then up at the high site. "It . . . Maybe. But could it be any less accessible?"

He grinned, bringing out the slight indentation in his left cheek. "The Templars were hiding a very valuable treasure. They weren't going to make the task easy."

She returned his smile. "You have a point."

"Ready to find a treasure?" William stood and waited for Siobhan to return the scroll to its leather casing, then slide it into the secret pocket in her gown. When she was done, she stood, and together they hiked up the steep mountainside.

Finally, they reached the lip of the cave just as the pewter gray skies opened wide, sending a hard, steady stream of rain to the earth.

"Luck seems to be on our side," William said as he set his saddlebag down and rummaged inside until he withdrew a flint stone, a tallow candle and the lantern. With a flick of the stone, he sent a spark onto the wick. The spark became a flame, and soon light spilled into the darkness, illuminating the cave's interior.

"Ready to continue?" he asked.

She reached for his free hand. "Thank you, William, for helping me and my father."

For an instant a shadow crept into his eyes, and then it was gone. "We'll free your father." He gently squeezed her fingers, then released them. "Let's find the Spear."

Side by side they moved deeper into the cave. Siobhan's heart raced as they descended the downward slope. "Will there be another trap?" she asked, giving voice to her fears.

"Anything is possible. Stay alert."

They passed through a long tunnel. William stopped and pressed his hand to the smooth stone walls. "These walls were shaped by man's tools, not by nature." He lifted the lantern to reveal a face carved into the wall above them.

Siobhan's hand clutched William's arm. The image was of an old man's face surrounded by greenery. "What is it?"

"A Green Man. They're nothing to fear. They're pagan in origin and were sometimes used by the Templars as a symbol of rebirth. The faces should grow younger in appearance as we progress. It also means we are going the right way."

They headed deeper into the coolness of the cave. As they headed downward, Siobhan would occasionally spot another face peering out of the chipped stone. The faces did appear to be growing younger as she and William moved deeper into the mountain.

The farther they went, the more silent the air became. They rounded a bend in the rock and came to a large open area. To the right were four colonnades carved from the mountain rock, almost like a temple. Beside each colonnade stood a statue of a knight wearing a Templar tunic and holding a sword across his chest. "What does it mean?" Siobhan asked.

"I believe we have found the entrance," William replied. "What else could it be?"

"A trap?" she suggested as an odd sensation rippled across the back of her neck. "It looks too perfect, too splendid." Siobhan retrieved the scroll from her pocket and set it on the ground. She smoothed the surface and studied the three lines she'd noted earlier. "We're missing something." She stood. "Can I have the lantern?"

He gave it to her. Slowly, she walked past the colonnades and around the open area, pausing every few steps to illuminate the high rock walls. She tried to remember her father's stories. Then it was there. A fragment from a tale he'd told her about entering God's treasured kingdom.

"Most people anticipate walking through Saint Peter's gates," she said out loud, "when sometimes it's down Saint Peter's stairs that will take you where you want to go."

Siobhan's mouth went dry. How had she remembered that? Instead of looking at the ceiling, she dipped the lantern toward the floor as she continued her progression along the walls until she came to a dip in the ground. She dropped to her knees, and with one hand dusted the loose earth aside from between the dip and the stone wall to reveal a carved step. "Hidden stairs."

William joined her, and together they brushed the earth back away from the wall to reveal not just three stairs, but an archway set back into what she'd assumed was more of the stone wall. The hardened dirt fell away to reveal the passageway.

"Do you think this is it?"

Siobhan sat back on her heels and smiled. "This is it. I can feel it. That doesn't sound logical, I know. But the temple is wrong. I feel that just as strongly."

He reached out and grasped her hand with his. "I believe you."

Warmth crept through Siobhan at the three simple words. Together they set to work clearing the stairs. The earth was loosely packed, and it didn't take long before they stood in yet another small chamber, at the bottom of ten stairs that had been carved into the rock.

William held the lantern aloft to reveal three slabs of rock, also cut from the stone. Two stood vertically, with a smaller slab perched across the top—just as the drawing indicated. Placing the lantern on the ground nearby, William and Siobhan brushed away the last of the dirt to reveal a stone door.

William pulled his dagger from his boot and chipped away at the seal until the last piece fell away. The sound of crumbling mortar hitting the earth echoed in the silence. "This is it. We are here." Excitement danced in his eyes.

Her heart beat so fast she could scarcely breathe—not from fear, but from the fact that they had found the treasure room by putting together the clues her father had left.

"Are you ready to look upon what has not been seen for many years?"

She nodded. It took their combined strength to push the solid rock door aside. "Get the lantern," she said breathlessly.

He got it and stepped inside, illuminating the dark cavern behind the door. Siobhan followed close behind. Stale air greeted them as they stepped inside the chamber. William set the lantern down, allowing their eyes to adjust to the half light. As her eyes adapted, she could see a long chamber, but no treasure. In fact, there was nothing at all, except another arched doorway on the opposite side. Determined to find something of use, she searched the walls for paintings or more carvings but could find none.

William drew an unlit torch out of a metal holder on the wall. He touched the tip to the flame of the lantern and illuminated the opening of the chamber with light. He handed her the torch, and they entered the chamber together. They walked farther, shining the light over every surface, but found nothing. "Looks like the journey continues," he said with a touch of disappointment.

"We'll find it," she said, reassuring him even as doubt pierced her prior certainty. They had to find the Spear, or her father would die. Siobhan tightened her hand around the torch and moved slowly forward into the darkness.

Siobhan stopped. "Listen."

William paused beside her. A low, deep hissing issued from the darkness ahead. "Sounds like water."

Siobhan smiled up at him. "It sounds like a waterfall. Come on," she said, hurrying down the passage. As they continued toward the sound, the walls came alive with bright, vivid paintings of men on horseback, wearing tunics bearing the Templar cross, charging into battle against a turbaned enemy. "Scenes from the Crusades," William noted as they hurried past.

They went on, eyeing the paintings as they did, until suddenly without warning, the floor slanted sharply down. Siobhan dropped her torch. She cried out as she slipped. She grasped for the walls, but the path was too steep, and she felt herself sliding over a precipice and into the darkness ahead.

Chapter Seventeen

"Siobhan!" Panic gripped William. He braced himself against the wall and made a wild lunge down the steep slope for Siobhan's arm. He couldn't lose her. He connected with something solid. Her fingers wrapped around his. He held tight and pulled with all his strength.

When her head appeared above the level of the floor, he grasped both her arms and tugged her beside him. They collapsed back against the floor, breathing heavily. "I thought I'd lost you again." He pulled her into his arms.

"I didn't expect the floor to just fall away like that." She rested against his chest until her own breathing and the beat of his heart returned to a normal rhythm.

"Another Templar trap. Just like the Egyptians in their burial chambers, the Templars were fond of traps to protect their treasure."

"What will we do now?" Siobhan asked.

William sat up, bringing Siobhan with him. Together they gazed off into the darkness beyond the tunnel. "Once again you were clever enough to discover the trap that was set here. Now all we have to do is figure out a way across."

"What was the second clue that Brother Kenneth decoded from the scroll? 'Only the faithful . . .'"

William picked up the lantern from where he'd tossed it to the ground. He held it out before them, illuminating a ten-foot drop that plunged into a pool of water. The water came from the waterfall on the other side. Between the pool and the more distant waterfall lay an island. They had to somehow bridge the divide between themselves and the island.

" 'Only with faith and might can one leap the divide to part a mother's tears,' " William said, recalling the phrase from the scroll. An idea took root. He hurried back to the colorful images that lined the walls. Holding the lantern high, he searched each scene. Templars engaged in various battles lined one side of the wall, while Templars at prayer lined the other. Faith and might. "Siobhan, run your hand over the wall and look for anything not as it seems."

She nodded and headed to the wall depicting men at prayer, while William skimmed his fingers over the rough rock on the opposite side. At a drawing of a knight holding his sword across his chest in salute, his fingers felt a rough cut in the stone that did not appear to be anything more than a part of the drawing. Upon closer examination, however, he could see that the cut encircled the drawing, as though designed to conceal something more.

"I found something," Siobhan called over her shoulder. "This image of a Templar on his knees is cut away from the rest of the stone, as if it would move if I pushed it inward."

"Press it, hard," William encouraged her, at the same time depressing the image he'd found. The stone sank into the painted image. In the next moment, a grinding sound filled the confined space of the tunnel. Farther down toward the ledge, a slab of stone slid sideways to reveal a winch set back into the carved stone. "Your father is a wise man to conceal the winch in such a way," William exclaimed as he scooted on his knees toward the device. He twisted it to the right again and again as the mechanism moved something at the base of the ledge Siobhan had nearly tumbled off.

The ground beneath them began to shake. Grinding sounds filled the air. A heartbeat later, a two-foot-wide wooden plank slid out of the solid rock beneath them, creating a bridge to the island beyond.

"Templar brothers have provided safe passage." William stood and offered Siobhan his arm. She accepted with a smile as he guided her across the bridge.

At the end of the bridge sat two giant urns filled with oil. William touched the candle from the lantern to them both. They caught fire and filled the underground cavern with a warm golden glow. The cavern's ceiling extended high above them. Crystalline formations in the rock walls and ceiling caught the flames and sparkled like a thousand stars overhead.

"It's beautiful," Siobhan breathed beside him.

They were deep inside the earth, yet a sense of peace, of restfulness and welcome, filled William to the core. "Your father is a true talent, Siobhan."

She looked at him, then back at the waterfall that spilled down a rock face that lay beyond the opposite side of the island. "My father?"

"I can't imagine how long it took him to build this place. And he would have had to do it in complete secrecy, too."

"Do you really think the treasure is here behind the waterfall?"

He grinned. "Do you want to find out?"

At her nod, they hurried across the island until they came to the water's edge. More than a hundred yards separated them from the base of the waterfall. A light mist hung in the air as the water rushed over the falls with a soft roar. Siobhan had started for the water when he held her back with a touch on the arm. "It would be easier for our return if we left our dry garments behind on the island."

A flush of color stained her cheeks before her lips worked into a smile. "What a clever ruse, sir, to get me out of my clothing once again." Her tone was playful as she reached for the ties of her gown.

"Allow me." He reached around her and made short work of the lacings until her gown dropped to her feet and she stood in her shift before him.

"Seems only fair that I should help you with your tunic and mail." She looked at him inquiringly. His breath caught at her expression, and a surge of heat shot through him. By the time she had removed his garments down to his braies, he was trembling with need. He fisted his hands. *The treasure*, he reminded himself. They were here for the Spear.

Regaining control of his senses, he reached into his saddlebag for his flint and a tallow candle, then grasped his sword. Offering her his other hand, they entered the softly churning waters. He pushed through the current that dragged against their flesh the closer they got to the falls.

William stopped at the base of the falls and turned to Siobhan. "Take a deep breath," he shouted above the crashing of the water. As soon as Siobhan's chest expanded, he plunged them forward into the stream.

The falling water hit them hard, nearly knocking Siobhan off her feet, but he held her tight against his side and moved them steadily forward into the heaviest part of the flow. The need to draw breath grew stronger with each labored step.

They broke through to the other side. He drew a gasping breath, as did Siobhan. "We made it."

She dragged several sharp breaths into her lungs. "There *is* a cave." They kept moving through the water until they stood upon dry land.

"Aye," he replied, peering into the darkness. He handed her the candle. "Hold this while I try to dry off the flint." He bent to the dirt beneath his feet and rubbed the stone along the surface, hoping the earth would absorb some of the water. Slowly his eyes adjusted to the darkness until he could make out the outline of Siobhan's body before him.

Her wet shift clung to her legs. She plucked it away from her skin, causing a pool of water to drip onto the dirt floor. Despite her soaked clothes, she wasn't cold.

"Bring the candle down here," he instructed. "The wick will be easier to light against the ground." He flicked the flint against his sword. Over and over he repeated the process, until finally a spark came forth. He had to create a spark several more times before one caught the wick. A wisp of smoke curled up from the fiber, then a sputtering flame that built in intensity.

Siobhan shielded the delicate flame with her curved fingers, protecting it, nurturing it, until it burned steadily. "Can you see any other urns? If they left them at the entrance, why would they not leave some here?"

"Over there." William motioned to the left side of the water where a giant urn stood as though waiting to be lit. A moment later, a bright golden light spilled across the inner chamber.

"We found it!" Siobhan gasped.

William uttered a cry of wonder and disbelief. Riches spilled over every surface. He took two halting steps toward the enormous wooden cases inset with jewels from an early period in Egypt's history. A painted dragon ship of Viking origin. A gilded chariot from Roman times. Statues made from marble, obsidian, limestone and granite from every culture—Babylonian, Egyptian, Greek, Viking, Roman and more. Jewel-encrusted chests brimming with gold bracelets, necklaces, crowns.

"Herod's crown," Siobhan breathed, her gaze fixed on the bejeweled chest that held it. "I recognize it from my father's stories."

William turned to Siobhan to see her eyes wide with wonder as she looked around. She moved with awestruck deliberation about the chamber. "All these things . . . I know them from the stories my father used to tell me." She paused beside four silver trumpets. Her hand reached out, hovering above them, but not touching the precious treasure. "The trumpets used to herald the coming of the Messiah."

She moved beyond to a gilded throne. "The throne of Constantine." As though in a trance she continued. "The Athenian Sword of Pericles. The girdle of Hippolyta, the Amazon queen." She moved about the room naming things as she went, "Ramses' golden chair. Octavius's goblet. Excalibur." She paused, her fingers suspended over the blade. "It does exist." She drew back her hand and continued about the chamber. "Penelope's spindle. The Tablets of Thoth." She paused, her breath coming in ragged gasps.

William rushed to her side, supporting her in the cradle of his arms. "What is it?"

"I never thought . . . My whole life I've heard about these things in the stories my father told me. The details he used to reveal . . . I always assumed he had a vivid imagination, but in reality he knew so much about these artifacts because he had touched each and every one of them." A smile lit her face. "My father *was* Keeper of the Holy Relics. I know that now without a doubt." Her breathing steadied. She grasped his hand. "Let me show you." Excitement laced her words as she pulled him toward the north wall, which was lined with shelves from ceiling to floor and filled with scroll upon scroll. "These are some of the rescued scrolls from the library at Alexandria. And here . . ." She pointed to others. "From the community at Qumran."

She hurried across the chamber and paused before a large bejeweled table. "The Table of the Divine Presence." On the table sat a chalice. She stared at the unassuming goblet as though caught in some spell. The chalice appeared to change colors before her eyes. Siobhan reached her fingers out toward it, then pulled them back, as though afraid to touch something so precious. "The Holy Grail."

Her excitement fueled his own. They were so close. "Help me find the Spear of Destiny."

"My father used to tell of a Roman spear made of iron. Over the centuries, the tale has changed. It is said that a nail from the crucifixion was hammered into the blade and set off by tiny brass crosses. The blade itself is sheathed in layers of silver wrapped with gold," Siobhan explained as she progressed about the chamber, searching.

"Here!" William exclaimed when he caught sight of the very object Siobhan had described. The Spear, its blade sheathed in gold, leaned against the chamber wall, toward the back. He made his way to the weapon. It seemed regal yet harmless, set among the other treasures in the room. But its history gave testament that it was anything but ordinary. "They claim the Spear of Destiny has been carried into battle by some of the greatest military minds to date."

"You found it." Siobhan stood beside him. "My father is saved."

William turned to her. "Siobhan, we cannot go to your father straight away. It'll be nightfall soon. Traveling down the mountain is far too dangerous in the dark."

Some of the joy left her face. "I understand, but that doesn't stop my worry. What de la Roche could be doing to my father . . ."

"De la Roche won't kill your father until he knows the Spear is within his grasp."

"I am counting on that," she said with a half smile. "Are you going to touch the Spear?"

Despite her worries, she stared up at William with a tenderness that touched his soul. This was the moment they had hoped for since joining forces outside her burning home.

And still he hesitated. Touching the weapon meant a return to the world they had set aside on their journey here. He would have to go back to his brothers. The ache of indecision centered in his chest. He was torn between a world he knew and a world he hardly dared to believe he deserved. Could he give up the Templars for this woman?

He sighed, suddenly feeling lost. The last few days with Siobhan had been a gift. He'd seen for the first time in his life that he was loveable, that happiness could exist for him, no matter how short-lived. He was lucky to have had this time with her—whether it evolved into one night of passion or six. He'd been given a wonderful, irreplaceable gift. And he intended to make the most of it in the here and now.

He grinned down at her. "The Spear isn't going anywhere. There are other things in this chamber that intrigue me more." William took Siobhan in his arms as strong emotions tightened his chest—an overwhelming sense of joy and rightness.

He'd never felt this way before, not with anyone. Making love with her had been more soul-touching than he dared put into words. It went deeper than that, though. He had known her only a few short days, yet it felt as though he had known her forever, that she was inexplicably a part of himself.

William brushed his face against her hair and smiled, remembering that his first impression of her had been of a plain-faced nobody. With the golden light cast from the urns brightening her face and gilding her hair, she was anything but plain. She was beautiful.

He tightened his arms around her as he thought about the night before, when she'd whispered his name in the darkness, when she lay trembling in his arms.

He breathed in the scent of her hair and felt his body tighten with desire. "We are safe here. Would it disturb you to stay in this chamber tonight, surrounded by the treasure?"

She shook her head. "With you, I feel safe."

He pulled back, his gaze intent on her face. "Don't feel too safe. My motives are not entirely pure. I don't want to have anything to do with the Spear this night."

Her eyes widened with awareness. "What would you like to—?" Her words broke off as he reached out and cupped her breast with the palm of his hand. He could feel her nipple through the sheer, damp fabric of her shift. He rubbed the tender peak until it beaded beneath his hand.

"Does that answer your question?" He released her and gently tugged the bodice of her shift down until her breasts were exposed. He leaned forward and licked each nipple lazily, feeling a hot shiver run through her. He pulled back. "Hmm. Something's missing."

She looked at him skeptically. "What could be missing?"

He took her hand and drew her toward one of the ornamented chests. He reached for a long, gold necklace set with rubies and placed it around her neck, allowing the gems to slide into the valley between her breasts.

She drew a sharp breath as the cool metal touched her skin.

"Allow me to warm those," he said, pressing his lips against her flesh at the side of her neck. He followed the path of the gemstones, moving behind her to kiss the back and then the other side of her neck. From behind, he reached around her and pulled her back against the solid wall of his chest. His hands stroked the necklace as it draped down her chest, until he moved them over both her breasts. He caressed her, stroked her, until she leaned back against him as though her legs could not support her any longer.

He reached into the chest once more, withdrawing a circlet of gold, which he placed on her head. Slowly, he unlaced her hair from its plait. With each unfurling tendril, he felt a longing that gained in intensity until it was almost unbearable. His gaze lingered on the bare flesh of her breasts tinted gold in the firelight. Suddenly he needed to see all of her. He loosened her shift until it fell to her ankles.

"William." His name trembled on her lips. She turned around and released his braies until they joined her shift on the floor of the cavern. The blood pounded in his veins and quickened in his loins. He felt as though his next breath would shatter what remained of his composure.

Siobhan must have felt it too, because she bent to retrieve her shift, then took his hand and pulled them to an open space among the treasure. She spread her shift on the ground. When she finished, he slipped his hand around to the back of her neck and pulled her toward him.

The air in the cavern was cool and soft, the light a muted gold, and the steady rhythm of the water falling in the background filled the cavern with serenity. They were alone, at peace, and naked to each other. He bent to kiss her, slow and easy, because he wanted to relish each taste of her, to memorize each nuance.

He touched the side of her face as he broke the kiss, then sat upon the shift she'd spread on the ground. "Come to me."

Siobhan drew a shaky breath as William pulled her onto his lap. He was ready, pulsing, engorged. Her legs felt weak as she gazed at him. He guided her slowly down onto his manhood, letting her feel every ridge, every dimension. A cry of satisfaction broke from her lips as he finally filled her.

They stayed like that for a moment, allowing her to adjust to the sensation. She watched the desire build in his eyes. She could feel the tension in his muscles as she clutched his shoulders.

"Move up and down slowly."

She did just that, needing to feel the length of him as he retreated, then possessed her once more. The rubies about her neck swayed against her flesh as her slow rhythm grew into a desperate need for abandon.

He leaned forward and took her breast into his mouth, his tongue flicking against her rigid nipple. Fire streaked through her. The rubies warmed against her skin. She could feel the hot column of his manhood filling her, stretching her, as the suction against her breast continued, intensified.

Tension mounted within her. He released her breast to lavish his attention on the other one. Again, he played her to a fever pitch. She began to shake, as tremor after tremor moved through her. "William, please," she cried out as the tension became unbearable.

He moved his hands to her hips and pulled her down, firmly against him, filing her fully. She gasped and arched her head back in response to the hot, convulsive shudder that tore through her. "I need you."

"I need you, too, *ma chère.*" He lifted her, and in one fluid movement laid her down upon her shift. Scarcely had her back touched the ground before he filled her again.

She was lost, consumed by him, as she lifted her body to his. Every sense heightened. She heard the heady rush of the water. Smelled the earth beneath their bodies. Felt the warmth of the rubies as they rolled against her breasts with each frantic stroke.

Their lovemaking was hot and wild, and the release that followed dragged a cry from her lips. William captured her frenzied cry with a kiss. He tightened his hands on her hips and plunged against her, exploding with a moan of pleasure that echoed through the cavern.

When it was over, Siobhan pulled him down against her chest, her breathing ragged as the rubies settled between them. She lay limp, unable to move.

He looked down at her with a smile, his eyes twinkling. "You look like the goddess Venus with your crown of gold, your swollen lips and the passion still lingering in your eyes."

She brought her hand up to stroke his chest. His heartbeat pulsed beneath her hand. A heady feeling moved through her. She was free to explore him in the firelight— every muscle, every ridge. The satisfaction of her body, mixed with the sense of power she held over him, gave her the courage to ask the question that had been turning through her mind since last night. "What happens next, William? How do we free my father without giving de la Roche the Spear?"

His muscles tensed beneath her hand. "We'll need troops. Men who will be willing to go up against de la Roche."

"How long will it take to raise a sufficient army?"

"A few days. I can persuade some of the Highlanders to join us, but those men who have been forced into hiding by de la Roche will be most eager to join the battle."

Siobhan's fingers stilled on the ridges of William's chest. "A few days? My father suffers each day that we wait."

"Without adequate men we are no help to your father.

Attacking now would just cost more lives." He reached out to comfort her. "Sir John's knowledge of the Spear will keep him safe. When de la Roche has all he needs, that is when we need to worry about both you and your father."

Siobhan shivered. In some part of her mind, she had realized when she'd started this journey that she could die. But she'd never considered the possibility of how death would happen. She didn't want to be tortured or burned alive, as many of the Templars were.

"I won't let anything happen to you," William said thickly, as though reading her thoughts once again. "I shall not fail you. I have failed too many others."

She frowned. "Whom?"

"Peter, for one. My brothers in the Scottish Templars who died on our journey to the Holy Land. My own mother and father . . ." His words faded.

"You couldn't have stopped a single one of those things, William. You were but a child when your uncle killed your family. And how were you supposed to stop an army of Saracens all by yourself? Perhaps your brothers died defending your life so that you could go on for them. And de la Roche took Peter's life, not you."

"I could have prevented it."

"How?" She sat up beside him. "By hiding him or other Templars away from their enemies? What kind of life is that? People need to be free to live their lives, regardless of the risks."

He sat up, his body stiff. "This from the woman whose entire life has been nothing more than to support her father's work. Where is your risk, Siobhan? How free are you?"

Siobhan's throat tightened at his accusation. He was right, of course, but hearing the words spoken so plainly made it seem as though she'd wasted her life. "I made my sacrifice willingly."

"Just as I shall accept the responsibility for my failures."

She reached up and took the gold circlet from her head and set it back atop the bejeweled chest, where she also placed the ruby necklace. She crossed her arms before her, feeling suddenly exposed in the golden light. How had they gone from such tender lovemaking to bitter argument in such a short span of time? She knew the answer even as she finished her thought. Because he'd put into words the realization she'd held in her heart for the last several years. She wanted her life to matter. "My father and I are not your responsibility."

"Siobhan," he said, moving his body to retrieve her shift, which had cradled them in their lovemaking only moments before. He shook it out, then offered it to her.

She plucked the damp garment from his fingers and turned her back to him before sliding it over her head. "You take the Spear to wherever you need to take it." She turned to face him. "I'll go to de la Roche with the scroll. That should be enough to convince him to release my father. He won't know you already have the Spear. You can make certain the Templars move the treasure before he finds the hiding place. Of course, he'll think he has what he wants." She turned to face William. "I'll have my father."

His lips were set in a grim line. "Nay, Siobhan. Not that way."

"Then where does that leave us?" she asked as emptiness settled inside her.

"Our original plan still makes the most sense. We leave tomorrow morning together. We'll take the Spear to de la Roche, supported by an army of men. We need to fight him, Siobhan. The man will remain a threat until we drive him back to France."

She sat down on one of the chests and pressed her fingers against her suddenly throbbing temples. "Will he burn my father at the stake?"

"Given the chance, aye." He took an impulsive step forward.

She stayed him with her hand. "Don't come any closer. I lose perspective when you're nearby."

"We need to stay united on this," he said hoarsely.

She closed her eyes and drew a deep breath. Had she made a terrible mistake by accepting his help? Could she negotiate with de la Roche on her own?

She opened her eyes and stared at the knight before her. Never in her life had she felt more confused, lonely or vulnerable than she did right now.

And it suddenly felt as though more than just her father's life was at stake.

Chapter Eighteen

He had disappointed her, but better disappointed than dead.

William watched Siobhan settle in for the night in the hull of the painted dragon ship. His hands curled at his sides. Her cool remoteness told him he wasn't welcome beside her. 'Twas probably for the best. The overwhelming passion they'd had for each other these last few days had to end.

An empty ache centered in his chest. He forced the pain away. He had to keep his head if they were both to survive. Acquiring the treasure had been the easy part of this adventure. Rescuing her father from de la Roche would be difficult indeed.

He had no choice but to gather an army before they proceeded. To do anything else would be madness. But her father could die in the time it took to amass the troops they needed. In reality, her father could be dead already. De la Roche usually spared his victims none of his displeasure.

William's gaze lingered on the length of Siobhan's body. He would make it up to her. When this was all over, he would find some way to set things right between them.

For now, he had to keep her near his side. Even that had dangers, as she had already proved twice. But with her nearby, he could at least minimize those dangers and find comfort in her presence, no matter how remote she was to him. Suddenly, being without her company seemed unfathomable. They needed each other.

And that was the way it would be.

Lucius writhed against the tree Brother William had tied him to in the woods. Darkness enveloped him. He couldn't breathe. He struggled against his bonds. The bark cut into his flesh as he pulled and pushed against the bindings at his wrists. Damn William Keith for leaving him here, alone.

Lucius stopped to rest a moment, fighting the suffocating fear of the blackness. He'd always been afraid of the dark. It was a weakness that only Peter had known about. And while Peter had lived, they'd fought his fear together.

But now Lucius was alone in the dark once again.

He drew a sharp breath, filling his lungs. He could get through this if he stopped thinking about the blanket of black that threatened to choke him. Leaning back against the tree, he tipped his head toward the sky. Bright white lights glittered overhead. Stars. Light. Safety.

Lucius focused his gaze on the light, let it fill him. His heart rate slowed, and soon he found himself relaxing against the wood at his back. His anger and his fear faded as the chill night air crept over him.

He drew a deep breath, filling his lungs as he kept his gaze on the stars overhead. Peter was up there. At the thought, instead of the pain that had been his constant companion the last few days, a sense of calm descended.

Did his brother watch over him still? The thought startled him. Could Peter see the horrible lengths Lucius had gone to in order to exact revenge for an unjust murder?

He hung his head as remorse washed over him. Peter would never have approved.

Lucius's behavior was no more honorable than de la Roche's. Lucius had wanted the Spear. He would have done anything to get it. But for what? A revenge Peter would have disapproved of?

A groan slipped through his lips, filled the quiet of the night. Brother William was right. Revenge wouldn't bring Peter back to him. It wouldn't bolster him so that he no longer feared the dark.

Lucius considered for the first time what Peter would have done if their places had been reversed. No doubt, his brother would have joined Brother William to see that justice was served.

Little good the realization did him now. It was his own foolish behavior that had brought him to this moment. He didn't blame Brother William for tying him to a tree. And tied to that tree he would stay until the knight either came back and untied him or sent someone else to do the deed.

And Lucius knew without a doubt Brother William would do just that. An honorable man like William would never abandon his friends, no matter that they had betrayed him.

Mournfully, Lucius shook his head and stared into the darkness. He let the blackness seep around and through him, no longer fighting his fear. The inky black was the penance he would have to endure. And with the morning light, perhaps he would find himself renewed, if not freed from a fate he had brought upon himself.

Siobhan lay silent and still inside the Viking dragon boat. She needed William to think she had drifted off to sleep. In truth, she felt anything but sleepy, as tumultuous emotions crowded her thoughts.

She never would have imagined a week ago that she would care about anything as much as she cared about her father and his work. But she did. Her whole life had been turned upside down by a gallant knight who had charged into her life on the back of a white horse.

It was the making of a perfect fairy tale. But the pain that tightened her chest and brought the sting of tears to her eyes felt anything but perfect. Siobhan squeezed her eyes shut, forcing back the tears that threatened. They had needed each other to find the Templar treasure and locate the Spear of Destiny. But now that he had the artifact, he didn't need her anymore. He'd proved that with his change in plans to rescue her father.

Or had he changed his plans? They had never truly discussed what would happen after they found the Spear. She had assumed they would leave for her father right away. Every moment he remained in that madman's hands . . .

Siobhan remained curled against the wooden hull for what seemed like ages, until the soft sound of William's steady breathing came to her. He was finally asleep. She sat up and peered out of the boat.

William sat no more than ten paces away, with his back against one of the jeweled chests. His eyes were closed and the sounds of his slow, steady breathing remained unchanged. Carefully, she slipped out of the ship. Her bare feet made no sound as they hit the ground. She stopped, not daring to move or breathe until she knew he still slept.

He didn't stir, except to release a deep and untroubled breath. How different he looked while asleep. Gone were the lines of worry that creased his brow, and his firm jaw had relaxed. The thick golden crescents of his lashes lay like fallen wings on his cheeks, and his hair, swept back from his forehead, looked like silken gold threads that were as much a part of the treasure as anything else in the room.

Her gaze wandered lower, to the sheer physical beauty that was William Keith. He was bare except for the braies, which covered his groin, and cast in the golden glow from the lit urns.

Dozens of scars, both fine and wide, threaded the surface of his arms and chest. The scar he'd acquired recently looked slightly redder and shinier than the others that rippled across the hard surface of his flesh. His ribs, belly and thighs also bore telltale signs of a hard, sometimes brutal life.

What right had she to cause him even more pain? Going against de la Roche without an army would most definitely gain this man even more scars on his body and on his soul. He'd shared with her the pain of his failures, and she had cast them aside with thoughts of herself and her father's needs.

Siobhan bit her lip to keep herself from crying out, so great was her remorse. She didn't want to cause him any more pain. But she also needed to save her father.

If she left tonight on her own, taking the Spear with her, it would indeed hurt William, but not in a physical way. Perhaps in time, he would forgive her. She drew a deep, painful breath. It was better this way.

Moving quietly so as not to disturb him, she slipped toward the back wall. She hesitated, her hand outstretched before the Spear. Did it hold special powers? If she touched it, would it somehow change who she was or what she wanted?

She swallowed roughly as she grasped the wooden shaft, and waited. No frisson of power came to her, nor did anything shift in her mood or outlook. Nothing happened at all.

She drew the Spear to her and silently headed for the entrance of the chamber. At the edge of the waterfall, she cast a quick glance behind her. William remained asleep. Nothing had changed inside her when she touched the Spear, but this man's presence had changed so many things.

Never had her heart beaten so wildly out of control at anyone's approach or at the sound of anyone's voice as it had with William. Her very bones seemed to melt at his slightest touch. All these things had happened with shocking intensity from the first moment they had met. She could no longer deny she was completely, painfully and utterly in love with him. It was a sweet pain that she would endure for the rest of her days. Because once she left here, she would endure them alone. Her deception would see to that.

Her heart pounded in her chest. She took a deep breath to steady herself, then plunged into the back side of the pulsing waterfall. Without William's help, it was more difficult to navigate through the waterfall and then the pool beyond, but she managed to pull herself up on the opposite bank. She quickly dressed in the clothes they'd left, then patted the pocket of her gown to make certain the scroll remained safe. Reassured, she headed for wooden plank they'd crossed last night.

It took all her strength to climb the ramp, then hoist herself up the lip of the ledge she had almost tumbled over. Finally, tired and grateful she'd managed the feat alone, Siobhan paused in the long hallway that led back to the main cave.

"Good-bye, William," she whispered. Firmly clutching the Spear, she ran down the hallway, past the paintings, up the stairs they'd uncovered, past the pillars and statues of Templar knights. She kept on running through the cave and out of the opening in the mountainside, before she was forced to slow her pace by the treacherous, rocky path.

The first hint of morning light filtered across the land, illuminating everything in shades of pink and gray. Siobhan reached a small band of trees and bracken that lay just ahead of where they'd left Lucius, when she heard footsteps coming quickly behind her. She took a deep breath and prepared to confront William.

She turned. It wasn't William who skidded to a halt behind her. It wasn't William who wrenched her into his arms, forcing her to drop the Spear. It wasn't William who clamped a brutal hand over her mouth to stifle her scream.

Siobhan. William sat up, instantly sensing something was wrong. He shot to his feet, his hand on his sword, and searched frantically about the chamber. The boat was empty. Siobhan was nowhere is sight. The Spear was gone.

She'd left on her own with a weapon she had no idea how to control. The power of the Spear was great. To one so innocent, it might also prove deadly. And if de la Roche came upon her before William could intercept her . . . "God in Heaven," he groaned. He had to find her—fast.

William grabbed his sword and Excalibur before he ran to the waterfall. He moved through the barrier as if no water could hold him back. Nothing would keep him from finding Siobhan and containing the power of the Spear. Some legends claimed that it gave men power in battle. Others spoke of how it took over one's mind, sending the owner in search of a constant flow of blood.

He ran through the pool on the other side, sweeping his garments up as he continued to run. At the ramp that led up the ledge he stopped and hastily donned his clothing, mail and boots. It wouldn't help Siobhan if he wasn't prepared for whatever might await them. When his armor was fully in place and his sword strapped to his side, he ran up the ramp and through the hallway, not bothering to conceal the stairs once more. He raced out of the cave and into the early-morning light.

As he ran, he replayed her impassioned speech from last night over in his mind. He was entirely to blame for her leaving this way. If only he'd taken the time to discuss his plans for rescuing her father more fully. Instead, he'd allowed his pride to get the better of him. When would he ever learn to overcome his pride? He should never have let her stew. He should never have done a lot of things where Siobhan was concerned, like staring into her bright green eyes, or kissing her, or touching her satin-smooth skin. He'd allowed his own emotions to go too far, needing to connect with her in a way that he'd never connected with a woman before.

There had been other women, and some equally as lovely and seductive as Lady Siobhan Fraser, before he'd taken his vows. And afterward, he had never been tempted. Not once. So what made her different? Why had he tossed aside everything he held dear for her?

He had wanted her so badly, had needed her as he'd never needed another person before in his life. He'd needed her in ways he hadn't even dared to consider until this very moment.

"Siobhan?"

He listened for a reply, but there was only the sound of the birds twittering high overhead. A prickle of sensation brought up the hair at the back of his neck. He forced his anxiety away. Siobhan was safe. He would reach her and all would be well.

With his heart hammering in his chest, he continued

his descent across the steep and rocky terrain. Was it fear that made the beat pound in his ears, or a message from a part of himself that he had denied for too long—a part that he'd kept prisoner since he was a child?

As he reached the trees, he slowed his steps. "Siobhan." The uneasy feeling he'd tried to ignore crossed the nape of his neck once more. He stared hard into the trees and bracken, searching for any sign of which way she'd gone. The breeze stirred softly around him, rustling the leaves, but he heard nothing else.

His hand fell to his sword, as much for comfort as protection, when he noticed a splash of color on the ground ahead. He raced to it and bent down beside one of Siobhan's half boots. He clutched the boot in his hand as he spotted the freshly scuffed earth that gave evidence of a struggle.

There was no movement other than the leaves jostling in the trees and the bracken beyond. No sound other than the breeze. Glittering slivers of sunlight illuminated the forest beyond.

William felt as though someone had slammed him in the chest with his own sword. Someone had captured Siobhan. The question was, who?

The thought of Siobhan in the hands of someone, quite possibly de la Roche, made him physically ill. He wanted to hit someone, to yell and rage and slam his fist against a rock. What was she going through right now? She must be wild with fear.

William tried to get control of himself. He wouldn't be any help to Siobhan if he didn't. He had to be calm. He had to think clearly. He had to find her. If de la Roche had found her . . . If he did anything to Siobhan . . .

Nay, he could not consider the possibility. He would find her. He had to.

And he knew just where to locate someone who would help him.

The Spear fell from Siobhan's hand. In only a matter of moments, she'd lost her one bargaining tool. She had no time to scream before the stranger removed his hand and stuffed a length of foul-smelling linen into her mouth. He tied the mass securely behind her head. The need to gag overwhelmed her, but she pushed it aside and lashed out against her attacker. He might have silenced her, but he had not won the battle.

He retrieved the weapon with his free hand, and Siobhan knew a moment's despair. How easily she had fallen into this trap. William wouldn't have succumbed to anyone or anything, especially with the Spear in his possession.

She kicked and writhed, desperate to find a way to freedom despite the heavy arm clamped around her waist dragging her backward into the woods. Who was this man? A rogue Highlander? One of de la Roche's men?

The tall, muscular young man who pinned her to him grinned down at her. "Quit fighting me and this will go a lot easier for you," he said in a thick French accent.

She dug her fingernails into the viselike grip that held her until she drew blood. The man grunted, then brought the hand holding the Spear down against the side of her head. The staff of the Spear connected with her skull.

The impact sent her senses reeling. Black edged her vision. She drew several short, sharp breaths through her nose, trying desperately to stay conscious. She tripped over a rock. The hard edge scraped against her leg, her ankle, and pulled the boot from her foot.

Without missing a beat, the arm about her waist hauled her to her feet and propelled her into the woods toward a waiting horse.

The Frenchman tossed her onto the animal's back, then mounted behind her. Instead of heading back toward the first waterfall that she and William had discovered, the man rode to the south, deeper into the Cairngorms's steep and rocky terrain.

At their rapid pace, Siobhan could do nothing but grasp at the horse's mane and hold on. Her captor seemed unimpressed by the steep cliff off to their left and the loose path beneath the horse's feet as he encouraged his mount to greater speed. Siobhan turned away from the steep ledge, which only brought a sharp chuckle from the man behind her.

"If you are frightened by the cliff, then you best faint now before my lord gets his hands you."

Fear roiled in Siobhan's stomach, but she lifted her chin and boldly met his gaze.

"You're a cheeky one, I can tell by the fire in your eyes." His grin was little more than a dark, evil slash. "De la Roche will like that even better. He likes nothing more than to break your kind."

She dropped her gaze so that he couldn't read her emotions. *De la Roche.* She didn't know if the name brought more a sense of relief or fear. At least she was on her way to her father. And the Spear, while not in her control, was still with her. She would have to find a way to use it to her advantage when they arrived.

A shiver of apprehension moved through her. She knew who had abducted her. She also knew why. Where they were going remained a mystery, except that her father would most likely be there as well. *If he still lived.* She thrust the thought away without further consideration.

What de la Roche intended to do with her once they arrived at their destination was something she didn't dare contemplate.

Chapter Nineteen

William didn't stop to think about what he was doing. He ran through the woods to where he'd bound Lucius.

At his approach, Lucius straightened. "You came back."

Without breaking his stride, William reached for his sword.

Lucius's eyes flew wide. "Nay! William, stop. I've changed—"

The ropes that imprisoned him dropped. "Where is your horse, Lucius?"

The man didn't move. He stared at William, his mouth slack.

"Where is your horse?" William repeated more harshly.

Lucius grasped his hands before him, rubbing his wrists. "I can't feel my arms."

"Lucius, please. I don't have time for this," William growled, gripping the man by the throat. "The horse."

Lucius motioned to the right with his eyes.

William released him. "Show me."

After sucking in a breath, Lucius frowned and rubbed his throat, which now bore the red imprint of William's hand. "Brother, I'm sorry I challenged you. I deserve your anger, but know that I've changed. I want to help you."

"Then lead me to your horse."

Lucius frowned. "Did you not find the Spear?"

William sheathed his sword. "The Spear is gone. Quite possibly to de la Roche or his men. I need to recover it."

Lucius's face paled. "Where's the girl?"

"She's missing," William said, striding in the direction Lucius had indicated.

"Was she abducted? Or did she steal the Spear out from under you?" Lucius said as he leapt through the underbrush, trying to match William's stride.

William stopped. "Don't push me." His tone was hard, harder than it had ever been with any of his men before. "Lady Siobhan has been abducted with the Spear. And for every moment we waste with useless discussion, the men who took her gain precious time on us. Now, for the last time, where's your beast?"

"Follow me." Lucius darted ahead of William and led him down a steep incline. "I had to leave Ares at the bottom of the cliff."

After several long moments, Lucius paused. "I apologize, William, for being so difficult. I miss my brother."

William frowned. "Loss is difficult, but villainy and deceit will never take the pain away."

"I realized that last night." Lucius sighed. "As much as I hated being tied to that tree, the time alone with my thoughts helped me see things more clearly."

"I appreciate your change of heart, but we need to hurry. Can we not discuss this later?"

Lucius nodded and moved down the mountainside once more until, finally, a large black horse came into view. "We ride together," William said, mounting, then offered Lucius a hand up to sit behind him.

Lucius had barely settled against the animal's flesh before William set the horse in motion, heading south. It was the right direction. He could feel it in every muscle of his being.

"Where are we going?" Lucius asked.

"To de la Roche."

Lucius tensed. "We're going to see the devil himself? Let me off. I want no part of it without the Spear for protection."

"What happened to your need for revenge?" William asked as he flew through the trees, feeling the occasional sting of pain as the branches lashed at his legs, his arms, his face. The pain was nothing compared to the constriction in his chest.

Siobhan needed him.

"With the Spear, there was a chance I could triumph over de la Roche. Without it, I'd best put the flames to my own feet. We'll be walking directly into a trap if we proceed without help."

"I'm going to de la Roche. You're going back to the monastery to gather the men."

Lucius gasped. "You'll go to him alone? He'll kill you."

William kept his gaze fixed on the land before him. He knew it was dangerous to go it alone. "I must do something."

"What is it about this girl that has changed you so much? You're not yourself. You're not thinking rationally."

William frowned. "I feel different when she's near. Through her, a part of me came back to life, the part that I thought I'd left in Teba."

But it was more than that. Her presence warmed the places in his heart his uncle had crushed so many years before. "I can't lose anyone else I care about. I can't stand by and let something happen to her, not even if I have to fight my way into the devil's den myself."

There was silence between them filled only by the rhythmic sound of the horse's hooves. Then Lucius spoke, his tone gentle, understanding. "You've told me more than I deserved to know. We'll catch de la Roche and get the Spear back." He brought a hand up to rest on William's shoulder. "You'll never have to fight alone. Not while there's still a Templar with breath in his body."

Some of the tension drained from William's taut muscles. "My thanks, Lucius."

"Since we are in this together, I know another way across this pass. 'Tis shorter, but a lot more dangerous."

"Tell me." William didn't care about the additional risk. If it closed the distance between himself and Siobhan, he was most grateful.

Siobhan was faint from cold and terror as they dismounted outside an isolated tower from ancient Viking times. The cylindrical broch sat at the edge of an inlet to the North Sea. Her abductor dismounted near the structure with the Spear in his grasp, then pulled her to the ground beside him. Her legs would have given out beneath her had he not had a firm hold of her arm.

The imposing structure loomed before her. "I wish to see my father," she demanded with a lift of her chin. She couldn't let this man see how frightened she was to be there alone, without the Spear in her hand to offer as a trade.

"We are not at court, milady," the young man scoffed. "You'll do what you're told. And you'll see your father when de la Roche says you can."

He drew her forward with a painful grip on her arm, toward the thick gray stone walls of the broch. They walked around the tall structure until they came to an opening, a doorway no more than four feet high. He released her arm only briefly to force her head down to clear the low structure, designed no doubt to make those who entered feel vulnerable.

He clamped her arm again when they proceeded to the ground gallery. An older man of medium height turned to greet them. His eerie light-colored eyes gleamed with appreciation as he appraised Siobhan. "Marcus, what have you brought me?" the man said in a thick French accent.

"Monsieur de la Roche." The younger soldier offered the man a quick bow. "The daughter of Sir John Fra—"

He held his hand up, cutting the younger man's words off as his gaze shifted to the Spear. His pale eyes widened, and he took several halting steps forward until his hands clamped around it. He held the Spear before him. His pale eyes filled with an almost fanatic gleam. He stood barely breathing, frozen in place, caught in a trance for several long moments. "The power of the centuries is mine," he said at last.

His eerie gaze landed on Siobhan once more. "Sir John's daughter."

Making an effort to appear undisturbed by the calculating way de la Roche looked at her, Siobhan straightened. "Where is my father?"

"Things are as they should be." A smirk came to his lips.

"Yes. You have the Spear. Now I want my father in return."

He crept closer and ran two fingers up the length of her arm. "I made you no promises."

A shiver coursed through her.

He must have felt her response, because he drew closer and ran the same two fingers along her jaw.

"Where is my father?" She twisted her head away from his touch.

"Why the haste?" He sneered and brought his fingers to rest along the ridge of her collarbone.

Siobhan drew in a slow, steady breath, trying to contain the terror that pounded in her chest. Why had she thought she could handle de la Roche on her own? Once again William was correct. Why had she not listened to his wisdom? "I ask you humbly, take me to my father," she said with calm civility.

His fingers dropped from her. He turned away. "He's not here."

"What do you mean, he's not here?" she said, surprised and not caring if he detected her displeasure.

He twisted back toward her, the Spear pointed at her chest. "The Spear wants blood. Your blood. Your father's blood. Even William Keith's blood." He pressed the tip against her chest.

She gasped as the Spear pricked her. A blotch of red appeared on the bodice of her gown.

"I do thank you for bringing me the Spear." He pulled the tip back and ran his finger along the blade, gathering a drop of her blood. He brought his finger to his mouth and licked the droplet with his tongue. "Sweet, so sweet, but a heretic nonetheless," he sneered. "And heretics must die."

She bristled. "I've done nothing wrong."

"No, you've done everything I'd hoped you would. I know William Keith well enough to suspect that he'll follow you anywhere and gallantly try to save you."

"You had no intention of releasing my father, did you?"

He smiled an evil smile. "None. He's a Templar and deserves to die a slow and painful death."

"He still lives?" There was still hope to save him.

De la Roche's gaze narrowed on her. "And now that you are in my possession, he'll tell me everything I wish to know about the Templar treasure when he watches me question you most thoroughly."

A chill flew up her spine. She could guess what the methods for thoroughly questioning a woman might be.

Her father would go wild with impotent fury if forced to watch such a thing. He'd grow angry enough that he just might surrender the secrets he'd kept hidden for so many years.

Not only that. Also because of her impulsiveness, William would come looking for her instead of trying to move the treasure.

William will come looking for me. Most likely out of anger at her deception. Siobhan raised her chin. She could handle William's anger. She might also be able to endure de la Roche's interrogation. But she couldn't allow either of the men in her life to die because of her mistakes.

She had to do something quick. The doorway was blocked by the young man who'd captured her—but she saw a set of stairs to his left.

She sped to them, reaching them with ease before either man reacted. She surged into the dark stairwell, unable to see where she was going. Stumbling over her skirt, she darted up the stairs, deeper into the blackness.

Footsteps sounded behind her as she passed a second floor. She kept going until she hit something hard in front of her. A door? She fumbled against the wooden surface, searching for the latch. Her fingers located cool metal. She sprang the latch free and stepped out onto the parapets.

"Get her," de la Roche growled. "I want to know where that treasure lies."

In the open, she searched frantically for an escape. There was nowhere to go but down. She looked over the edge of the broch. A wave of dizziness swamped her. The ground lay far below. Could she throw herself over the edge and survive with nothing to break her fall?

Did she have a choice?

The trail Lucius and William followed had deteriorated to nothing but a sheep track along the edge of a cliff.

Below them the earth fell away at a sharp angle that dropped onto jagged rocks far below. William had never feared heights, but a less-needful man might sanely have turned back to more steady ground.

"'Tis called the Devil's Lip," Lucius said.

It didn't make William feel any better. The horse stepped with care onto a ledge no wider than three of his own feet placed end to end. He willed all his thoughts to surefootedness and balance for the beast that carried them both near the abyss.

Hazy clouds scudded across the sky, and William almost prayed for darkness. At least then he wouldn't have to see what they traveled through at a slow and steady pace. A dozen ravens circled the sky above them, possibly searching for prey or waiting for any misstep to supply their supper for the night.

Halfway across the ledge, the wind picked up, and William was forced to lower his head to protect his eyes from the bits of dirt and grit. He found he was holding his breath even as his heart raced, and that his skin had turned clammy and cold.

Step by step they made their way over the aptly named divide. They both breathed a genuine sigh of relief when they reached the other side.

"Hellish enough for you?" Lucius asked.

"Indeed." William drew his first full breath since they'd started across the side of the mountain, grateful to be on solid land once again.

William slid from Ares's back and began searching the ground for signs that Siobhan and her abductor had come this way. He forced himself to proceed slowly so as not to miss anything. His heart stumbled when he finally found the tracks. With a renewed sense of urgency, he remounted and continued down the mountainside. At the base of the mountain, William pulled the animal to a stop. "This is where we part," he said to Lucius. "You must head to the monastery on foot."

Lucius nodded and jumped down.

"Before I left, Brother Kenneth said he would have the monks assembled for when I came back with the Spear. They should be waiting for you."

"How many?" Lucius asked.

"Nearly two score at the monastery. And probably some Highlanders as well."

Lucius frowned. "'Tis not nearly enough to go up against de la Roche."

"It must be," William said. "We have no other resources."

"What about the girl? How will you get her away from de la Roche so that we can attack?"

"You leave that to me." With a parting nod, William put his heels to the horse's flanks. "Make haste, Ares. With all your strength, I beg you to get to Siobhan. I can't lose her."

The horse obeyed, charging like the wind across the open terrain and following the tracks that headed directly for a gray, stone broch in the distance. William neared the ancient fortress just in time to see Siobhan running across the parapets with de la Roche at her heels.

Before she could even react, de la Roche grabbed her arm in a viselike grip. "Oh, no you don't. I'll have my answers before you harm yourself." The younger man blocked the door, waiting to respond, should de la Roche need him.

Siobhan met the Frenchman's steady gaze. "You may ask anything you like, sir, but I can tell you nothing."

Tightening his grip, he pushed her back toward Marcus and the open doorway. "Torture has a way of changing a person's mind about what they will and will not say."

One man she might be able to resist. With two, she

would be overpowered. She had to break free before they reached the door and Marcus. She twisted and squirmed and dug in her heels until de la Roche lifted her off her feet. He carried her toward the door, despite her flailing.

Inside, she would have little hope of escape. She had to break free. Grabbing what she could of the Frenchman's hair, she pulled hard. "Put me down."

"*Sacre bleu!*" he yelled, dropping her to her feet and angrily reaching to make her release her grip on his hair. His hand clamped over hers.

She brought her knee up as hard as she could.

Recognizing her intent, de la Roche dropped the Spear he clutched in his hand and twisted. Her aim missed his manhood, but connected hard with his thigh. He grunted. His free hand swept up and struck her face, knocking her grip on his hair free.

Marcus lunged for the Spear.

Siobhan rushed to her feet, but de la Roche was upon her. He struck her again, sending her smashing against the stone wall. Her breath hitched and a wave of dizziness swamped her.

"There is no escape." He grasped the fabric of her gown and pulled her to her feet. "You'll tell me where that treasure is while we wait for William Keith to arrive. Soon, I'll have everything I want." His gaze moved back to Marcus. "Give me the Spear."

The young man handed the weapon to his master.

"I shall enjoy using this blade on your unspoiled flesh."

"If you want to use that blade, de la Roche, try it on me."

Siobhan recognized William's voice. De la Roche whipped toward the doorway. Marcus charged. With one mighty blow, William felled the young man. He lay on the parapet floor, unmoving.

The fury Siobhan saw in William's eyes sent fresh

waves of fear through her body. Who was that anger directed at? De la Roche? Her? Both? He drew his sword.

The sound of many footsteps echoed in the stairwell.

"Seize him," de la Roche snarled to the ten men who poured through the doorway. Complete chaos erupted all around. Siobhan broke free of de la Roche's grasp. She moved away, pressing herself against the wall, trying to be invisible. She wasn't. Two men charged her. Before they reached her, William attacked from behind. The two men fell. He pushed her into a corner so as to form a protective barrier between her and the fighting.

Siobhan pressed her hand to her lips as she watched the fighting from over William's shoulders. Three more men charged. William hit the first with the hilt of his sword, then thrust forward, driving his sword deep into the second man's body. He pulled his weapon free in time to catch the third man's stroke and disarmed him.

As William twisted free, two more men charged, catching him off guard, unbalancing him. The impact knocked the sword from his hands. It skittered across the wooden floor, out of reach. He grabbed one of the men by the shoulder and punched him hard. The other man he kicked in the stomach, sending him flying backward against the stone wall.

Before he could react, two men surged forward and grasped him by the arms. Two more men grabbed his legs. His eyes filled with fury. A roar filled the darkening evening air. William writhed against the hands that constrained him.

Siobhan moved toward William, but de la Roche grabbed her about the waist. She shrieked.

De la Roche brought the Spear up to Siobhan's chin. The pointed tip pressed cruelly against her flesh. "Take them belowstairs and tie them up. I have plans for them both."

William's gaze connected with hers. In his eyes she saw pain. She had betrayed him. Her throat tightened. And still he had come for her.

Tears sprang to her eyes. "I'm sorry," she mouthed.

He nodded stiffly.

She watched with a sense of horror as Marcus stepped up behind William and brought the hilt of his sword down hard against the back of William's head. William slumped forward, still supported by the men.

Siobhan eyed him frantically. "Don't hurt—" Marcus strode toward her and struck her brow with his hilt. Pain exploded in her head. Marcus's arms gripped her as her knees buckled and darkness consumed her.

Chapter Twenty

Siobhan woke up to pain in her arms. Her heavy eyelids struggled open. William gazed at her from across a short distance. His hands were bound together and he was suspended from a rope as she was, hanging over a deep open pit with sharp metallic spikes at the bottom. Above them were several beams of stout wood that made up the flooring for the room abovestairs.

A surge of panic shot through her. "Where are we?" she asked, pulling against her bindings.

"Don't struggle," he said calmly. "The men partially cut our ropes. If we move much, we'll fall."

The chamber was lit by a single torch set against the wall near the stairs. They were alone except for the scurrying sounds beneath them—almost certainly rodents.

Siobhan became chillingly aware of the dank earth that surrounded them, the scents of decay and death. She swallowed roughly. "A dungeon?" she asked.

"It would seem so."

"William, I am so sorry. I didn't mean for any—"

"Stop," he said gently. "I will accept your apology when we get out of here. Until then—" He stopped speaking at the sound of a latch moving across the door.

De la Roche entered, clutching the Spear. A lanky older man followed him, then Marcus. "You're awake."

"I suppose it's foolish to ask why we're here," William asked.

"Very," de la Roche replied with a slight smile.

The older man stood next to de la Roche's side, while Marcus moved across the chamber and drew a bolt onto the crossbow he carried in his hands. He aimed the weapon at William.

"You wanted a trade." Siobhan kept her features neutral. She was so scared, she was sick to her stomach, but she wouldn't let de la Roche know that. "You have the Spear. Release us."

"You expected a trade, milady. I gave you no such guarantee." His smile faded. "I'll give you both the end you deserve."

"You're going to kill us?" Siobhan asked.

"Not I." De la Roche waved at the man beside him. The older gentleman set a leather satchel he carried upon the ground at the edge of the deep pit they both dangled over. He flipped the bag open and uncoiled a long leather strap. He coiled the whip around his hand, then let it fly at William's face. The leather struck his cheek. William tensed but did not cry out. A red welt marred his flesh. The man lashed out at William several more times until his lip was split, his cheek and eye swelling.

William took the blows in silence. Each flick of the whip met with hard muscle. The tension in William's body pulled against the rope. Slowly, the frayed cord unraveled, leaving less and less of it to bear the warrior's weight.

"Don't hurt him," Siobhan cried out, unable to watch the abuse any longer.

"Tell me where the treasure is."

"Where is my father?"

"He lives," de la Roche said. "But not for much longer if you do not tell me where that treasure is located."

"If I tell you, will you release us?"

"Perhaps. Or perhaps no matter what you do, you'll end up pierced clear through by the stakes that line the bottom of that pit. The rats will feast upon you." De la Roche smiled. "Seems a fitting end for you, Keith. Too bad for you, Lady Siobhan, for getting involved with this Templar. Now you must die as well. That is, unless you tell me what I want to know."

"Nay, Siobhan." William's voice was icy and sharp. "He will kill us no matter what we tell him."

De la Roche frowned. "So little faith . . ."

"In you. Aye," William ground out as the whip bit into the flesh of his arms, his neck.

Pain contorted his face as he suffered silently. Siobhan knew he would take it all into himself rather than let de la Roche experience any sort of pleasure from his torment.

"Does it bother you to watch him suffer?" de la Roche asked, no doubt picking up on the horror and fear she failed to disguise.

"Yes. Please. Stop." The whip fell still, and Siobhan heaved a relieved breath.

De la Roche nodded to the older man, who coiled his leather strap. "Good. Because it was never my intention to torture William in such a way."

The old man sent the whip flying. The strip connected with Siobhan's back. She released a startled cry and arched against the pain. The rope partially gave, and she slipped closer to the opening of the pit.

A snicker echoed about the small chamber. "It was always my intention to make this Templar watch while I tortured you. Now that he knows the pain you'll endure with each stroke, my own satisfaction will increase ten-fold."

Siobhan couldn't speak. Her throat was locked in terror as she stared into de la Roche's pale blue eyes. He nodded his head. "Whenever you are ready, Lemar." The older man let the whip fly. He struck her again and again. Siobhan bit down on her lip to keep from crying out.

"Cease!" William's roar filled the chamber.

De la Roche's lips thinned. "Then tell me where the treasure is hidden."

"Why?" William asked. "You won't let us live anyway."

"No." A flicker of disgust passed over his face. "But you might save yourself some suffering."

The Frenchman reached up to Siobhan's rope with the Spear and poked at what remained of the fiber with the weapon. Several more strands gave way.

The rope jerked above her. Siobhan gasped. She glanced up. Only one section of rope remained whole. She closed her eyes. Regardless of everything she and William had already suffered, they were going to die.

Agony tore through William as he watched de la Roche's henchman strike Siobhan's back, her shoulder, her neck. He took each strike into himself, feeling her pain. Rage burned in his chest as he watched the rope stretch as a result of the abuse the older man inflicted upon her.

His own rope continually unraveled beneath his body's tension. Only a few more strands remained between him and certain death. His arms and shoulders were numb. Yet the places where the whip had ripped his flesh burned.

Icy fury consumed him. William forced himself to breathe. Siobhan might be in pain, but she was not dead. He forced his gaze away from the abuse. He had to think.

He had to stay in control. Only then could he reason a way out of this trap.

He concentrated on the younger man, Marcus, on the opposite side of the pit. The crossbow remained aimed at William's chest, but the warrior was transfixed by what was happening to Siobhan.

William felt his pulse pound in his jaw. If he did nothing, de la Roche would prevail. Damnation! It wasn't right for de la Roche to succeed after all that they'd gone through to defeat him. He closed his eyes for a simple, desperate prayer, then opened them once again.

William coiled his body, bringing his legs to his chest, and shifted his weight in one heaving motion. He heard the rope snap and the floorboard crack as he flung himself to the side of the pit.

He hit the ground, and hot blinding pain stabbed through his shoulder. In the space of a heartbeat, William grasped Marcus's ankles with his bound wrists and twisted him to the left. The crossbow fired.

Using what he could of his hands and his legs, William pulled Marcus to the ground. He brought his elbow up into the young man's nose. Marcus collapsed as a cry of pain rent the air. The bolt hit its target. The old man dropped the whip, midstrike. He crumpled to his knees, clutching the bolt in his chest.

De la Roche roared and surged toward William.

Siobhan screamed.

The sound of her rope snapping filled the chamber. Sheer terror tore through William. He reached down with numb fingers and plucked the dagger from his boot, quickly slashed through the ropes at his wrists, then sent the dagger flying across the pit to imbed itself in de la Roche's thigh. The man dropped to his knees with a howl of pain.

As though in a slowed stream of action, Siobhan fell.

William got to his feet. He took a step toward her, then another.

The pit gaped wide below. He snatched the whip from the older man's fist and sent the leather flying. With a smack the leather connected with Siobhan's waist. "Grab on!" Her bound hands reached out. Connected.

Her weight and the momentum of her fall propelled them together toward the pit. "Let me go, William. Save yourself."

"Hold tight. Hold on," he chanted over and over. He jerked the rope, hard.

With a mighty heave, William pulled her back to the surface. She scrambled onto the ground, trembling. Tears filled her eyes. "That's the third time—William!" Her eyes focused behind him, wide with terror.

He twisted. His hands came up. With his forearm, he blocked the blow de la Roche aimed at his chest with the Spear. William brought his fist up and connected with the man's chin. De la Roche staggered backward and shook his head, then took several more steps back, toward the stairs. "Let's see how you fare against my troops, Templar!" de la Roche snarled as he fled to the main level of the broch.

"My lord," the younger man called after de la Roche. The Frenchman paid him no heed. Marcus staggered to his feet. Blood streamed down his chin and onto his chest from the blow William had planted against his nose. The young man's legs buckled and he collapsed back against the ground in a faint.

William knelt beside Siobhan. He grasped the dagger de la Roche had removed from his thigh and tossed to the ground. He sliced the rope at Siobhan's wrists. "Are you well?" He gave the dagger to her.

"Scared, but whole." She grasped the dagger in her right hand. "This is all my fault. If I'd only listened to you,

you never would've been endangered. Why didn't you stay where you'd be safe? Why did you come after me?"

"Hush." His finger touched her lips, silencing her. "How could I stay away when I knew you were in trouble? We're in this together. But it's not over yet. Can you stand?"

She nodded. "We have to get out of here."

He helped her to her feet, then moved back to where Marcus lay on the ground. William seized the sword from the downed man's scabbard, pleased to see that it was William's own. The man had taken it when William was unconscious.

"Ready?" he asked when he returned to Siobhan's side. "We'll have to fight our way out of here."

She nodded. "We have to find my father."

"We'll find him, Siobhan. We will." With his sword at the ready, he made his way up the stairs. Siobhan matched him step for step. She wore one half boot. Her clothes were slashed, and blood showed through. He knew she had to be in pain, tired and terrified of what lay ahead for them. And yet she refused to give up.

Admiration tightened his throat as they made their way up the steps. At the top he paused and turned to her. "Let's do this together."

She nodded.

Together they burst through the doorway.

They paused in the doorway side by side as the main floor of the broch filled with de la Roche's men. "Take my sword. Remember what I taught you." He took the small dagger from her fingers and pressed the hilt of his sword into her hand.

"You'll fight with only a dagger?" She tried to keep the fear from her voice, to remain calm. Inside she quaked. Forty men stood before them.

"Trust me," he said calmly, tucking the dagger into his boot.

She clamped her fingers around the hilt of his sword. Her heart raced. "I trust you."

In a blur of motion, William shot forward. He grasped the man in front of him by the throat and tossed him backward so hard he took four other men with him when he fell. A heartbeat later, William had pulled two swords free from the men's hands and set upon the others.

"Stay behind me, lass," he called out as all the men in the room rushed forward. A broadsword came crashing down, slashing in an arc close to William's head. Siobhan's shriek alerted him to the danger. He easily spun away, but into the path of yet another challenger. The steel of the blade barely missed his neck and shoulder, slicing harmlessly through the air. William kicked the man in the stomach and sent him back into the fray.

Two warriors made it through the melee and closed in on Siobhan. Their eyes told her they had more than combat in mind if they caught her. She raised William's sword. One man lunged. She brought the heavy sword down, yet kept it close to her body as William had taught her. When her attacker left himself open with the swing of his blade, she brought her weapon back up and clipped the man in the chin. He roared and fell back through the open doorway.

The other man charged, his sword at the ready. Siobhan prepared for the impact. As he rushed forward, she easily stepped aside, then brought the edge of the blade down against his back. He collapsed at her feet.

She stepped over the man and the trail of bodies William had left in his wake. Her heart thundered in her chest. They were halfway to the door. The floorboards beneath their feet groaned.

William dispatched one warrior with the sword in his

right hand, then struck another with the sword in his left. His strokes were swift and clean. The men before them charged. William struck out. He sliced the ear off one man and hit another in the neck. The first man roared in pain and fell back, while the second man's eyes widened, his fingers clawing at the hole that was left when William pulled his sword back. He staggered back several paces before he toppled sideways as a sickening hiss and gurgle of air escaped his throat.

They had advanced to the center of the room. Twenty or more men still blocked their exit, pressing in on all sides. She twisted around, positioning her back to William's. They would never make it. Not this time.

The cracking of wood broke through the clang of steel that echoed in the chamber. Siobhan turned to William. He glanced back at her. In his eyes she saw a plea to once again trust him as he fended off one attacker with one sword and struck the floorboards with the other.

Another crack sounded, this one more ominous than the last. He struck the floor hard once more. A terrifying groan filled the space. For a heartbeat, the men ceased their fighting and confusion settled over their faces.

William reached back, grasped her by the hand and hauled her with him to the door just as the center of the room dipped. Two of the floorboards cracked. The floor suddenly sloped down. The men scrambled to follow them to the door. The floor fell away, and the men along with it.

She and William burst through the door into the night air, the roars of fear and deep-chested cries of outrage echoing behind them. Hoofbeats sounded off to their right, and they could barely discern the shadow of a horse and rider fleeing in the distance.

De la Roche.

"This way," he said, racing for the horse he had left hidden in a grove of trees up the bank from the shore. He tossed his borrowed swords on the ground and untied Ares' reins from the bushes.

When he returned to Siobhan, she handed him his own sword. "This is better in your hands than mine."

He accepted the weapon and returned it to his scabbard. "I don't know about that. You did well." He mounted behind her, tucked her safely in his arms, and with a jerk of the reins, set off in rapid pursuit into the dark, mottled shadows of the night.

Ares flew across the terrain. The sound of hoofbeats echoed in the night ahead of them, and although they could not see de la Roche clearly, they could hear him.

"Where's he headed?" Siobhan asked.

"Most likely to wherever the other half of his troops are located."

"Do you think my father will be there?" Siobhan's voice was serious but steady. Truly a surprise, for all they'd just lived through.

"Aye."

"Make this horse go faster."

He put his heels to Ares' sides, encouraging him to greater speeds. "Is there anything I can say that will dissuade you from coming along with me? I could send you back to the monastery. Lucius is gathering men to fight. You'd be safe there."

"Would I?" she called out as the wind whipped her hair about her face. "It's obvious de la Roche wants not only the Spear, but the entire treasure. He'll do anything to get what he wants."

William frowned into the darkness ahead. He had considered the possibility that separating the two of them was exactly what the Frenchman hoped for. He could get Simon to watch over Siobhan while he followed de la

Roche, but he knew he'd still be frantic with worry all the time she was out of his sight.

"I'm going with you," she said as though reading his thoughts.

"We started this adventure together. Let's end it that way, too." He tightened his grip on her. He had no right to dissuade her from finding her father. He knew how important it was to her. He could only try and protect her from any more harm.

Chapter Twenty-one

William could tell by the untamed breeze that they were nearing the coastline once more. The air smelled wet, and oddly sweet. A familiar scent? He wasn't certain why.

He scanned the ghostly scenery of trees and rocky outcroppings as they flew past on horseback. His mind wandered, remembering the courage in Siobhan's soulful green eyes as the leather whip had sliced into her flesh and as they fought together in an attempt at freedom.

She hadn't blamed him for her torture. Instead she'd tried to apologize for something his stubbornness had forced her to do. "Siobhan?"

"Yes," she replied.

"You are not to blame for what happened back there."

She tensed. "The Spear is in that evil man's possession because of me. I was so desperate to help my father, I never fully considered what would happen as a result of my actions. I wouldn't blame you if you no longer wished to help me. I betrayed you."

"We can't change what has happened. I admit I was upset when I woke and found you gone. That you had gone off alone hurt me more than that you'd taken the Spear."

"I felt I had no choice." Her words sounded tortured.

A familiar sting pierced his pride. "I gave you no choice. I understand that."

"I am sorry that I disappointed you. I made a bad

decision. One I wouldn't make again if given the opportunity."

He gently caressed her cheek with the back of his finger. "Life isn't always filled with decisions or moments that are simply good or bad, black or white. It's in the shades of gray where most of us live, Siobhan."

His mind moved back to the battlefield at Teba. It had been a massacre. There had been no hope for any of them to survive, and yet some of them had done just that. They'd defied the odds and lived.

He'd never been happier about his survival than he was at this moment. He brought her body back against his chest. His heart beat firmly against his chest, and in some mysterious way through him and into her, as though they were one. She was part of him. He was part of her.

They were together in this moment because he *had* survived. And they hadn't gone through all the struggles and traumas of their lives just to have it end in defeat. "We'll get the Spear back and save your father," William said.

The light of dawn began to press against the darkness, painting the world around them in hazy shades of gray and pink. In the distance he could see the outline of a man and horse riding along the cliff that dropped into the water far below.

A feeling of unease passed over him. He recognized those cliffs. He recognized the ocean beyond. "I've been here before," he said.

Siobhan straightened in his arms.

"Something is amiss."

"What?" she asked.

William slowed the horse, then pulled him to a stop as a large fortress came into view. A muscle in his jaw tensed.

"A castle." Siobhan's voice was laced with confusion.

"Not just any castle." William's heart pounded as anger and shock took root inside him, growing to colossal proportions. "The castle my uncle stole from my father and me."

Siobhan gasped.

In that moment, William knew to the depths of his soul that his uncle was responsible for de la Roche's presence in Scotland. He also realized his uncle had encouraged de la Roche's attack on the Templars in an effort to keep William from going after what had been stolen from him as a child.

But William was no longer a child. He was an adult with resources at his disposal. "My uncle and de la Roche are in this together." As the sun started to rise, William gazed upon the home he'd been forced to flee.

The castle was perched on a spit of land thrusting into the Atlantic Ocean. Its tall, stark fortress walls rose sheer from the edge of a bluff, and the cold, gray stone facings presented a monstrous and deadly fortification incongruously nestled in a setting that looked almost idyllic—though William's uncle had seen to it that his memories were less than idyllic. The castle itself consisted of four round war towers capped with turrets. The inner rooms were long, and carefully designed to fit one upon the other in staggered tiers. Rounding the whole were crenellated battlements where the sentries could see the terrain in all directions.

The castle was approached along a well-packed road of earth and stone that seemed to go on forever. De la Roche traveled upon that path now. He rode furiously to the entrance of the castle, to the gates set between two enormous barbican towers, and vanished inside. The clang of a heavy iron portcullis sounded in the morning air.

"What do we do now?" Siobhan asked, turning to face him. "We can't breech those walls without help."

"We'll have help." William gazed down at the woman

in his arms. She looked tired, her dress was shredded and splotches of blood stained the fabric from hem to bodice. She hadn't eaten or slept for nearly two days. Even so, determination shone in her eyes.

"I'll do whatever you need of me," she said.

He leaned forward and kissed her lips. She responded instantly, softening beneath him. He drew in the sweet, honeyed scent of her, taking it into himself, using it to soothe his emotions and bolster his resolve. "Since we now know where de la Roche and presumably your father are, we must go for help."

Siobhan nodded. "Then let us go."

"You don't wish to rest a while?" They had been riding for the better part of the night.

"I couldn't sleep now if I tried."

William smiled. "Then we ride for the monastery."

At nightfall they reached the monastery. The journey had taken some time because of the need to rest the horse. William had walked at times, allowing Ares a break from carrying two riders. And after a full day on horseback, Siobhan struggled to keep her head up, so great was her exhaustion.

The wooden gates of the monastery flew open at their approach. Brother Kenneth rushed out to greet them. "Praise the saints," he said as he helped Siobhan to dismount. "I had feared for both your lives when Brother Lucius returned and told us what had transpired."

"We are safe," William said, coming to stand beside her.

Brother Kenneth frowned as he took in their tattered and bloody clothing. "What has happened?"

"De la Roche has the Spear and Sir John, two things that will soon change. But for now, Siobhan and I need a good soak and a hot meal." With a hand on the base of her back, William guided her into the monastery and down a long hall.

"Where are you going, William? Shouldn't you be heading for the dormitory?" Brother Kenneth followed behind.

"We go to the baths."

"You cannot take her there."

William stopped. He turned to face Brother Kenneth, his gaze hard. "I can. I will. Her skin is torn and bleeding. The baths will help."

"But they are only for Templars," Brother Kenneth said, shrinking back from the anger that radiated from William.

Siobhan placed her hand on his arm. "It's all right. I can use a washbasin."

William ignored her. "She is the daughter of the Keeper of the Holy Relics. That gives her access, does it not?"

"She's female." The abbot's eyes went wide.

William's frown turned dark. "And God does not accept females in the holy waters?"

"William," the abbot pleaded. "You know it's not done."

"Everything changes. Perhaps it's time for the baths to change as well." William turned back around, encouraging her to do the same. They stopped in front of an overly large wooden door carved with the face of Christ in the center, his hand raised in blessing, surrounded by alternating rows of five-pointed stars and roses.

William pushed the ornate door aside to reveal a large room with a black and white mosaic floor. He waved her inside. "This is the changing room."

He stepped into the chamber. He pointed toward a set of stairs off to the right of the door. "Down there is the cleansing pool. You need to start there. The waters there will cleanse the impurities from your body."

Siobhan peeked down the stairs to see a round, white marble bath at the base of the stairs.

"After you finish cleansing, you will pass through the warm room to the calidarium, the hot bath. Once you feel relaxed proceed to the frigidarium, or the cool bath." He handed her a long length of linen. "Dress yourself in this between each bath."

Offering her his arm, he guided her to the changing room. "Stay in the cool bath as long as you can tolerate it. The healing waters will help your wounds." He released her arm.

"William, I—"

"I'll meet you when you are done." Before she could stop him, he vanished into the inner rooms of the bath.

Siobhan pressed her lips together as she looked around the beautiful chamber. Blue and green and yellow mosaic tiles lined the floors and walls, bringing a sense of peace to the chamber.

She looked down at the brownish red blood on her gown and reached for the ties. The sooner she cleansed the memories of today's events from her mind and body, the better. She dropped the gown on the floor, then wrapped the linen around her body and headed down the stairs to the cleansing bath.

Siobhan proceeded through the rooms, taking time to relax in each of the baths. In the hot bath, wisps of steam floated up around her. The pleasant heat brought her out of her exhausted lethargy. Her body tingled with an awareness that she hadn't known until William had entered her life. That awareness was longing. A dull ache throbbing between her thighs had nothing to do with any of the abuse she had suffered today. She stood and proceeded to the next bath.

In the cool bath, her body came fully alive, tingling and throbbing as the waters bathed her flesh. A sense of sacred calm descended over her. By the time she stepped from the cool waters, not only did she feel refreshed, but her muscles no longer ached. The red welts that marred her skin had grown angrier at first, but were already fading. And the deep gashes upon her body no longer pained her in any way.

William had mentioned holy waters. Had the baths helped to heal her in some way? Would he use them as well? The thought had barely materialized when William appeared behind her draped in a sheet of linen much like hers. He had followed her through the cycle of the baths.

"Better?" he asked.

"Much."

"Then allow me." He scooped her into his arms and carried her out of the room and down the long hallway.

At the end of the hall he stopped and pushed the wood door open with his foot. He stepped into a small chamber like the one she had inhabited earlier, then set her on a small cot. He tucked a woolen blanket around her. "I apologize for the lack of clothing. I have sent one of the brothers to the nearest town to find a woman who will part with one of her gowns for your use. Until then . . ."

She reached up and touched his cheek, which no longer bore the red welts that had marred it earlier. "What magic did those waters contain to take away the pain and evidence of what we endured today?"

"No magic." He reached down and smoothed the damp strands of her hair away from her cheek. "It is faith alone that heals us. Sleep now. I'll be in the chamber across from yours, should you need me." He turned to leave.

"William?"

He turned back to her, and she could see tension in his face and desire flaring in his eyes. "Aye?"

"Thank you."

His gaze traveled over her wet, tousled hair, her bare shoulders, to her body hidden beneath the heavy wool. "I must go, Siobhan, or something that should not happen in a monastery will happen here this night."

At the heat in his eyes an answering warmth flared within her. Her body tingled, throbbed—not from the effects of the baths, but from the look in his eyes that said he wanted to consume her. She bit down on her lip to keep from calling him back.

William returned to his chamber and quickly pulled on a fresh linen shirt, breeches and his boots. Once dressed, he strode down the hallway in the opposite direction from Siobhan's chamber. He had to move away from the temptation she posed—from his own desire—until he could get himself back in control.

He proceeded to the chapel and forced himself to slow his steps as he made his way to the altar. At the stairs of the dais, he fell to his knees before the crucifix that hung upon the wall. He allowed the burden of what he'd done, of what he'd turned away from, to swamp him.

Many years ago he'd knelt in this same place, filled with purpose and determination to change the world, to right the wrongs that he saw all around him.

But something had changed. He had changed. His ideals had taken the lives of so many others that he loved. Could he sacrifice any more and still remain whole?

He stared up at the image upon the cross. "My vows to you, Lord, were the reason I lived for so long. You protected me in my childhood and as a warrior. But now I find myself pulled in another direction. I feel as though you are guiding me to another purpose, that I can serve Your will more fully by protecting Siobhan from those who would seek her knowledge of the treasure."

He dropped his gaze to the hands he held folded in

front of him. "My loyalty, my life, will always be yours, Lord, but my heart calls me to another path. Please give me the strength to do what must be done." Crossing himself, he rose.

He turned to find Brother Kenneth standing ten paces behind him. The man offered William a gentle smile. "As you stated earlier, things change. Change can be good."

"That wasn't meant for your ears."

"My ears are God's ears," Brother Kenneth replied.

William frowned. "My path in life calls me in a different direction."

"As it should. You came to us as a boy, William. I've often wondered if you chose this life with us because it was before you. That's why I forced you to go away as a young man, to go to the king's court, to find who you truly were. When you met the Bruce and became his guardsman as a Templar, I knew your heart was in your commitment, but still something of your soul was missing from your choice. I could see it in your eyes every time you looked at me."

Brother Kenneth came to stand before him, searching his face, his eyes. "That emptiness is gone, William. Lady Siobhan is the reason."

With a fatherly smile he said, "There are many sacraments in this world. Service as a lay monk, to your faith, as a Templar, is only one of those sacraments. Love and marriage are another expression of the sacrament made flesh."

William paused, considering his brother's words. He placed a hand on Brother Kenneth's shoulder. "What a wise man you are. My thanks."

He nodded his head toward the door. "Go to her, with my blessing."

William didn't hesitate. He hastened for the door, then down the hallway. At Siobhan's door he tapped softly. The door eased open. He pushed it farther. Siobhan was no-where inside the small chamber.

His heart stumbled, until he reminded himself she was safe within the walls of the monastery. Making his way through the refectory first, he proceeded outside. He found her in the garden, sitting upon a bench, staring off into the darkness.

"When you weren't in your chamber, I knew I would find you here." A midnight breeze brought with it the scent of heather from the hills beyond.

Siobhan had found and donned an unattended cloak on her way out and now wrapped it closer about her body as he sat down beside her. She stared at him uncertainly. "I couldn't sleep."

He nodded and passed her one of the two apples he'd picked up on his way through the refectory.

"My thanks." She bit into the sweet, crisp flesh. He did the same. When they finished, he brought a finger up to her lips to wipe a wayward drop of juice from the corner of her mouth.

Her eyes drifted closed. She leaned into his touch. He pulled her into his arms as naturally as if he'd done it a thousand times before. He nestled against her, drowning in the feel of her warmth, the sweet scent of her hair, her skin.

He pulled back. Their eyes met. "I asked you to come to me if you needed me, *ma chère*. But I find it is I who needs you."

Chapter Twenty-two

•

Siobhan couldn't breathe. She couldn't look away from William's eyes. In their depths she saw a vulnerable man who had survived a hellish childhood and the horrors of war. He had emerged strong and vital, yet remained on his guard about risking his heart to any further damage.

"Siobhan?" He stroked her cheek, tracing a line down to her throat.

A primal shudder went through her. She raised both arms and curled them around his neck, then brought her lips to his, pressing her breasts against his chest.

Desire flared in his eyes as he returned her kiss with a passion that engulfed them both. He lifted her in his arms, then stood, carrying her toward the stable. Inside the door he set her down. With hands far steadier than her own, he saddled Phantom. When he was done, he lifted her into the saddle and mounted behind her. With a flick of the reins, they left the stable and rode through the monastery gates.

A nearly full moon cast a silvery glow across the land, casting the world around them in shades of black and gray. The shrubs that had looked friendly in the daylight were now stark and menacing. Yet Siobhan did not feel unease, not with William's arms around her. "Where are we going?" she asked, leaning back against William's chest.

"A special place, where we'll be free to do as we desire."

They rode in silence for a distance until he brought Phantom to a halt at a copse of trees. William dismounted and tied his horse's reins loosely to a bush. He plucked her out of the saddle and carried her across a grassy area to a small stone cottage with a thatched roof. He kicked the door aside and carried her into the single room.

The musty smell of dust greeted them, and cobwebs hung from every corner. He batted them away and proceeded across the room to a small wooden bed. He set her gently down on the dusty quilted bed linens. "I apologize for the chill, and the state of dilapidation. I haven't been here in quite a while."

"You said this was a special place. Why?"

"I used to come here when I needed to escape the rigidity of the monastery. Brother Kenneth knew about it. He encouraged me to come, to discover who I was truly meant to be."

"Did you?" She reached up and stroked the length of his arm, pausing as she came to the cuts left behind by the whip.

"I thought I'd found myself. Now, I am not so certain."

"What is it that you want?" Siobhan asked.

He stared down at her, the line of his cheeks hollow with tension. "I won't lie to you. In my head, I'm still confused as to what I want. But in my heart I know. I want to experience your sweetness, to take you into myself, to lay beside you in this bed."

"Bed of cushions or bed of leaves, it matters not to me." She offered him a smile that faded a moment later. Before they went any further, she had to ask him the question that burned inside her. "Have you truly forgiven me, William?" Tears blurred her vision, and there was a thick twisted knot in her throat. "I betrayed you."

William said nothing as he studied her face.

Siobhan felt the thudding of her heart. The sound pounded in her ears like the hammering of a nail into wood. *Please forgive me. . . .* The formless prayer circled through her brain with dizzying repetition as she waited for some sign that he would, someday.

A heartbeat later he scooped her into his arms and held her close against his chest. "I forgive you—for the Spear and for every other misunderstanding that may happen between us in the future."

"Truly?" She pulled back, memorizing every detail, every nuance, every line of the face before her—a face she loved. A man she loved.

"Truly." He kissed her then, a slow, gentle, loving kiss that set her heart and soul afire.

When he released her lips, she opened her mouth to speak, but he silenced her with a finger to her lips. "No more talk. Let me show you how much I forgive you." His hands fumbled with the fabric of her cloak, with the linen sheeting she'd wrapped around her body, until she lay naked before him.

It took him only a moment to disrobe. Then he too was naked, and boldly aroused.

She opened her arms. He came into them, pressing her naked breasts hard against the coarse hair of his chest. He rubbed against her, making low, groaning sounds deep in his throat.

He rolled so he was beneath her, settling her atop his thighs. She could feel his pulsing manhood against her own apex, but he did not penetrate. Instead, he first took one, then the other of her nipples into his mouth, teasing each straining peak.

Heat flashed through her. The muscles of her stomach clenched. She arched her head back and cried out as his teeth closed gently on the small nub, nibbled, then pulled. She cried out as sensation after sensation burned through her.

Her fingers stroked his chest, gently, as she could feel the cuts in his flesh beneath her fingertips. The healing waters had worked their magic on him as well, but it would be several days more before he fully recovered.

His muscles bunched and relaxed as she moved her fingers across his chest. Again, she marveled at her power, at the way she could please him with a simple touch. She stroked each of his nipples, gaining a deep-throated groan for her efforts. She brought her hand lower, down the ripples of his abdomen, to where his rigid manhood pressed against her.

"Please, William," she pleaded, hoping he understood what she needed. His hands moved from her ribs to her waist. He lifted her and guided her slowly down on him. Heat engulfed her as he filled her. She clutched desperately at the bed linens. Holding her hips, he moved her up and down, the tempo wild, exciting.

"Only like this can two people take up the same space and become one," he said in a strained tone. "We are one, you and I, in this moment." He lifted her up and then lowered her until she took all of him inside her.

"We are one." Siobhan gave a low cry of wild satisfaction.

He stopped, gazing up at her with eyes that glittered with primitive pleasure. "I've never felt like this before."

"I never imagined it could feel so good," she replied, her heart beating so rapidly she could scarcely breathe.

With a low growl, he flipped her onto her back. His hands delved beneath her body to cup her buttocks, to pull her against him as he thrust into her with frantic urgency.

She moved against him, trying to meet his passion.

He thrust desperately, wildly, beyond control, as she slipped over the edge of the abyss. She climaxed, the tension exploding with a force that sent a fiery release through every muscle in her body. She opened herself to him until his life force pulsed and throbbed deep into her very soul.

A heartbeat later she could feel William spasm again and again within her, shuddering with the force of his release. He collapsed on top of her, his heart racing in his chest, his breathing ragged. As they lay there, contentment seeped into all the places his passion had touched.

Finally, when their breathing slowed, he lay back, pulling her against his side as though yet unwilling to release their bond. He had said they were one. In that moment they had been.

His breathing slowed, and he drifted off to sleep with an arm tucked securely about her. Siobhan smiled as she felt herself slipping into utter contentment wrapped in his warmth.

"Why is my nephew not yet dead?" Alasdair Keith growled as he strode through the great hall toward where de la Roche waited. His dark eyes glittered in the candlelight.

De la Roche narrowed his gaze on the tall and imperious older man. How dare the Scottish bastard talk to him in that way! He was master of the Spear, ruler of the world, an unstoppable force.

His lips tightened as Keith, dressed in black breeches and a plain linen shirt and tunic, came to join him on the dais at the front of the chamber. The bastard didn't bow to him, merely stared into his face as though expecting an answer to his ridiculous question.

De la Roche held his tongue. If he'd been able, he would have delivered William Keith's head on a platter when he'd arrived here. But the Templar had outmaneuvered him at the broch. And de la Roche now needed Alasdair's troops if he was to succeed in massacring the Templars—William Keith included. "Soon you'll have what you desire," he said.

"'Tis not soon enough," Keith said coldly with a thin, contemptuous smile.

De la Roche's gut twisted in anger and he gripped the Spear tighter. If he didn't need the man's troops so much, he would take great pride in skewering him through the heart right now. His fingers itched, but he forced himself to hold back.

The doors to the great hall flew open. The ranks of his own and Alasdair Keith's men filed into the chamber until nearly two hundred men stood before him. A rush of excitement replaced his earlier anger.

It was time to put the Spear to the test. Informants had sent him word that Templars traveled from all areas of Britain toward Crosswick Priory.

De la Roche intended to capture all those men before they could get that far, crippling William Keith and annihilating the Templars once and for all. "Hear me out, men. Hear me out," he shouted above the din of voices.

One by one the voices in the chamber fell silent, and the earnest faces turned toward him. "I need four groups of twenty-five soldiers to head north, south, east and west. Your mission is to capture any armed men you come across. They are our enemy. Treat them as such. The rest of you, prepare for an attack on the castle."

De la Roche smiled as he thought of how angry William Keith would be when he discovered his men had been slaughtered like sheep.

Everything that he wanted would come to him without effort and with great efficiency—all because of the Spear. With the Spear he would triumph over anyone and anything. With the Spear he was a god.

"How much longer will I have to wait for you to hold up your end of this bargain?" Alasdair Keith's grating voice cut into his thoughts.

De la Roche muttered an obscenity as fury filled him. How dare the bastard interrupt his thoughts? The tip of the Spear edged in the older man's direction. A heartbeat later, de la Roche forced his arm to stop, his anger once again in control.

Even so, something had become abundantly clear to him this day. Once he'd wrung all he needed from the irritating Scotsman, the man would have to die.

The thought was all that comforted him as he sent his troops out to do his bidding.

Siobhan drifted back from a dreamless slumber sometime later. Faint pink light filtered into the room through the cracks in the shutters and from beneath the door. She and William were still curled together. She drew a deep, contented sigh.

"Siobhan?" His voice was steady, as though he'd been awake for some time, waiting for her to open her eyes.

"Yes."

His hands played with her breasts, stroking, cupping them in his callused palms. His fingers moved lower to stroke her belly. "Do you think I've given you a child?"

She came instantly awake. "A child?"

"Had you not thought of a child? There is a possibility—"

"No, it couldn't be." She sat up, her mind spinning. She should have started her flux a couple of days ago. Yet she hadn't. In all the chaos, she hadn't even considered it. Panic thrummed within her. Sweet Mary! How could she have not considered a child?

His hand came to rest upon her belly once more. "More than anything else in the world, I want my child to be within you, here." His voice was tight. He shifted his body to gaze into her face. The fierceness that usually existed there faded to tenderness. "I don't know what it is I feel for you, Siobhan. But every time I think about life without you, I feel empty and confused."

Siobhan stared at the man beside her. Heaviness consumed her. A child? Why had she never considered such a fate? God would never be so cruel. Would He?

He smiled. "Why do you say nothing?"

"I don't know what to say."

"Say you'll marry me."

She stared at him, stunned. "What about the Templars? The treasure? Your vows?"

His face became shuttered. "I have work to do there still. But know this, my desire for you is honest."

"I have no doubts about your honesty or your desire, but you are not free to ask me such a question." She dropped her gaze to her hands. "You belong to the Templars, just as my father still does. Even though he wanted to be free from them, look what happened. He never managed to sever the ties. Would it be the same for you?"

"I don't know."

"I lived in absolute isolation with my father. It was my choice to remain, I realized in the later years. But I don't want that for my children. I want any child of mine to have experiences, to know the world. To be free, not fearing discovery of some Templar secret or that someone like de la Roche might someday take their father away. As a Templar, you can't be committed to me or a baby."

Siobhan reached for the linen that had served as her gown and pulled it over her breasts, no longer comfortable with her nakedness.

"You are refusing me?" He frowned.

"I've never spent much time thinking about marriage,

although I knew the possibility might exist someday soon."

"That someday can be with me. I've realized over the past several days that my vows are to the Lord, not necessarily to the Templars. I could never separate the two before, but I can now. The Lord has led me in a different direction. Once I leave the Templars, I will reclaim all that I have in the way of worldly possessions. I'm a very wealthy man, Siobhan. You'll never want for anything."

"You're not free of the Templars, William. Until then . . ."

With a finger beneath her chin, he brought her gaze back to his. "You're right. I'm not free to ask you to share my life. But I shall be soon. I've served out my purpose with the Templars. A new calling beckons." His voice vibrated with emotion. "Then I'll have you, Siobhan. I'll persuade you to my way of thinking."

"So much remains to be done," she said, not knowing how else to respond to his words.

The gentleness she had witnessed earlier returned to his eyes. "Aye, it does." He bent down to brush his lips sweetly, tenderly against hers. The kiss had just begun when he moved away, leaving her longing for more. She drew a sharp breath. That was exactly as he'd planned. He wanted her to crave his taste, to yearn for his touch so that when the time came, she would surrender herself freely.

She wrapped herself in the linen, then pulled the cloak around her shoulders while she watched William dress. Marriage? She had never considered such a thing until her father had brought up the subject just a few days ago. Her existence had always been devoted to helping him.

Her father.

Pain centered in her chest at the thought of what he'd

suffered since he'd been abducted. "William, do you think my father is still alive? After what de la Roche did to us in only one afternoon . . ." Her words died off.

"Your father is a strong man."

"He's been gone for days."

Again the vulnerability she'd seen earlier emerged from the tough exterior he tried to present to the world. An answering ache awoke within her, and she moved to his side.

"The men are assembling. We'll ride out as soon as we are able, *ma chère*. Have faith that all is well."

Faith.

She had faith in William, and in the troops he would mass. But she also knew from her own experience that de la Roche would do anything he could to get what he wanted from her father. What had he divulged already under the torture he no doubt had suffered?

Faith. She had to have faith.

Chapter Twenty-three

Upon their return from the cottage, Simon met Siobhan and William at the monastery gate. He held an amber-colored gown, a linen shift and a pair of boots. When the two of them approached, Simon assisted Siobhan down from the horse, then handed her the garments. "For you, milady."

"My thanks," Siobhan said. A flash of eagerness filled her eyes.

William dismounted. "Go change," he encouraged her.

She darted into the monastery, no doubt eager to shed her makeshift garment for something more acceptable.

"What brings you out here? It is unlike you to play the greeter."

"Templars are coming from Wales, Ireland, the Isles to join your forces."

William nodded. "That is good news."

Simon's features remained pensive.

"What aren't you telling me?"

"De la Roche must have anticipated that the men would come to you, because our scouts report his troops are everywhere. They're arresting men before they can reach us," Simon said tightly.

"How many men do we have?"

"No more than forty-five."

"Damnation! So few?" William snapped. "But we must go. We'll prepare to leave with what we have."

"De la Roche has the Spear," Simon countered. "Does that not mean anything to you?"

"It means everything to me. It's why we cannot risk staying here and doing nothing."

" 'Tis suicide. And you know it."

William narrowed his eyes. "No man is all-powerful, not even with the Spear."

"But the legends—"

"Say that the bearer of the Spear can conquer all. But now that I've actually held it in my own hands, I believe the Spear reacts to the person who possesses it. It is a neutral force until it picks up the character of its bearer— whether good or bad."

"De la Roche will use the weapon for ill."

"Against us, first, before he ventures anywhere else. 'Tis up to us to take the weapon away from him."

"Much easier said than done."

William nodded. "Nothing that we have ever done together, Simon, has been easy. Yet we prevailed."

"What then?" Simon asked. "Will we hide the Spear once more?"

"Nay, the Spear's place is in the world, not hidden away. We will see the Spear into the hands of good people who will use the weapon for good causes." William placed a hand on Simon's shoulder. "We have always fought for what was right."

Simon straightened. "And we will continue to do that." William patted Simon's shoulder, then drew his hand back and put it on the hilt of his sword. "Aye. The Brotherhood will preserve justice and protect the innocent." He offered his other hand to Simon in a salute often used by the Templars to show affection and respect.

The two shook hands just as Siobhan returned. She strode toward them. She moved with grace, her shoulders back, her spine straight. Elegant yet strong. She stopped before Simon. "Thank you for the gown. It's the finest garment I've ever worn."

William took in the sight of her. The unadorned and simply cut velvet gown the monks had found for her in the village was a rich amber shade. The sleeves hugged her arms from shoulder to wrist. Her gown was straight and graceful, falling from the low, square neckline of the bodice, which revealed the soft swell of her breasts and the long line of her throat against the rich fabric. Her hair fell in loose waves across her shoulders. Beneath the fading light of day, her tresses shimmered like fiery gold. "You are a vision."

She dropped her gaze and curtsied, but not before he saw the pleased little smile that tugged at her mouth. Hope blossomed inside him. She wasn't entirely impervious to his charms.

"When do we leave?" she asked.

"As soon as the men can gather." He reached for her hand. "Would you not rather stay behind, where it is safe?"

"No," she said with determination. "I'm as much a part of this as you are. I need to see it through."

"Aye, you are." William squeezed her hand before releasing it. "May we find only success in the trials that lie ahead."

"We are united in purpose and spirit," Simon said.

"To the end," Siobhan added.

Gooseflesh pebbled William's skin at the eeriness of their chosen words. Similar words had been spoken by the Brotherhood on the eve of the Battle of Teba.

No such disaster would befall them at Stonehyve Castle. William closed his eyes and said a silent prayer.

The massacre could not happen again.

Fate would never be so cruel twice.

Twenty-five men managed to make it past de la Roche's patrols and joined the twenty already at the monastery. As soon as the men arrived, William and Siobhan rode out.

What their small army lacked in number, they made up for in strength. The air fairly crackled with hope and a renewal of spirit that William hadn't seen in these men for years. The Templars might be disbanded, but they were not destroyed.

The mists were reluctant to leave the coves and the inlets near the shore as the men, some on horseback, others on foot, followed William's lead. Once, as they approached Stonehyve lands, he glimpsed the distant silhouette of the battlements. His home. A home he'd been forced to leave. And one he was willing to attack to bring peace back to the Brotherhood.

They reached the inlet below the castle just as the sun dipped low against the blue-black Cairngorm Mountains. "We'll make camp here for the night," William announced, reining in his horse. He wanted the men rested and well fed before they made their attack in the morning.

The men set up camp at the edge of the inlet, where they couldn't be seen by the castle towers. It wasn't long before watch fires bloomed against the gray of dusk that cast Stonehyve Castle in shades of angry, unyielding black.

When the campsite had been settled, the men gathered near the fires, eating bowls of a hearty rabbit stew they had brought with them. William stood near his own fire, staring not into the flames, but at the sky. The moon perched heavy and full over the mountain peaks. Stars hung suspended by the millions, but the light they shed did little to alleviate the growing tension that stirred within his chest.

"You look as far away from here as those stars," Siobhan said, coming to stand beside him.

"I feel far away." His attention shifted to her and he felt a sudden calm come over him. Curious that on the eve of battle, he would find comfort in anything, let alone the woman whose very presence usually distracted him.

"Are you worried about the morrow?"

He shook his head. "Just thinking about how we'll force our way inside." His eyebrows came down in thought. "I've been trying to remember if there are ways to enter the castle other than through the front gate. With our limited numbers, it would be wiser to pursue a less direct approach."

Simon came to sit beside William. "I've been giving that some thought as well." A sudden hush went out over the camp as every ear turned to their conversation.

"Gather round, men," William called out. If they were to put their lives on the line tomorrow, they deserved some say in their plan of attack.

They abandoned their campsites to huddle around where William stood. Momentarily his breath quickened as he thought back to the last time he had gathered around a fire with other Templars. It was the last time he had seen some of his brothers alive.

Simon caught William's gaze across the fire. "We are on our homeland, the land of our ancestors, of our fellow Templars," he said, knowing as he always did where William's thoughts had gone.

William looked at the faces of the men gathered round. In their gazes he saw confidence, and no fear. He shook off his memories of the past and focused on the here and now. "Our enemy rises before us like a hissing serpent, which we must either capture or remove from this world if we are to protect our brothers, as well as our countrymen."

"How will we do it?" one of the men opposite William asked.

Red-orange flames licked greedily at the wood in the fire, casting all who gathered in a warm, golden glow. "I was hoping to avoid a direct attack. Our numbers would be better used in some sort of ploy."

"Can we enter through the moat and into the drainage system beneath the castle?" Lucius asked.

"And then enter through the garderobe?" another man beside him countered. A general roar of disgust followed the suggestion.

"Is there a sally port somewhere along the castle walls?" Simon asked. "We could use a crossbow to send up a rope. With luck it will anchor in the wall, and we can pull ourselves up the side."

"Without being seen?" Robert Tam asked. "Too risky. We will be too visible."

"Perhaps we could try that approach at night?" another man suggested.

One of the monks from the monastery stood. "We have everything we need here in the nearby woods to build a trebuchet. With that we could break through the outer walls."

Simon shook his head. "We don't have time to build a trebuchet. Besides, as soon as they see us building such a weapon, they will charge us. If our scouting parties are correct, de la Roche's men outnumber us ten to one."

"A Trojan horse." A female voice cut through all the others.

When silence fell, Siobhan repeated, "What we need is a Trojan horse, the ploy used by the Greeks to enter the city of Troy."

"If we don't have time to build a trebuchet, why would we have time to build that?"

"We don't need to build anything." Siobhan stood and moved away from the fire to where William had left his saddlebag. She returned a moment later with the leather casing and scroll in her hands. "I shall be the Trojan horse."

Murmurs arose from the men. William silenced them with his hand, even though the very idea made him more than a little uneasy. "Let her continue."

"You'll all hide against the castle wall or in places where you cannot be seen by the sentries during the night. At first light, I'll approach the gates and demand to see de la Roche, saying I'm ready to trade knowledge of the Templar treasure for my father."

Siobhan pulled the scroll to her chest. "From what I've seen of de la Roche's hunger for the treasure, he'll not refuse. He'll order the gates be opened, and then you'll attack."

"Nay," William said with force. "Too many things can go wrong. I'll not put you in danger like that again."

"I'm putting myself in danger." Siobhan's tone was suddenly fierce. "I may not be able to fight like a Templar Knight, but I'm strong enough to do this one thing."

William softened his voice. "I know you're strong, Siobhan."

"Then let me do this."

"It might work," Simon acknowledged from his seat nearby. "We could hide in trenches alongside the drawbridge. As soon as the gate is open, we could attack." His eyes brightened. "It just might work."

"How do we dig trenches under the light of a full moon without the guards seeing us?" William asked, still adamantly opposed to risking Siobhan's safety.

"You leave that to us," the Dunn brothers chimed in.

"We are quite adept at distracting the nightwatch. You could dig a tunnel, and they'll never suspect a thing when we get going."

"Is this a plan we can agree to?" Lucius asked the others.

A hearty cheer of "Aye" rose from the men. Siobhan met William's gaze. "You're always asking me to trust you. For once, please trust me on this. It will work to get you all inside the fortress."

William inclined his head. The men had already decided her plan was a good one. He could say nothing to counter that argument. But there was no reason he couldn't go to extraordinary means to keep her safe regardless. In keeping with that notion, he moved back to his saddlebag and reemerged with the sword he had taken with him from the Templar treasure room.

He handed the sheathed blade to Siobhan. "Take this. Promise me you'll wear it as we proceed with this plan."

Her eyes glittered as she accepted the weapon with her free hand. "Excalibur?" She offered him a brilliant smile that alleviated some of the unease in his chest. "Thank you."

"For when I cannot be near to protect you."

She brought the legendary weapon to her chest. "I'll treasure it always."

Treasure. Their journey began with treasure. It seemed only fitting it should end with treasure as well.

"To our success." William unsheathed his sword and raised it in salute to his comrades.

Every weapon joined his in salute. "To success," the others chanted as one.

Siobhan rose before dawn. William had encouraged her to rest while everyone else worked through the night. The others were now gone, set in their places. Before beginning her part of the plan, she knelt upon the ground of the campsite. She listened to the sound of her heartbeat, feeling her breath, letting her courage flow through her.

She reflected on the past ten days she'd spent with William. So much had changed in her life, in herself, during that time. Despair no longer settled inside her, making her doubt her decisions. She no longer feared the unknown, for the unknown made life an adventure. Every day could be filled with excitement and joy if she just left her heart and mind open to the possibility, and if she believed she was strong enough to handle whatever came her way.

Like today. She had told William she was strong enough to go up against de la Roche on her own. She rose. She was that strong and more. Siobhan retrieved Excalibur and secured its scabbard about her waist.

Dawn approached. Siobhan could see the first shimmer of light through the hazy clouds above. Picking up the scroll, she made her way up the long path to the castle.

The castle was strangely quiet as she walked down the broad approach. There were no signs of William or the others as she stood at the edge of the moat that separated the pathway from the castle gate. She and William had shared their parting words earlier. He'd wished her success after he'd given her multiple tips on how to keep herself safe. She smiled at the memory.

William cared for her, whether he had expressed it in words or not. She knew he did; his every action told her so.

She stopped at the edge of the deep moat. It was time to begin. She straightened her shoulders. "Greetings," she called out.

"State your purpose," a deep voice high above responded.

Her smile slipped as the gatekeeper poked his head from the gatehouse. Beady eyes fixed her with a stare that even at this distance raised the hairs on the back of her neck.

"I've come to see Monsieur de la Roche. I want to exchange the map to the Templar treasure for my father."

The man disappeared. All remained silent. A moment later he reemerged. "His lieutenant will see you."

"No," Siobhan stated boldly. "I shall see de la Roche and no other."

The man laughed, the sound harsh in the still morning air. "You are hardly in a position to demand anything as you stand there alone. The men of this castle could be upon you in a moment."

Siobhan set the scroll at her feet, then unsheathed her sword and fingered the flint she had taken from William's saddlebag. She drew the stone against the blade, sending sparks toward the ground. "I could burn this scroll before you could so much as lower your gate."

Silence filled the air as he vanished inside the gatehouse once more. After a long moment, chains rattled inside the castle and the groan of gears sounded as the drawbridge came down. It settled against the ground with a thump, and the gates to the castle opened to reveal de la Roche.

Siobhan picked up the scroll and waited until the portcullis had fully risen before she started across the thick wooden structure that provided access into the fortress. With each step, her heart pounded in her chest. She tried to keep her expression neutral as she continued forward.

De la Roche remained where he stood, inside the gate, with the Spear clutched in his hand. A flicker of grudging admiration crossed de la Roche's face as he studied her. "You are a surprise, my dear."

"How so?" She had to keep him talking, distract him, until William and the others were ready to proceed.

His thin lips pulled up in a smile. "To have you show

up here, to offer me the scroll, all for the sake of your father's pitiful life."

Siobhan drew a slow, steady breath as she allowed the abuse to slide over her. She had to stay in control. "You may have the scroll and the treasure, but first I want to see my father. Bring him to me."

"Now I understand William Keith's interest in you. You're far more daring than one expects. Unfortunately, that interest also makes you one of them. You'll die like all the others." His laughter boomed out in the empty bailey.

The empty bailey. Where were all the warriors? How could William's men attack if there was no one to attack? A sick feeling centered in her stomach. Had their ruse somehow been discovered? Siobhan forced her breathing to slow and her mind to stay focused.

De la Roche's smile vanished. "If you want to see your father before you die, you'll have to come with me." He reached for the scroll. "I'll be taking this from you."

She held the scroll tight. "If I am to die, then kill me now."

His gaze narrowed. He brought the tip of the Spear to rest against the underside of her neck. "Don't issue a challenge you aren't prepared to fulfill."

Siobhan's hand tightened on the scroll. Her other hand drifted to her sword. As William had taught her, she drew the sword swiftly and knocked the Spear away from her neck. De la Roche was thrown off balance. He stumbled.

Siobhan shuffled back, placing the length of the Spear between them.

De la Roche roared a deep-throated call to arms.

Out of nowhere, men erupted from within the bailey—from behind walls, towers, across the top of the battlements. They charged Siobhan, their swords raised.

Her breathing stopped. Her heart thundered. She hugged the scroll to her chest like a shield. She prepared for battle, her sword held high. De la Roche glared at her with his pale, eerie eyes. He pulled his arm back, ready to thrust the Spear at her.

A single shout of challenge rent the air. Footsteps sounded behind her.

Siobhan dared not take her gaze from her foe as they charged forward. One warrior bore down on her and hit Siobhan hard. She absorbed the strike with her own sword. Before she could complete her parry, the man flew backward with a slash to his chest.

William.

She could feel his presence at her back. "Well done, *ma chérie*." Savage satisfaction tore through Siobhan at the sound of his voice.

At William's command, the Templars surged forward from the hidden depths of the trenches they had dug the night before. On foot, they charged through the open gates, once again proudly wearing their Templar tunics. They surged through the bailey like blood-flecked waves of the sea.

William led the charge as he struck one man's sword, then another's, taking them both down in a single hit. The battle raged around him. His men were holding their own against de la Roche's and his uncle's forces. He slashed, severed an arm, stabbed a thigh.

Simon charged forward, his sword ever in motion. "Glad to see we've not forgotten how to fight." He ducked as a blade aimed at his head hacked down in an arc. The blade missed. Simon brought down the attacker instead.

"Aye," William agreed. His eyes were on one target: Siobhan. He threw himself against the ground, rolled and came up instantly to pierce the man who charged her. The man stumbled backward and collapsed, undone.

The screech and clangor of steel, along with noisy grunts of exertion, filled the bailey. De la Roche charged William. Spear down, he thundered forward. "I'll kill you and have your head on a pike, Templar. I'll burn what's left of you later."

William braced himself for impact. De la Roche wouldn't triumph. Not this time.

De la Roche struck. William twisted to the left, sending de la Roche behind him. Two warriors charged William. He caught one in the stomach with his foot and plunged his sword through the chest of the other.

On the offensive now, William forced de la Roche back. Anticipation flared in his belly as fear entered the Frenchman's eyes. De la Roche stepped back, hesitating. William pressed forward. A stroke of his sword took the blade from the Frenchman's hand. A second stroke caught the man in the chest and sent him flying backward against the ground. He lay there stunned or hurt. William wasn't sure which.

From out of nowhere, another swordsman appeared. This warrior was older, with gray hair and a full beard. "Damn you for interfering," a familiar voice called out.

William hesitated. The sword before him came down and caught him in the chest. His mail held, but the impact stole his breath for a heartbeat. His gaze locked on his attacker's face. Those gray eyes were so familiar, so like his father's had been.

His uncle. Alasdair Keith.

They faced each other. Thrust. Parry. Engaging each other, counterthrusting without a break in their strides or in the rhythm of their movements. Out of the corner of his eye, William could see that de la Roche still remained on the ground.

William lunged, caught his uncle in the thigh. The man stumbled, went to one knee. Dropped his sword.

Empty-handed, he stared up with a mixture of anger and fear in his eyes. "Why come back now?"

"I would never have returned had it not been for your helping de la Roche."

His uncle remained on his knees, his chest heaving as he tried to catch his breath.

"Why did you kill them?" William nicked the flesh at his throat. Fear pervaded his uncle's tired, watery eyes.

Alasdair stared into the face of death, and he knew it. "I wanted what your father had." His mouth twisted. "This castle, your mother. But they chose death instead of surrender."

William clenched his jaw as he cast yet another quick glance at de la Roche, who struggled to sit up as he caught his breath. "Why help de la Roche?"

A warrior charged William. He caught the movement out of the corner of his eye. His gaze never left his uncle's as he pierced the man clear through, then kicked his body aside.

"Why?" the word was as hard as his gaze.

"I needed you out of the way." His uncle shrugged. " 'Tis not complicated."

Not complicated? Hope, betrayal, fear, anger mixed in caustic turmoil through his chest. Should he take this life? The murderer of his family? His own uncle? A man who clearly held no affection for him?

If he did, would that make him the same kind of savage that his uncle and de la Roche had become?

His uncle laughed. "You've got no backbone, boy! Your conscience will be the end of you, mark my words."

William clutched the hilt of his sword. Pain radiated through his grip. His breath ran harsh in his throat. He was different from these men. He couldn't kill just to solve a problem.

A scream tore William's attention from his uncle.

Siobhan. She fought against two men. From the look on her face and the angle of her sword, he could see fatigue setting in. He had to help her. William turned back to his uncle.

The man had retrieved his sword. "You're a fool," his uncle ground out.

William spun. Too late. The blade cut into his forearm, yet he managed to hold on to his sword. Drawing on every fiber of strength he possessed, he hurled himself forward.

He caught his uncle by the shoulders, and together they slammed into the rocky ground. William's arm bled as they rolled together, each trying to gain the advantage.

"You should have killed me when you had the chance, boy," his uncle roared. The older man rolled with him until they came up against the bailey wall, trapping William momentarily.

Seeing his opening, his uncle raised his sword high into the air.

William rolled to the side, missing the blow by a hairsbreadth. The blade clanged against the rocky ground, sending sparks flying. William gripped his sword, surged to his feet, and in a downward lunge canted the blade forward until it bit into the flesh of his uncle's outer thigh.

His uncle screamed as hot blood spurted from a severed artery. Fired with the need to reach Siobhan, William grasped the dagger from his boot and thrust it deeply into his uncle's chest.

Alasdair slumped forward, his gaze fixed on William's, then on the handle of the blade protruding from his chest. His hands clawed upward and curled around William's throat, but there was no strength left there to do more than mark the skin with bloody smears.

William supported his uncle's weight in his arms as

the life drained from him. "I knew . . . I couldn't keep . . . what wasn't . . . mine." With a soft rasp of breath, he went limp. William lowered him to the ground. He would grieve later for what he'd done.

Siobhan needed him.

Frantically he fought his way to her side, tossing warriors out of the way. He reached her. Two swipes of his sword later, the men who'd challenged her fell to the ground.

Off to the side of the most vigorous fighting, Siobhan sagged with relief at the sight of him, then tensed as she saw his arm. Without hesitation, she set the scroll on the ground and reached for her hem. Using Excalibur, she sliced off a length of her new velvet gown and tied it around his wound.

"My thanks," he said as he scanned the battleground. Blood turned the bailey into a bog as de la Roche's troops collapsed. Flesh was torn, bones shattered, men died.

But William and his men lived. These men were no match for the young and powerful fighters trained to fight the Saracens. Even his uncle's men, some of them Scottish, had been shredded with deadly efficiency.

Some of Alasdair's men had noticed his body upon the ground and had abandoned the fight. They ran for the open gate. Other's shouted with triumph at the death of their lord. Cries of "Justice has been served!" filled the bailey as the castle residents who had once attended his parents turned their allegiance to William.

Harver Cates, the man who had once been his father's steward, led the charge, and the huntsmen, the knights and the archers followed suit. Warmth flared in William's chest at the sign of devotion to his parents. With the Templars and the castle's residents fighting de la Roche's troops, the battle would soon be at an end.

William took Siobhan's hand. "We must find your father." He led her in the direction de la Roche had disappeared. Together, they raced up the stairs to the keep's entrance.

"Follow me," William said, recalling from his youth the layout of the castle. The dungeon lay low in the northern reaches of the castle. He hurried through the empty great hall and down the north corridor. The castle's staff huddled into the rooms as they passed, trying to stay out of harm's way as the battle raged outside.

Much had changed in the castle since William had left. His mother's tapestries had faded, or hung in tatters from their mountings. The wood panels were dingy and dull. The rushes on the floor reeked of decay.

A surge of emotion burned in his chest as memories both good and bad assailed him. He clenched his jaw, forcing the emotions back. He couldn't give in to thoughts of the past. It was the future that mattered now.

When they came to the end of the hallway, he guided Siobhan down the stairs. Halfway down, he grabbed a torch from an iron holder. Two more turns of the staircase and they arrived at the door of the dungeon.

A howl of pain crept past the closed door. William grasped the latch and threw the door open. His heart plunged at the satisfied grin on de la Roche's face.

Sir John Fraser hung by his bound hands from a hook in the ceiling. His body dangled limply, his head lolled against his chest. He gasped for breath—still alive, but just barely.

"You're too late," de la Roche sneered as he pulled the bloody Spear free of Sir John's side.

Chapter Twenty-four

Siobhan rushed toward her father's abused body, her heart in her throat, only to pause a moment later as the Spear turned in her direction.

"Want to join him?" de la Roche taunted, his lips pulling back in a feral grin.

Her father's eyes drifted open. Their gazes connected. "Siobhan. My dearest."

"Father." The word emerged raw, agonized.

William started forward, his sword drawn, but as the Spear pointed at his chest, he stopped. "What purpose does his death serve?"

De la Roche laughed. The sound echoed in the dank and desolate chamber. "It will motivate you to hand over that scroll. I don't need him or the girl if I have that scroll." His gaze shifted back to Siobhan. "Give me what I want, or you'll all die by the Spear."

Siobhan held the scroll in front of her. She threw the protective leather casing aside and let the open scroll flutter to the ground at her feet. "Hand over my father," she said in a steady voice. "Or there will be no scroll." She stepped back and plucked the torch from William's hand. She held the torch over the papyrus.

De la Roche's eyes narrowed on her. "You wouldn't dare."

"Wouldn't I?" She dropped the torch. The paper caught. Greedy flames lapped at the dry papyrus.

"Stop!" de la Roche shouted, thrusting the Spear at William. In a blink of an eye, William dropped his sword and clasped the Spear's bloody head between his two bare hands.

"I'm invincible with the Spear," de la Roche roared.

William held tight, twisting the blade with sheer brute strength. How would the Spear interpret ownership now, with two men vying for it? For a long moment the two men stood face-to-face, eye to eye, the muscles of their arms bulging in their battle for control.

"No man is invincible, regardless of his weapon." Sweat broke out on William's brow as the struggle continued.

Siobhan tensed. She had to help. Her fingers drifted to the hilt of her sword. She pulled the weapon and sent it forward into de la Roche's gut.

De la Roche gasped. He released his grip on the Spear. William twisted it free, the Spear now in his possession.

De la Roche jerked backward, freeing himself from the blade. His hand pressed against his wound. Blood seeped from between his fingers. In the next instant, he shot forward. "You can't kill me!"

Siobhan brought her sword up to strike once more, but de la Roche was faster. He knocked Excalibur from her grasp. The weapon tumbled to the dirt with a thump. She shrieked as his hand clamped tight around her throat. She kicked out, trying to break his grasp, struggling for air.

Out of the corner of her eye she saw William toss the Spear to the corner of the chamber and charge toward them. He grasped Siobhan's shoulders, effectively knocking de la Roche aside without sending Siobhan to the ground as well.

Siobhan caught her balance, then moved to the burning pages. She grasped the hem of her gown out of the way, then tapped at the flames with her booted feet, smothering the flames.

William charged the Frenchman. "It's time to end this."

De la Roche bolted for the door.

His hand on his sword, William hesitated. His gaze shot to Siobhan's.

"Go," she called, waving him on. "I can take care of my father and the Spear."

William disappeared.

Siobhan stepped over the ash that used to be the scroll to her father's side. Blood seeped from his wound into a pool beneath his feet. On a surge of anger at what de la Roche had done, she retrieved her sword and severed the ropes that bound his wrists together. Siobhan tossed her sword down and grasped his body as he sagged against her. She nearly tumbled beneath his weight, but managed to keep from falling and set him gently upon the soft earth.

"Father," she whispered as she knelt beside him, stroking the matted strands of gray hair away from his brow. When he didn't respond, her heart missed a beat. Were they too late? Her shoulders doubled over under the weight of her grief. A single sob escaped her lips.

"Don't . . . cry." The brittle sound of her father's voice caused her heart to soar.

"Father."

His head turned to the sound of her voice. His eyes were slits he struggled to open. "Shouldn't . . . have . . . come."

"Hush," Siobhan murmured as she grasped the hem of her dress, ripping off another large portion. She balled it up and pressed it against her father's side.

He flinched, and brought a trembling hand up to rest

atop hers. Their fingers grew red with blood. New tears sprang to Siobhan's eyes at the sight of his bloody, mangled and smashed fingers.

"What have they done to you?" she whispered as she shifted her knees under his head. Her arms wrapped around him.

Her father stirred in her arms.

"What can I do? How can I save you?" Her gaze moved to the Spear. She released her grip on her father long enough to grasp the weapon to her side before tightening her arms around him again.

"If this Spear holds any kind of blessing, I pray that it work now." She clenched her fingers around the shaft. "My father did everything in his power to protect you for years. Please, I beg you not to let him die like this."

Tears flowed freely down her cheeks, falling onto her father's face, mixing with the smears of dirt and dried blood upon his cheeks.

"You found . . . the treasure."

"Yes, just where your map indicated."

He patted her hand. "Smart girl." He drew a long, ragged breath. "Siobhan, I need . . . to tell . . . you." His voice faded as he struggled for another breath.

She brought her fingers up to caress his face. The jaw that had seemed so strong to her all her life now trembled and looked too pale.

His eyes opened. He glanced into her eyes, his gaze tender and wise. "I will . . . always . . . love you."

She smiled down at him, forcing her tears to stop. "I love you, too."

"Must . . . go." He coughed, blood splattering from his mouth onto his chin.

She tried to hold back her tears. "Nay," she pleaded, smoothing his cheek. "Stay with me."

"Be . . . happy. Do not . . . blame the Spear." He coughed again and struggled for each breath of air that filled his lungs.

"Don't talk. I'll send for help. We can help you," she pleaded.

He shook his head slowly. "The Spear . . . thirsts for blood." His breathing slowed. His body sagged in her arms. "Keep it . . . from . . . others like . . . him."

"Father." Her voice was raw with pain. "Stay with me."

"Must go." He squeezed her fingers. "Not afraid." His eyes closed and his head lolled to the side, his last breath rattling out.

Siobhan's heart stumbled. She drew a ragged breath, then another. Tears spilled past her lashes. She shut her eyes against a rising tide of grief.

He was dead.

The Spear had not saved him. It had ended his life instead.

William broke into a run, taking the stairs two at a time. He had to stop de la Roche. If the man escaped, the danger to Siobhan would continue. Even if the Templar treasure was moved, de la Roche would not know that. He would always pursue the two of them, a Templar and a keeper of Templar secrets.

The two of them would never have a moment's peace.

William ran faster. He raced down the hallway, through the great hall and out of the keep. In the courtyard William came to a stop. His gaze passed over the bailey. No sign of de la Roche, but the battle had ended. Only his men, dressed in their Templar tunics, stirred in the aftermath of the battle as they separated the wounded from the dead.

At the sight of him, Simon hurried to William's side. "Where's de la Roche?"

"He has to be here. I chased him from the dungeon."

Simon shook his head. "The men and I would have seen him." With fingers to his lips, he sent up a shrill whistle, signaling a dozen men to join the two of them.

"What would you have us do?" Simon asked.

William started barking orders. To the men closest to him, he said, "The two of you, close the gates." He motioned to the men on his right. "You go in pairs to search the castle. The rest of you, continue to assist the wounded."

They sprang into action, executing his commands. William remained where he stood, his body stiff with tension, every nerve stretched. He would find de la Roche. If he had to search the entire country for the man, he would do just that.

"De la Roche!" William's voice rose, filled the bailey, echoed off the stone walls. If de la Roche was not out here, that meant he'd never left the castle. William startled as a thought struck him. Instead of exiting the stairwell on the main floor, what if the man had kept on going?

His gaze shot upward to the closest tower. That had to be where he'd gone. Without explanation to Simon, he raced inside the castle, up the back stairwell, and erupted onto the tower's roof walk.

"Hello, Templar. I knew you'd be the one to find me." De la Roche stood halfway across the rooftop with his back to the crenellations. The wind whipped across the top of the castle, ruffling the Frenchman's graying hair against the collar of his bloodied doublet.

"You've lost, de la Roche," William said, his tone even, steady. "You've lost everything."

"Nonsense. Nothing has changed. I've more men who'll join me. The Spear will be mine again. And the treasure," de la Roche laughed. "You can't keep that from me either." He took two steps backward. "Soon I'll have everything I ever wanted."

"You're through. The treasure is safe from you and the world." William walked slowly toward him, his hand on his sword.

"You can't defeat me," the Frenchman scoffed.

"Look around you." William's hand encompassed the view for miles, as well as the bailey below. "There's no one here to help you. My men will have you surrounded if you try to leave by way of the stairs. Surrender. Things will go easier for you if you do."

Anger blazed across de la Roche's features a moment before he drew his sword and slashed at William's chest.

William jerked back out of harm's way.

De la Roche twisted toward the crenellations.

Finding his balance again, William ran after him.

The Frenchman dashed across the tower toward the openings in the crenellation.

William refused to let de la Roche get away. He grasped the Frenchman's shoulder just as he made to jump up on the waist-high opening.

De la Roche snarled. He turned and struck out with the hilt of his sword, hitting William in the chest and at the same time kneeing the knight in the groin.

Agony and pain shot through William. He staggered back as his chain mail absorbed the blow to his chest.

De la Roche jumped up onto the crenellated wall.

Forcing the pain back, William sucked in a breath and lunged for de la Roche as he jumped into the nothingness that existed beyond the battlement.

William slammed against the side of the stone, his gaze following the Frenchman.

De la Roche hurtled over the edge, toward the dark, murky waters below.

A cry of frustration was rent from William's lips. He couldn't follow the man over the side, not if he wanted to live.

De la Roche hit the moat with a splash.

William's fingers bit into the stone wall as he searched the depths of the moat for some sign of de la Roche's body. Had he survived the fall?

Nothing surfaced. William thrust away from the wall and dashed down the stairs. His shouts roused the men to his side. He ordered the portcullis to lift, explaining what had happened as they waited for an opening large enough to squeeze through.

The men followed William to the moat's edge. "We'll conduct a search. I won't be satisfied until we've retrieve his body, dead or alive," he said, desperately searching the silent, murky waters of the moat.

"Is there any way he could have survived that fall?" Simon asked from beside him. His gaze shot up to the tower overhead. "That's a big drop."

William shrugged, still staring at the waters. He should be feeling satisfaction. Most likely de la Roche was dead. Justice had been served. And yet a part of him refused to believe without the proof of de la Roche's crumpled body. "Ask the men to be thorough. That is all we can do."

Simon's gaze shifted from the water to William. "Your uncle is dead."

"I killed him myself."

Simon's only response was to raise an eyebrow. "That must have brought you some sense of peace."

"Nay," William said sharply. "I'll grieve his death, but not the evil that led to it."

Simon nodded, shifting his gaze to the men dredging the waters of the moat with long poles and nets. "What will you do now? As leader of the Keith clan, this castle is yours."

William frowned, suddenly unsure of everything in his life. For the first time he had options. He could resign as a Templar and take over the leadership of Stonehyve Castle. He could stay with the Templars and help relocate the treasure. He could continue to search for de la Roche if no body was found. Or he could spend the rest of his days in Siobhan's arms, making certain that no harm came to her and their future children. He wanted a life with Siobhan. He wanted to keep her safe. Forever.

He allowed the words to sweep over him with their sweet shattering power. *I love Siobhan*.

He inhaled a sharp breath, feeling suddenly renewed. He had to tell her. He had to ask her to spend every day with him for the rest of their lives. "Take care of things here. I need to return to Siobhan."

He hurried back through the castle gates, through the bailey, into the keep and down the stairs leading to the dungeon. His steps were fueled by thoughts of the last several days. He would trade not a second in her arms, not one word spoken between them, not the passion they shared, not one of her smiles for anything else in the world.

He loved her.

A part of his soul had died along with his parents, and half his heart had died on that battlefield in Spain with his Templar brothers—and then she'd entered his life.

Something new had grown inside him, something he no longer wanted to turn away from.

He was no longer afraid.

Chapter Twenty-five

Death. Death was all around her. Siobhan knew her father was gone from this world, but she couldn't let go of his body. She cradled him in her arms as she never had while he was alive. She felt heavy inside, weighed down with tears she couldn't shed, not yet. If she started crying, she might not be able to stop.

"Siobhan." She lifted her gaze to William's pale gaze. "Is he—?"

"Dead."

"Let's get you both out of here."

Siobhan hesitated as her gaze moved to the pile of ash that used to be the scroll. She hesitated.

"You did what was right." He strode to her side, extending his hand to help her up. She reached out with trembling fingers to grasp it. At his touch, the pain that pierced her soul receded.

William released her, then bent down to retrieve her father's body. Her father's face was at peace. William took a moment to close the eyes before he lifted the older man, nestling the limp body in his strong and capable arms.

Siobhan drew a shaky breath at the image. Her father must have cradled her in the same protective way when she was young. Now the roles were reversed. It was she who would care for and protect his body as it journeyed on to his final resting place.

"What about the Spear?"

"Leave it here. I'll come back for it."

"I can carry it." At William's questioning gaze, she straightened her shoulders. "It wasn't the Spear that killed my father. It was de la Roche." She retrieved the weapon from where it lay on the dirt floor.

Slowly, the three of them moved together up the stairs to join the others in the bailey. The sun overhead peeked down through scudding clouds, yet no warmth covered the land. Only a chilling wind rustled through the yard.

William set her father's body down next to all the others who had died. He came back to her, wrapping her in his arms. Gently, he stroked her hair. "You should rest."

She allowed herself a moment in his arms, taking what brief comfort she could from his touch. "Too much remains undone. We must bury the dead, and say good-bye to my father." Her voice cracked.

William pressed a kiss into her hair. "You're right." He held her tightly. "Sometimes it helps to keep busy."

She nodded, thankful he understood. She couldn't stop moving, couldn't let her emotions through the barrier she'd erected, because if she did, she would have to consider what came next for her. Life without her father was too difficult to fathom at the moment.

Siobhan moved by instinct over the next several hours as she and other women of the castle helped wash the bodies of the dead. William and his warriors dug graves in the kirk yard. The men had given up their search for de la Roche's body long ago. They'd found nothing—no sign of his survival or of his death.

Dusk had fallen over the land when they placed the final dirt atop Sir John's grave. Siobhan stood at his grave site, looking down at the freshly turned earth. It seemed right to leave him here, buried next to William's parents.

"Is there anything I can do?" William asked, gently touching her arm.

Siobhan shook her head as she cast one last glance at the grave site. "There's nothing anyone can do. He's gone. Everything is gone." She closed her eyes.

"I'll miss him too, Siobhan."

She opened her eyes and stared up at William. He still wore his blood-spattered clothes. The bandage she'd placed around the slash in his arm remained where she'd tied it. Dark shadows hovered beneath his eyes.

"Thank you, William, for being so kind to me and my father."

"Kindness shouldn't end in death." His words were angry, hard.

"Don't blame yourself. That de la Roche did not kill him sooner was a miracle. At least, I got to see him one last time. To be with him in the end."

William groaned and pulled her into his arms. He held her there for several long moments as though nothing else in the world mattered, as the light of day faded all around them.

He offered comfort to her, but as he drew several ragged breaths and tightened his arms around her, she realized he needed the comfort she could give.

"William," Siobhan said, interrupting the moment. "Everything will be all right, especially now that your uncle is dead. He can't hurt you anymore."

He drew back to gaze into her face. "I hadn't let myself think about that yet. So much has happened."

"Stonehyve Castle rightfully belongs to you."

William's gaze shifted to the bailey, to the castle's residents and the members of the Keith clan who had helped bury the dead and set the castle back into some semblance of order. "My parents were happy here. . . . Their deaths have been avenged."

He returned his gaze to her face. "Things are as they should be, I suppose."

"Except with the Spear. What's to come of it?"

Gently, he brushed the long strands of her loose hair back from her cheek to tuck them behind her ear. "It must be taken somewhere safe."

Siobhan nodded, dropping her gaze to his chest. "Then you'll be leaving soon." She couldn't let him see the sadness she knew must be reflected in her eyes. "With my father gone, it is only natural that you would step into his role as Keeper of the Holy Relics."

With a finger against her chin, he lifted her gaze to his. "I'm uncertain what role my future holds."

"What could be more important than the treasure?" she asked, breathless.

"You." He gave her a tender smile. "Come with me. Stay by my side while we rescue the others who were taken by de la Roche's troops."

"And after that?"

"Then I must go to Edinburgh to fulfill my duty with the Spear. Templars who must hide to protect themselves are no guardians for such a powerful weapon. There is a man there I trust, Archbishop Lamberton. I've met him many times while at the Bruce's court and feel confident in his ability to assist the Templars with the task of keeping the Spear safe. Only Archbishop Lamberton can see the relic returned to the mother church in Rome. There, among other holy relics, the Spear will be safe from men like de la Roche."

"And the rest of the treasure?"

"Simon will see that it is moved and secured once again."

Still she hesitated, though she wasn't certain why.

"Will you come with me? We started this adventure together. Let us end it that way as well." He held out his hand.

Siobhan stared at the calluses and silver-threaded scars

that marked his palm. Strong and capable fingers waited patiently for her decision.

So much had changed between them from the first time they'd met outside her father's home. She'd been filled with dreams of adventure then. Over the last few weeks, those dreams had come true because of the man before her. But with those dreams came pain and loss. Never could she have imagined a life without her father. It had been just the two of them for so long.

Everything changed, William had said. Her fingers drifted down to cover her belly. Her father's life had ended. Would another life fill that void?

Everything changed. Did it change for the better?

She accepted his hand. His fingers curled around hers, enveloping them in warmth. "Yes, I'll go with you."

With the Spear clutched in his hand, William rode out the following morning with Siobhan tucked safely in his arms. Not only did the Templars who'd helped defeat de la Roche at Stonehyve Castle follow him, but many of his clan members had joined their ranks as well.

He still couldn't believe how accepting they had been of him after he'd killed his own uncle. Revenge never made things right. But his clan seemed eager to aid him and pleased to welcome him back into the fold, despite the fact he couldn't promise them he would return to the castle or to them. He still had a lot to accomplish.

William led the way along the shoreline to the first campsite of de la Roche's men. His scouting parties had kept watch over the troops that had captured Templars trying to join the battle at Stonehyve Castle.

William came to a halt at the top of a rise, just out of sight from de la Roche's troops, who spread like a blight across the gently sloping land. Smoke from their camp-fires filled the air.

His grip tightened around the Spear. For a fleeting moment, he felt a surge of power move through his body. Not malevolent power, but a calmness of spirit, of rightness, of hope.

Siobhan turned to look at him. "What is it, William?"

He returned her gaze. "I think I finally understand the power of the Spear."

Her gaze turned questioning. "In what way?"

"The Spear is not an evil thing that hungers for blood. It longs for transformation within its carrier. The Spear triggered the original transformation with the resurrection of Christ. The weapon guided Herod in his rule over Judea. It helped Boadicea triumph over the Romans. It helped Constantine accept Christianity and brought triumph to Charlemagne in forty-seven battles."

She frowned. "What effect did it have over de la Roche? He did not triumph in the end."

"Nay," William said. "Had he remained in possession of the Spear, terrible things could have happened here in Scotland and wherever else de la Roche carried it. We changed that outcome, along with your father."

"I'd like to believe that my father died for a noble reason," she said softly.

"He died for the noblest reason, Siobhan, even without the Spear. He died for the love of his child."

She swallowed roughly and nodded.

"And I must protect you and our child."

"We don't know—"

"Hush," he said placing a finger against her lips. "I know, and I want you safe. So I'll leave you here with a contingent of men while I lead the others. Please don't deny me this."

"I won't," she agreed.

He kissed her gently, then set her off the horse. He signaled to ten men to stay back with her while the others rode down the gentle slope to engage their target, their war cries slicing through the silence of the morning.

After three more conflicts with other factions of de la Roche's men, all the Templars were freed from captivity, and de la Roche's leaderless troops marched toward the shore and the ships they had moored there.

In the aftermath, William stared at the Spear in his hand. The Templars hadn't lost a single man in any of those battles. The Spear had to be the reason why.

With their purpose complete, William thanked the men who'd joined him and sent them back to their homes. With the Templars still hunted by those like de la Roche, they had no other option than to keep their presence in Scotland secret.

Only his own men followed him now. As they rode through the countryside on the morning of the third day since they'd left Stonehyve Castle, William looked fondly upon one warrior in particular: Lucius. The man had lived up to his declaration of change. He had become all that a warrior should be—faithful to his duty, dependable to his brothers and humble about his prowess. He had proved his worth, and William intended to recommend to Brother Kenneth that Lucius be allowed to assist in the relocation of the treasure when the time came.

Returning his attention to the scenery around him, William reined Phantom to a stop at the top of a ridge. The rest of his men followed his lead. He tightened his hold around Siobhan's waist as they took in the gorge below them. Sparkling, swift-flowing waters of the South Esk River cut across the land. To his right, the jagged crest and fertile glens of the Grampian Mountains stretched before them. To his left, set against the clear blue vaulted sky, were the Sidlaw Hills. Behind him lay the Firth of Tay.

"Why are we stopping?" Simon asked, bringing his own horse alongside Phantom.

"It is time for us to part ways," William said.

"Where do you go? Edinburgh?" Simon gazed thoughtfully at Siobhan.

"The Spear must be placed safely into Archbishop Lamberton's care."

"And after you finish there? Where will I find you? At Stonehyve Castle? At the monastery?"

"I haven't decided yet."

A sudden warm smile lit Simon's face. "I have a feeling I know which way the wind blows for you."

William frowned. "If I do not—"

"Farewell, my brother." Simon turned his horse around and signaled for the men to follow him down the slope toward the fertile glens below.

"You love him well," Siobhan stated as they watched the others ride away.

"I do. We've been through much together."

"He is the brother you never had."

William's arms drew her back against his chest, against the sudden emptiness there at the thought of not seeing Simon on a frequent basis.

"The wind is cold. Let us go," he said, suddenly filled with the need to finish the rest of their journey. "To Edinburgh."

William turned Phantom toward the Firth of Tay. There, they would hire a ship and head for Edinburgh.

From atop his horse, Navarre Valois, Pierre de la Roche's captain, scowled at the retreating lines of his own men as they turned back from their mission and toward the

Scottish coast. Three double-masted carracks waited there to take them back to France.

De la Roche must be dead. In his place, Valois was now in charge. His lips twisted in anger. De la Roche's failure to bring back the Templar treasure to their king would fall on his own aging shoulders.

Navarre waited as the last man left the campsite to follow the others. He'd given de la Roche the best years of his life. He'd followed the man across miles of land and over seas to flush out the Templars. He'd thought his life had held a purpose until this morning, when he'd come face-to-face with William Keith bearing the Spear of Destiny. The Templar had been unstoppable in his efforts to free his men.

Navarre's men had had no option but to let them go. They had lost the treasure, the Spear and even their honor. None would return to a hero's welcome.

"Damn you, de la Roche, and your failure," Navarre muttered through clenched teeth.

Behind him a branch snapped.

He twisted to peer behind him. The windblown trees at the edge of the incline appeared unchanged. He frowned at the sudden silence as the last of his troops moved in the distance. Putting his heels to his horse's side, he began to join them.

Another rustle sounded behind him.

His hand slid to the hilt of his sword. He turned to look behind him once more.

Nothing moved. Nothing stirred. Even the wind had died down for the moment.

"Who are you to blame me?" A voice came from the tree to his left, but there was no one there.

Navarre frowned. "Show yourself."

"I am everywhere, and I am nowhere," the voice came again.

Fear brought a chill to his flesh. "De la Roche?" he asked in a near whisper. How could it be? The men had reported their leader dead. Drowned in the moat of Stonehyve Castle, or broken by the fall beneath those waters.

A ghost?

Navarre shook himself. He did not believe in such things. There was no danger here. He turned back around and continued down the rise of the hill.

A sting centered in his back. He arched against the pain, but it spread until it consumed him.

Two heartbeats later, he fell off his horse.

Dead.

Chapter Twenty-six

Siobhan stared out over the ship's edge, allowing the vigorous wind to brush her cheeks, to catch her hair and whirl it about her face. The wind, the water . . . She loved the sensations they carried and the newfound sense of freedom they brought to her.

Siobhan had never been on a ship before. It hadn't taken but a moment for her to find her sea legs. She tipped her head back, up toward the rays of the afternoon sun. Vitality flowed through her, and joy.

She'd had three days to adjust to the idea of her father's death. And though she'd thought she would never be happy again, instead she found she looked forward to each day with William. Each day held a surprise she had never counted on, the constancy of his love. He had yet to tell her the words, but his every look, his every touch spoke volumes.

Her hand drifted down to her abdomen, to the slight rise she would feel there soon. She was with child. The prospect suddenly didn't seem so terrible. This wasn't just any child she carried. It was William's child. And she loved him.

Her gaze fixed in the distance where the sea met the sky, and some of her excitement faded. She couldn't tell William about the child until he'd decided the path his life would take. One path led to the Templars. The other to her and her child.

The choice had to be William's. She wouldn't come between a man and his dreams. Not ever.

The symmetry between her own situation and that of her mother's brought a tightness to her chest. Was this what her parents had had to face? After their joining, her father had chosen to return to the Templars. And her mother had remained behind, silently bearing the burden of raising a child alone. Her mother's death had been an unforeseen variable that had brought her father back into Siobhan's life.

Now that she knew the truth about her father, she could recall times in her past when she'd seen a deep sadness in his eyes, a longing she could do nothing about. He'd expressed feelings that had been stifled sometimes by their need to live in isolation. She'd known nothing else.

Because of her, her father had been forced to live in a state of limbo—stuck with her in the secular world, with his heart firmly in the religious past.

Siobhan gripped the edge of the railing. She could never do the same thing to William, baby or not. She would not sway him in any way. The decision he made had to come from his heart. And his heart alone.

With the Spear of Destiny clutched in one hand and his Templar tunic in the other, William stood before Archbishop Lamberton at the altar of Saint Giles's Church in Edinburgh.

"So good to see you again, Sir William," the archbishop said, smiling a greeting. "I've missed our long discussions since you left Edinburgh."

"Important things drew me away."

He nodded. "I am aware of your attempted journey to the Holy Land and the outcome of that battle. I prayed quite diligently for your safe return."

"Thank you, my friend."

"What brings you back to my altar?"

William cast a glance over his shoulder at Siobhan as she stood at the back of the church. Sunlight shone through the stained glass behind her, stroking her auburn hair with flame.

A pang of tenderness stirred within him. He knew what he wanted. He'd never been more certain of anything in his whole life.

"We have much to discuss," William said, turning to face the holy man, who was dressed in a black cassock. The archbishop had a deeply creased, heavily jowled face, with clear and kind blue eyes.

"Indeed we have," he said with a touch of awe as his gaze shifted between William's face and the Spear. "Is that what I think it is?"

"Aye. The Longinus Spear, the Spear of Destiny, the Holy Lance. Call it what you will. The Templars have kept this artifact hidden for many years. It's time to send it home. And although the pope may see me as a criminal, I still hold the Church in the highest esteem. I want the Spear returned to Rome, where the Vatican can oversee its care and protection."

The archbishop's jaw slackened. "You found the Templar treasure."

William smiled. "All of it."

"And you need my help because . . . ?"

"I trust you more than any other to see to the Spear's safe return."

"You honor me, William." His brow creased as his gaze searched William's face. "There is more to your story than you are telling me. In your eyes I see more happiness than I've witnessed in many a year. But sorrow still lingers there as well."

William released a soft, almost inaudible sigh. In the

five years that he'd spent at court, he'd visited his friend the archbishop on a weekly basis. "You could always read me better than anyone else."

"I doubt that still holds true."

At the archbishop's laughter, William smiled.

"Is Siobhan the reason for your happiness?" the holy man asked, his gaze seeking her out at the back of the church.

William nodded.

"What do you desire?" the archbishop asked, returning his gaze to William.

He held out his Templar tunic. "To renounce my vows to the Templars."

The archbishop nodded and a look of understanding filled his gentle eyes. "Your vows are as a lay monk, William. Abandoning them does not mean you are abandoning our Lord. If you choose to follow another path, another vocation, then I'll make certain you are free to do so."

William drew a slow, steady breath. "I want that very much."

The archbishop accepted William's tunic. "What about the treasure? It must be moved if it has been discovered. Does Sir John Fraser know that you've found his storehouse?"

Deep regret washed over William. "Sir John is dead at the hands of Pierre de la Roche. The man used the Spear to send him to his eternal reward."

The archbishop genuflected. "My most sincere regrets. Sir John was a very good man."

William motioned to Siobhan with his head. "She is his only daughter."

The archbishop's gaze moved beyond William to Siobhan. "The last time I saw her, she was a wee babe in arms." He sighed heavily. "Is there anything I can do to assist you?"

"Marry us?"

The archbishop's eyes went wide, then laughter filled the church.

Siobhan twisted toward the altar, her expression uncertain.

"Consider your request fulfilled, my son." The holy man's smile increased. "When do I get to meet your lovely bride?"

William could feel heat rise to his face. "As soon as I ask her to be my wife." He held out the Spear to the archbishop. "Meanwhile, take this into your care."

The archbishop accepted the Spear. "'Tis an honor I do not take lightly."

William released a heavy breath, suddenly relieved to have the responsibility of the Spear out of his hands. He had more important tasks to deal with. "Wait here. I shall be but a moment."

The archbishop nodded. "Anything for your happiness, my friend."

Siobhan nervously smoothed the gently used midnight blue velvet dress William had purchased for her earlier this morning. As he strode down the long church aisle after speaking with the archbishop alone, a radiant smile lit his face. Gone were the lines of strain. Rugged power marked each step as he drew near.

Dressed in a wine-colored velvet tunic, dark trews and black boots, the sight of him brought warmth to the core of her being. There was an intensity and excitement in his expression that had never been there before. She felt herself melting as he stopped before her and took her hands in his.

" 'Tis done," he said, his voice soft.

"This is truly what you want, to be a Templar no more?"

He nodded. "In my heart I'll always be a Templar, Siobhan. I've been a warrior all my life. I cannot break away from what has formed me into the man I am today. But I no longer have formal ties to the Templar Order. And I feel at peace with that decision."

His hands moved up to cup her shoulders. "I want other things."

She swallowed to ease the tautness in her throat. "What do you want, William?"

"You tempt me so," he breathed as he brushed her hair away from her cheek, his fingers lingering on the curve of her neck. "I don't let my guard down easily. I haven't let anyone into my life in a long time. But somehow you slipped into my heart and soul. When we made love in the Templar treasure room, I knew you were the one— the one I would love forever."

The breath stilled in her chest as the words she'd longed to hear wrapped around her heart. She opened her mouth to respond, but he brought a finger to her lips, stalling her.

"I asked you before, when I wasn't free to do so. But today I stand before you an unencumbered man." He paused. "You would make me the happiest man in the world if you would wed me, here in this church, today."

Emotion swelled inside her. "Yes," she responded without hesitation.

"You agree?"

She nodded, no longer trusting her voice.

He captured her lips in a kiss that stole her breath and left her longing for more. "I love you," she responded when she was able, tracing her fingers over the sculpted muscle beneath his velvet tunic. His heart hammered beneath her touch. She was blissfully content to know a part of that heart belonged to her now.

William slipped his arm around Siobhan's waist. "You're trembling," he noted as he guided his bride up the long aisle toward the holy man who would wed them. "There is nothing to fear, *ma chérie*." He smiled down at her. "After you've braved the wilds of Scotland, torture and battles with de la Roche, marriage to me cannot be so terrible."

"It is not fear," Siobhan admitted. "I truly don't know why I feel suddenly so at ease."

He paused. "Are you uncertain about this marriage? If you feel I am rushing things—"

"I have never been more certain of anything in my life," she said, her tone fierce.

"Then what is it?" he asked, concern filling his sherry-colored eyes.

She worried her lower lip. "I am saddened my father could not be here with me."

"He is here with us." An understanding smile returned to William's lips. "He's in our hearts. He's in the afternoon sunlight streaming through the stained glass. He's in the silence that fills the church."

A mixture of warm sunlight and shadow created a mosaic on the marble aisle before her. The scent of flowers, incense and candles permeated her senses in a heady mix. And from high above, a bell tolled the hour.

"You're right. He is here with us." Siobhan smiled into William's eyes, suddenly filled with a sense of joy unlike any she had ever experienced.

This brave, strong, independent man would soon be her husband. She knew from their experiences over the past days that life wouldn't always be perfect, that they'd have their challenges. She'd learned that life and love were a series of peaks and valleys, euphoria and pain. But in the end, it was the constancy of love that mattered.

"You're the only man for me, Sir William Keith of Stonehyve. I shall be yours every day for the rest of my life."

"Treasure." He leaned forward and brushed her temple with his lips. "You're the only treasure I need."

Epilogue

Stonehyve Castle, Scotland
April 1332

Siobhan found herself at the gates of the kirk yard of Stonehyve Castle. She couldn't keep herself from visiting her father's grave, not today. Her father had died one year ago this day.

She threw open the gates, reveling in the pungent scent of the sea as it swept in with the rising of the tide. Over the past year she had come to love the smell of the ocean, just as she'd come to cherish her new life as mistress of the castle. William had also embraced his new life. Beneath his command, the castle and all its residents had flourished.

The most welcome addition to the castle she held cradled in her arms. "We're going to meet your grandfather," Siobhan explained to the four-month-old child, who seemed more interested in the tartan cloth Siobhan had wrapped around her than in the scenery.

Siobhan chuckled as she picked her way across the grave sites. At her father's resting place, she stumbled. Where only a week ago there had been a simple wooden grave marker, now rested a life-size reclining figure carved in stone. It lay next to the monuments of William's mother and father, which their staff had commissioned years earlier.

Instead of the sorrow she expected to feel at the sight of the newly capped year-old grave, joy bubbled up. Siobhan bent down beside the image of her father's face. She traced her fingers across the strong, noble jaw that the artist had captured from the days of his young adulthood, not at the time of his death. "Maggie, meet your grandfather," Siobhan said to her daughter, her words thick with emotion.

William was responsible for this precious gift.

"Do you like it?" a familiar voice called from behind.

Siobhan turned to face William. "What a lovely surprise."

He folded the two of them in his arms. He placed a kiss upon his daughter's head before he turned to Siobhan. His kiss for her was slow and gentle, setting her heart and soul aflutter.

He pulled back with a beaming smile, knowing the effect he had over her. "I wanted to do something special for you, something that would remind you of the man your father was, and give our dear little Margaret at least a small understanding of who her grandparents were."

Margaret cooed in response, reaching toward the effigies of his parents. Captured forever in stone, Sir Philip and Lady Eda Keith lay next to each other, their bodies close, eternally in love and at peace in each other's arms.

"I can think of no better way to leave this world than in the arms of the man you love."

"There are other statues I commissioned. Would you like to see them?"

Siobhan glanced around the kirk yard. Nothing else had changed.

"They're not here." William took the baby from Siobhan's arms and led her out of the kirk yard, through the bailey and to the courtyard that overlooked the ocean at the back of the keep. Throughout the past year, William had spent much of his time directing the changes to the formalized gardens. Now she understood why.

In the center of the courtyard rose an urn similar to

the one they had seen in the Templar treasure chamber. Flames danced in the metal urn, lending life and motion to the groupings of life-sized statues that stood at each of the courtyard's four corners.

"I left the Brotherhood behind, but I didn't leave my brothers. I placed them here so they could look out over the waters of the Atlantic and into forever." William guided her to one corner.

"Siobhan, this is Sir James Douglas, our leader. Beside him are Sir Walter Logan and Robert Logan of Restalrig."

"These are the men who fought with you in the Battle of Teba."

He nodded. "Over here we have Sir William Borthwick, Sir Kenneth Moir, Sir Alan Cathcart, and Mistress Brianna Sinclair."

"A woman?"

"Aye, and a brave one at that."

"How did she end up traveling with a Templar army?"

"That is a story in itself," he said with a laugh as they continued to the far corner of the courtyard. "Allow me to introduce Sir William Sinclair and his brother, John Sinclair of Rosslyn."

"Do the statues resemble the men and women you fought with?" she asked, curious as to how their images had been captured.

William nodded. "The death masks Simon and I made before their burials captured every detail. For those still living, I relied on past portraits."

Siobhan smiled up at the two Sinclair brothers. "We must invite all their families to come see this tribute you've given them."

William took her hand and walked with her to the final corner. He stopped before the two statues there. "Sir Simon Lockhart of Lee, and myself."

Siobhan remained silent as she stared at the lifelike images of Simon and her husband. Despite her attempt to keep her emotions in check, tears came to her eyes and slid silently down her cheeks.

"Does this upset you?" William asked as he pulled her against the hard length of his body.

"Nay, my love. I'm touched by their bravery." Looking up at him, she lifted her hand to his face and stroked his cheek. There was so much to this complex man she'd married. "You loved them all, didn't you?"

"Aye."

"Of these eleven, who is still alive?"

"Simon and Brother Kenneth you know, Sir William Borthwick and Brianna Sinclair. Alan Cathcart remains a mystery. His body was never found."

Siobhan closed her eyes. The statues were so poignant. William was everything to her, everything she'd ever dreamed of and more, yet if something was missing from his life, if he'd rather be with the Templars . . .

He touched her chin and forced her to look up at him. "I know what you're thinking, Siobhan. The answer is nay. I wouldn't trade one moment of my life with you and Margaret to be a Templar again."

"Just as I wanted to give our daughter a reminder of who her grandparents were, I needed to immortalize the Brotherhood to help me honor the past, both yours and mine."

Staring into his eyes, she suddenly understood. For him, the statues meant it was time to move forward with life, to let go of the past. For in his eyes she saw love, and hope, but there was something else there as well. A part of himself that had been a Templar, a part of himself he would never let go. The adventurer.

And that is when Siobhan knew the truth: the adventure of her life had only just begun.

Afterword

The Brotherhood of the Scottish Templars is a fictitious name for a group of men who truly existed in medieval Scottish history. The hero of *To Tempt a Knight*, Sir William Keith, was one of the knights selected by James "Black" Douglas at the time of King Robert the Bruce's death to take the king's embalmed heart to the Holy Land. Their mission was to place the king's heart in the Church of the Holy Sepulchre.

In the spring of 1330, the Bruce's inner circle of knights, supported by twenty-six squires and a retinue of men, set off on a Crusade from Scotland for Jerusalem, fighting the infidels along the way.

James Douglas wore the heart of the king in a specially designed cylindrical vessel about his neck, using it as a talisman as he and his men made their way through enemy territory.

On the morning of August 25, 1330, the Scottish knights joined King Alfonso of Castile in a battle that was intended to crush the Kingdom of Granada, which was held by the Moors at that time. A false battle cry sent the Scottish knights into battle before they had adequate reinforcements. They were outnumbered a hundred to one. And even with the heart of the king on their side, they were doomed to failure. The knights were crushed by the Moors, and their mission failed.

Five of the ten knights died, along with hundreds of

foot soldiers. Sir William Keith and Sir Simon Lockhart of Lee recovered the Bruce's heart and returned with it and the bodies of the fallen knights to Scotland.

There is no documentary evidence that shows that the knights who traveled with the Bruce's heart on Crusade were Templar knights. However, enough evidence exists to suggest Sir William Sinclair and his brother, John Sinclair of Rosslyn, were associated with the Templars. The idea of this association is not too much of a stretch for the time period, especially since their journey took them into lands once protected by the Templars.

It is recorded in French Masonic history that eighteen Templar ships left at midnight from La Rochelle, France, at midnight on October 11, 1307, reportedly heading to Scotland, the refuge place designated for Templar relics.

In the year 1331, when this story takes place, the Templars worldwide had been disbanded for seventeen years—everywhere, that is, except in Scotland. In those years, Scotland was seen as a safe haven for Templars, because Robert the Bruce never disbanded the Templar Order within his lands.

Another notable aspect of the Templars is their connection to the legendary treasure. Did it truly exist? What precious artifacts did it contain? No one knows for certain. In the pages of *To Tempt a Knight*, the Templar artifact the hero and heroine struggle to protect is the Longinus Spear, also known as the Spear of Destiny and the Holy Lance.

According to tradition, at the crucifixion of Jesus Christ, the Spear was in the possession of the Roman Centurion Gaius Cassius Longinus. It was Longinus who pierced Christ's side with the Spear. Eventually the Spear fell out of Longinus's care and into the hands of destiny.

Among those who are alleged to have possessed the Spear at one time or another are the following: Boadicea; Herod the Great; Saint Maurice of the Theban Legion; Constantine the Great, who carried the Spear into victory at the Battle of the Milvian Bridge, and also while surveying the layout of his new city, Constantinople; Theodosius; Alaric, who sacked Rome; Theodoric, the only man to force Attila the Hun to retreat; Justinian; Charles Martel, grandfather of Charlemagne; and Charlemagne himself, who is said to have carried the Spear through forty-seven victorious battles and died when he accidentally dropped it.

In early 900 AD, the Spear fell into the possession of the Saxon dynasty of Germany, passing from Heinrich I, who was victorious in his battle against the Magyars, to his son Otto I, who carried the Spear into victory over the Mongols in the Battle of Leck.

After the death of Otto I, there are conflicting stories concerning the fate of the Spear. Eventually, it fell into the possession of the house of Hohenstaufen.

Napoleon attempted to seize the Spear after the Battle of Austerlitz, but it had been smuggled out of Vienna just prior to the battle.

In the early twentieth century, the Spear was briefly in the possession of Kaiser Wilhelm II before eventually ending up in the Imperial Treasury (*Schatzkammer*) at Hofburg Palace in Vienna. It was there, in September 1912, where Adolf Hitler first laid eyes upon it.

Hitler seized the Spear in the name of the Third Reich on March 12, 1938, the day he annexed Austria. During the final days of the war in Europe, at 2:10 p.m. on April 30, 1945, Lieutenant Walter William Horn of the United States Seventh Army took possession of the Spear in the name of the United States government.

Within ninety minutes of the United States' capturing the Spear, Adolf Hitler committed suicide.

Generals Eisenhower and Patton decided to return

the Spear to the House of Hapsburg shortly thereafter. The Spear can once again be found in the Imperial Treasury at the Hofburg Palace in Vienna.

There are several Spears that claim to be the "true" Spear of Destiny. In addition to the Vienna lance, another lance discovered during the First Crusade exists in Echmiadzin, Armenia. Saint Louis brought another spear to Paris, following his return from the Crusades in Palestine in the thirteenth century. Another lance, known as the Vatican lance, was sent to Pope Innocent VIII by the Ottoman sultan Bajazet II in 1492. Some medieval scholars believe that this lance is truly the Echmiadzin lance, which fell into the hands of the Turks and eventually made its way to Bajazet, who sent it to Pope Innocent. The Vatican lance is encased in one of the pillars supporting the dome of Saint Peter's Basilica. Another Spear is kept in Kraków, Poland, and is believed to be a copy of the Vatican lance.

Which is the real Spear of Destiny? The world may never know.

Coming in Spring 2010

Seducing the Knight

Book Two of the
Brotherhood of the Scottish Templars

Jessamine Burundi knew it was pointless to run. Tears streamed down her cheeks. She hated to cry, hated it almost as much as feeling helpless. She raced through the stark white buildings of the small town of Teba, a town on the brink of war. The church lay ahead of her. Her mother's church. A place of refuge and peace.

She ran through the streets toward her only hope. The church had to protect her from the Conde of Teba. She would rather die than become his condessa. A quick glance over her shoulder as she cleared the open doorway showed her the Spanish pig's mottled red cheeks and blazing eyes. Maybe death would be her reality after all.

Her heart was pounding so hard she could scarcely breathe as she slipped into the church, one of the few Catholic churches her people had salvaged out of what had become a Moorish Spain. The heavy scent of incense assailed her. The scent of death. She stumbled, then caught herself. A funeral had no doubt taken place here earlier this morning.

Heavy footsteps sounded on the stone floor behind her. He gained on her. She ran toward the altar, toward the tall, thin man in a black robe who knelt there deep in prayer. He was her only salvation.

Jessamine's breath came in harsh sobs. Candles shimmered at the sides of the altar. Silent. Serene. So unlike the turmoil that tightened her chest. Someday she wouldn't have to run from anyone or anything. Someday, she, too could be silent and serene.

"Father!" she gasped.

Father Gabriel twisted toward her, then looked to the conde. He stood swiftly, his black robes rustling with the movement.

"Help me." She ducked behind the priest, praying he could shield her from fate.

The conde skidded to a halt before the priest. Beads of perspiration dotted the conde's temples. His black disheveled hair and his dark eyes, considered together with his black velvet jerkin, breeches and polished black boots, made him appear demonic. Only the redness of his cheeks gave the man any color. "Move aside," he demanded.

Wild despair tore through Jessamine. She'd been a fool to hope for rescue. Even Father Gabriel couldn't protect her from Conde Salazar Mendoza. She touched the side of her head where he'd struck her earlier, and winced at the pain.

"Whatever is going on here?" Father Gabriel questioned. He turned halfway toward Jessamine, while keeping his gaze on the conde.

"She is to be my wife," the conde said. "I have her father's consent." He lunged for her.

Father Gabriel shuffled backward, sheltering her with his arms. He reached for her hands. "Jessamine, explain." He startled at the sticky moisture between their joined hands. He pulled back and stared at the blood on his fingers. "You're hurt."

Hurt? The pain she suffered already was nothing compared to what the man intended. "My father did not willingly approve. The conde forced him to sign that document."

"This sounds like a matter of royal politics. . . ."

The conde growled. His hand moved to the blade at

his side. "Do not concern yourself in these matters, priest."

Father Gabriel flinched and pulled back from Jessamine. "Has he reached an agreement with your parents?"

Jessamine stared at the priest in disbelief. Would even he desert her now? "He held my mother at sword point until my father signed whatever contract he offered. No money was exchanged, just treachery and brute force."

"If you know what's good for you, Father, you will release her to me." The conde's eyes were fierce and filled with unchecked violence. "One word from me to the Moors, and you, along with this church, will be in ruins."

Father Gabriel turned pale and took another step back from her. "Jessamine, I'm sorry, but I cannot risk one life for all the others he might destroy."

"No," she gasped, feeling suddenly exposed. The conde gripped her arm and jerked her toward him. She slammed against his chest. The hilt of his sword bit into her hip. He twisted his fingers in the flesh of her arm, then smiled.

Jessamine gasped. Terror flooded her.

His smile broadened.

He wanted her fear. He thrived on it.

"Come along, my little flower. I have decided to take you as my bride without the formal vows. Once I taste that little body of yours, you'll be mine. No one can argue the point." He tugged ruthlessly on her arm. "I'll possess you right here in the churchyard." He propelled Jessamine forward, his grasp cruelly tight.

Jessamine knew she could never break free of his grip, but she could fool him. In a rare moment of compliance, she walked silently beside him.

In the middle of the cemetery, they stopped. The conde's lips tightened until they formed a thin line. "You're suddenly quite meek. I hope you will show me some of your headstrong spirit when I'm between your thighs."

Jessamine brought her heel down hard on the man's foot, then brought her knee up between the man's legs with all her might. He bellowed, relaxed his grip and clutched his groin. She jerked out of his grasp and streaked through the cemetery. She ran among the headstones, across a freshly turned grave of the newly dead.

A dull roar sounded in the distance.

The conde shouted something from behind.

Jessamine tore through the graveyard.

Footsteps sounded behind her.

The blood drummed in her temples. She headed for the shrubbery that boxed in the cemetery. Branches lashed her face and clawed her arms as she pushed through the bushes.

"When I catch you, you'll pay for your insolence." The conde crashed through the underbrush behind her.

Jessamine ran faster. She had to outdistance the demon in black. *Mother of God, I don't want to sacrifice myself to that pig.*

She broke through the other side of the shrubbery and into a dense copse of trees beyond. The shadows of the trees covered her in slivered light.

Her feet pounded the ground, her pace frantic.

She couldn't hear him any longer. Was it because he'd given up or because the soft earth absorbed the sound? She couldn't look behind her to find out.

Her heart pounded to the point of pain. She fixed her gaze on the morning light streaming through the trees at the opposite edge of the copse of trees. The edge of her town. Beyond the trees was only desert. But what choice did she have? She couldn't loop back without the conde capturing her. She broke through the trees and started down the hill on the other side, when her steps faltered.

Shouts of men mixed with the shrieks of horses, punctuated by the clang of steel upon steel. The acrid scent of smoke and the coppery scent of blood overwhelmed her senses. Her steps slowed. Her stomach lurched.

Blood. War. Death.

Heavy footfalls sounded dangerously close.

With nowhere else to go, no other means of escape, Jessamine stumbled down the hill, toward the fighting. A single sob escaped her throat. She would die this day. The choice was now whether her end came at the hands of the conde, or by the blade of a sword.

A sudden chill gripped her. She preferred the latter.

Bracing herself for the pain that was to come, Jessamine hurled forward into the fray of horses and men.

Sir Alan Cathcart, known to his brothers in the Scottish Templars as the Falcon, gripped the hilt of his sword and prepared for the onslaught as ten thousand Moors swarmed toward him. For a moment he wished he were more like his namesake, soaring high overhead, out of the danger and away from death.

Today, that was not his fate. Nay, his fate lay undetermined by the coming conflict. They were here to take back the Castle of the Stars from Moorish occupation at the request of King Alfonso XI of Spain. The Scottish Templars, under the direction of Sir James "Black" Douglas, and the Spanish had joined forces to rid the country of the heathens conquest.

Though the Templars had come through Spain intent on making their way to the Holy Land, Black Douglas and his men didn't mind a little diversion along the way. They would triumph. They always did.

Yet, for Alan, today had a different feel, compared to past conflicts. Could it be the number of Moorish forces lined up on the hillside opposite them? Could it be the high desert air that he and the other Templars were un-used to breathing? Or was his odd feeling just an omen of something he didn't understand?

He sloughed off the odd sensation and focused on the enemy. The sound of thundering hoofbeats and the swirl-ing of dust filled the air as men dressed in black robes and turbans bore down on him and his brothers.

"Hold steady," Alan crooned to the anxious beast be-neath him, as Shadow's muscles clenched and quivered. "We will get through this." They had to. Too much lay at stake.

Sir James Douglas sat upon his warhorse, clutching the silver vessel containing the heart of Robert the Bruce. The Bruce had promised to see them through to the Holy Land. He'd promised his heart would protect them.

And along with that promise, Alan had accepted an ad-ditional burden. Once they reached Jerusalem, an army of Moors would not stand in the way of that promise.

For a moment, Alan let his mind wander back to a more familiar land, that of his ancestors. Where the wind blew gently through the grass, where the heady scent of heather permeated the senses, where blue-black hills dot-ted the landscape and clouds roiled overhead, threatening rain. But not here in the land of his enemies. Nay, here the grass was dry and brown, the soil a rocky gray, the air heavy, and the constant heat prickled his skin beneath his white Templar tunic and heavy chain mail.

The hoofbeats drew closer. Alan could see the men's dark eyes framed between their turbans and beards. He clenched his sword and waited. He liked to play it close.

He could feel the air move past him as the Moors came within reach. One man on horseback brought his sword down at an angle, intent on slashing across Alan's torso. Alan matched his stroke, watching the sparks that flew from the metal as the blades clashed. As the attacker retreated, two more men approached on foot. Alan kicked one in the chest, sending him tumbling backward, a second before he struck the other man in the chest with his sword. The man dropped to the ground, dead.

The moment the two fell away, two more replaced them, in a tide of unending black. From the corner of his eye, Alan saw a speck of peach fabric moving through the throng. He snapped his attention back to the bright silver steel that came stinging through the air just a hairsbreadth above his head.

He ducked, shifted Shadow to the left and countered with a boot in the face of one man and the flat of his blade against the head of the other. In the span of another heartbeat, the flash of peach came to him again.

His breath caught. A woman? She ran with her dress hitched up to expose two shapely, honey-toned legs. Dark hair streamed out behind her as she pushed into the fray of swords and scimitars, men and horses.

Alan shifted his weight forward. His horse understood the command. Together they charged through the sea of black toward that strangely incongruous femininity floating in a sea of death. As he came ever closer, he could see a thin, graceful form, a riot of shining dark hair and wide, frightened eyes.

He sliced through the fighting, the carnage, almost as if his drive to reach her was aided by Providence. Never slowing his horse, he came up beside her and scooped her slight body up into his arms.

She screamed.

He kept on going, through the dead and the dying.

She struggled against his grip.

"Halt your writhing, woman, or you'll return to the sea of blood beneath us both." His voice was harsh, but at his words she suddenly ceased her movements.

"A sea of blood?" Her eyes, if it were possible, grew

even wider as her gaze dropped to the cross of the Templars upon his chest. "Turbans and crosses," she breathed in disbelief. Her gaze returned to his face. "It is just as the prophecy of my birth predicted." An instant later, an expression of profound relief lightened the tension in her face.

As Shadow avoided the worst of the fighting, Alan couldn't keep from looking at the woman in his arms. Her features were finely drawn. A pair of ruby lips, so full and tempting. Large almond-shaped eyes, their color an infinitely changeable medley of black and brown, set above high, chiseled cheekbones. Lush, dark lashes, a straight nose, all set into an oval of perfect honeyed skin.

The catalog of her features didn't do her justice. It was not so much her features that caught his notice, but the animation in her face—the hesitant smile that came to those full, red lips and the relief that entered her eyes. "Thank you."

Her voice was low yet melodic, with the slightest hint of a rasp. She leaned closer, and the faint scent of jasmine teased his nose. He tore his gaze from her at the sound of hoofbeats behind him. "Save your thanks until we are indeed free." As though in response to his words, a swarm of black-cloaked men moved toward them, surrounded them.

JENNIFER ASHLEY
EMILY BRYAN
ALISSA JOHNSON

Invite you to

A Christmas Ball

It is the most anticipated event of the ton: the annual holiday ball at Hartwell House. The music is elegant, the food exquisite, and the guest list absolutely exclusive. Some come looking for love. Some will do almost anything to avoid it. But everyone wants to be there. No matter what their desires, amid the swirling gowns and soft glow of candlelight, magic tends to happen. And one dance, one kiss, one night can shape a new destiny….

Coming this Fall! ISBN 13: 978-0-8439-6250-5

Dawn MacTavish

"...An enthralling, non-stop read. 4 ½ Stars!"
— *RT Book Reviews* on *Prisoner of the Flames*

Counterfeit Lady

"NO, MY LADY, I COULDN'T—"

But Alice could—and did. Against her better judgment, she allowed herself one night at a masquerade ball, playing the role of her mistress. When else might she, daughter of an austere Methodist minister and a servant, sample the pleasures of the ton? She had but one obligation: deter the coxcomb and would-be suitor, Nigel Farnham.

"WHEN HAS 'NO' EVER STOPPED ME?"

She vanished in a swish of buttery silk and left behind the scent of sweet clover and violets. Mischievous and bold, Lady Clara Langly was a chit who desperately needed to be taken in hand—but she had left Nigel abruptly, fled into the night, and he'd had no chance to see her pretty face unmasked. If he was right, and dancing was nothing but making love to music, their quadrille was just the beginning....

ISBN 13: 978-0-8439-6321-2

Award-winning Author

CAROLINE FYFFE

"The love that unfolds in this tender and emotional story will touch your heart. Don't miss this breathtaking debut."
—Patti Berg, *USA Today* Bestselling Author

Chase Logan liked being a loner, a drifter, free and clear as a mountain stream. But one look into Jessie Strong's sky blue eyes and in the span of a heartbeat, he found himself agreeing to be her husband—and a father!

Jessie knew it was all pretend. And only temporary. Just until the adoption went through for three-year-old Sarah. But the longer Chase stayed, the less she could imagine a long, lonely Wyoming winter without him.

Times may be tough—supplies short and danger just outside the doorstep—but with the strength of the pioneer spirit and the warm glow of love in their hearts, Chase and Jessie are determined to have a true family at last, no matter

Where the Wind Blows

ISBN 13: 978-0-8439-6284-0

MELANIE JACKSON

Author of *Night Visitor* and *The Selkie*

A ghostly hound stalks Noltland Castle. For years, such appearances have signaled doom for the clan Balfour, and there is little reason to believe this time will be any different. Wasn't their laird cut down while defending the Scottish king, leaving a boy to take a man's place?

Frances Balfour has done all she can, using guts and guile to keep her cousin safe in his new lairdship, but enemies encroach from all sides, and now the secluded isle of Orkney is beset from within. A stranger has arrived, and his green gaze promises to strip every secret bare. The newcomer is a swordsman, a seducer and a sometimes spy for the English king, but for all that, he seems a friend. And Colin Mortlock can see into the Night Side, that spectral world between life and death. He shall be the destruction of all Frances loves—or her salvation.

The Night Side

ISBN 13: 978-0-505-52804-9

LEANNA RENEE HIEBER

*W*hat fortune awaited sweet, timid Percy Parker at Athens Academy? Hidden in the dark heart of Victorian London, the Romanesque school was dreadfully imposing, a veritable fortress, and little could Percy guess what lay inside. She had never met its powerful and mysterious Professor Alexi Rychman, knew nothing of the growing shadows, of the Ripper and other supernatural terrors against which his coterie stood guard. She saw simply that she was different, haunted, with her snow white hair, pearlescent skin and uncanny gift. This arched stone doorway was a portal to a new life, to an education far from what could be had at a convent—and it was an invitation to an intimate yet dangerous dance at the threshold of life and death . . . .

The Strangely Beautiful Tale of Miss Percy Parker

"TENDER, POIGNANT, EXQUISITELY WRITTEN."
—C. L. Wilson, *New York Times* Bestselling Author

ISBN 13: 978-0-8439-6296-3

INTERACT WITH DORCHESTER ONLINE!

Want to learn more about your favorite books and authors?
Want to talk with other readers that like to read the same books as you?
Want to see up-to-the-minute Dorchester news?

VISIT DORCHESTER AT:
DorchesterPub.com
Twitter.com/DorchesterPub
Facebook.com (Search Pages)

DISCUSS DORCHESTER'S NOVELS AT:
Dorchester Forums at DorchesterPub.com
GoodReads.com
LibraryThing.com
Myspace.com/books
Shelfari.com
WeRead.com

☐ YES!

Sign me up for the Historical Romance Book Club and send my FREE BOOKS! If I choose to stay in the club, I will pay only $8.50* each month, a savings of $6.48!

NAME: _____

ADDRESS: _____

TELEPHONE: _____

EMAIL: _____

☐ I want to pay by credit card.

☐ VISA   ☐ MasterCard.   ☐ DISCOVER

ACCOUNT #: _____

EXPIRATION DATE: _____

SIGNATURE: _____

Mail this page along with $2.00 shipping and handling to:
Historical Romance Book Club
PO Box 6640
Wayne, PA 19087
Or fax (must include credit card information) to:
610-995-9274
You can also sign up online at **www.dorchesterpub.com**.
*Plus $2.00 for shipping. Offer open to residents of the U.S. and Canada only.
Canadian residents please call 1-800-481-9191 for pricing information.
If under 18, a parent or guardian must sign. Terms, prices and conditions subject to change. Subscription subject to acceptance. Dorchester Publishing reserves the right to reject any order or cancel any subscription.